Find. Wife. Find. Wife. Find. Wife.

Every time the soles of Gray's running shoes bounced against the narrow tree-lined path, the words seemed to echo in his head.

"Shut. Up. Shut. Up," he said under his breath.

"Find. Wife. Find. Wife," his footsteps answered.

He muttered an oath and picked up speed.

Everything that Gray had ever wanted to accomplish in life, he had. He was successful in every endeavor, because that's who he was.

But in this one…damned…thing…he was—

—barreling straight for a runner squatting in his path.

He tried slowing down, but momentum had him in its grip. "On the left," he barked, hoping the girl—oh, yeah, definitely a girl—would heed his warning and move to the side.

Instead, he got a glimpse of fair skin, wide dark eyes and flying dark hair as she rose and took the impact with a gasping "Oomph!"

Dear Reader,

Who doesn't love a fairy tale?

Well, of course, there are those who say they don't. But just between you and me, I have my doubts. Like his brothers before him, Grayson Hunt doesn't believe in fairy tales. Doesn't believe in love, in happily ever after. Yet those are the very things that he wants more than anything. And when, after having had a taste of that magic, he finds himself in danger of losing it, he's willing to give up anything to keep the magic alive.

That magic isn't just between the pages of a book. All we have to do is believe. And not forget to see the magic, even when it's hiding among the mundane details of everyday life.

Magic is all around us. In the people and the lives we touch. In a smile. In a hug. In a child's laughter and a parent's sigh. In a rainy day, in the scent of baking bread, in the stroke of a hand. Fairy-tale magic doesn't have to be wrapped in festive trappings, in animated movies or even in a romance novel. It just needs to be felt in your heart.

Wishing you magic,

Allison

ALLISON LEIGH
THE BRIDE AND THE BARGAIN

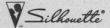

Silhouette®

SPECIAL

SILHOUETTE BOOKS

ISBN-13: 978-0-373-24882-7
ISBN-10:   0-373-24882-2

THE BRIDE AND THE BARGAIN

ALLISON LEIGH

started early by writing a Halloween play that her grade-school class performed. Since then, though her tastes have changed, her love for reading has not. And her writing appetite simply grows more voracious by the day.

She has been a finalist in the RITA® Award and the Holt Medallion contests. But the true highlights of her day as a writer are when she receives word from a reader that they laughed, cried or lost a night's sleep while reading one of her books.

Born in Southern California, Allison has lived in several different cities in four different states. She has been, at one time or another, a cosmetologist, a computer programmer and a secretary. She began writing full-time after spending nearly a decade as an administrative assistant for a busy neighborhood church, and she currently makes her home in Arizona with her family. She loves to hear from her readers, who can write to her at P.O. Box 40772, Mesa, AZ 85274-0772.

For my fellow Cinderella Hunters.
It has been a true pleasure working with you.

Prologue

July

Of all the things he might have foreseen, never in his life could Gray have imagined this.

No, he'd been more annoyed with the command performance his father had requested. In the month since Harry had suffered a heart attack, the man had been increasingly unpredictable. And the last thing Gray had needed was a trip out to the family's high-tech estate on Lake Washington when he had fifty million things to attend to back at the office in downtown Seattle.

Not that the distraction of his work was any excuse.

He was Grayson Hunt, president of HuntCom.

Whether or not he and his three younger brothers had been summoned to the shack—as they'd wryly dubbed the opulent family compound when they were young—he was supposed to be able to juggle any number of responsibilities. God knew that Harry had never let anything set *him* off track for any length of time. The only child of a storekeeper and his homemaker wife, Harrison Hunt had invented the computer software that had made HuntCom a household word. He'd turned an offbeat, fledgling company into a multinational, multibillion-dollar juggernaut that had set the computer industry on its ear.

Gray was forty-two, Harry's firstborn and supposedly just like him. The knowledge was as much a curse as a blessing.

Gray biffed another shot at the antique pool table and shook his head, surrendering the table to his youngest brother, Justin.

"Does anybody know why the old man called this meeting?" Without hesitation, Justin began pocketing balls, easily showing up Gray's less impressive attempts.

"He left a message with Loretta," Gray said. "Didn't give her a reason." When it vibrated silently, he pulled out his cell phone, glancing at the display. Another text from Loretta, his secretary, keeping him apprised of his ever-evolving schedule. He'd canceled six meetings in order to answer Harry's summons.

"Harry called you himself? Me, too." Alex was working his way through a bottle of Black Sheep Ale from his position in one of the leather armchairs arranged around the spacious library. At thirty-six, he headed up the company's philanthropic arm—the Hunt Foundation—and had probably canceled his own share of meetings, as well. "What about you, J.T.? Did you get the message from his secretary, or from Harry personally?"

A tumbler of bourbon in his hand, J.T. looked beat. An architect by training, he was in charge of all HuntCom properties and construction and was more often on the road than not. "From Harry. I told him I'd have to cancel a week of meetings in New Delhi and spend over half a day on the corporate jet to get home in time, but he insisted I be here." He peered wearily at Justin, the baby of the brothers at thirty-four. "What about you?"

"I was at the ranch when he called. He told me the same thing he told you. I had to be here. No excuses." Justin slowly rolled the pool cue between his palms. "He refused to tell me what the meeting was about. Did he tell any of you why he wanted to talk to us?"

"No." Gray was plenty irritated about it, too. Harry *knew* they were all busy. So what the hell was he calling family get-togethers for? And then to leave them cooling their heels in the library?

He looked at his vibrating phone again. Dammit. Another hiccup with their latest buyout. He started for the door. If he had to call and ream out somebody, he wanted some privacy. But before he could make it to the hall door, it flew open and their father entered.

"Ah, you're all here. Excellent." Harry waved his hand toward his massive mahogany desk at the far end of the room that faced the French doors overlooking their private beach. "Join me, boys," he invited, as if he did so every day.

Which he didn't. One thing Gray could not say about Harry was that he'd been a doting, hands-on kind of dad.

He faced Harry across the desk, ignoring the chairs situated in front of it. His brothers took no interest in the chairs, either.

Harry eyed the empty seats through his horn-rimmed bifocals. Despite hitting seventy on his last birthday, his dark hair was barely marked by gray. And his blue eyes were definitely looking peeved.

Gray could relate.

Harry shrugged impatiently. "Very well. Stand or sit. It makes no difference." He did sit, however, which was good because Gray would have told him to if he hadn't.

His father drove him around the bend, but that didn't mean Gray had no concerns for the old man's health.

"Since my heart attack last month," Harry began, proving yet again that Gray's mind often tracked along his father's, "I've been doing a lot of thinking about this family. I've never thought a lot about my legacy—"

At that, Gray's lips did twist, but he remained silent when Harry glanced at him.

"—nor about having grandchildren to carry on the Hunt name," the old man continued. "But the heart attack made me face some hard truths I'd ignored up until then. I could have died. I could die tomorrow."

Gray still had a hard time imagining that. Harry seemed too vital. Too stubborn. Still, though Harry was a machine in many ways, he was an aging one.

His father rose, pressing his fists against the desktop. "I finally realized that left to your own devices, you four never *will* get married, which means I'll never have grandchildren. I don't intend to leave the future of this family to chance any longer. You have a year. One year. By the end of that year, each of you will not only be married, you will either already have a child or your wife will be expecting one."

Gray stared, uncharacteristically nonplussed.

"Right." J.T. finally broke the stunned silence.

Harry ignored their general lack of response. "If any one

of you refuses to do so, you'll all lose your positions in HuntCom and the perks you love so much."

"You can't be serious," Gray finally said, focusing on the bottom line. Harry held controlling interest in HuntCom. Not even if everyone else on the board—Gray and his brothers, Harry's oldest friend Cornelia and Corny's four daughters—voted in accord against Harry could they outweigh his votes. He could do pretty much whatever he wanted, but that didn't mean Gray believed the old man would actually follow through with unseating them.

They were all too good at what they did for HuntCom and the family interests, and Harry—affected by his heart attack or not—knew it.

"I'm deadly serious." Harry's eyes didn't waver.

"With all due respect, Harry, how will you run the company if we refuse to do this?" J.T. asked. As often as Gray thought like Harry, J.T.'s thoughts were on the same wavelength as Gray's. "I don't know what Gray, Alex or Justin have going on right now, but I'm in the middle of expansions here in Seattle, in Jansen and at our New Delhi facility. If another architect has to take over my position, it'll be months before he's up to speed. Construction delays alone would cost HuntCom a fortune."

"It wouldn't matter because if the four of you refuse to agree, I'll sell off HuntCom in pieces."

Gray went still, ignoring his vibrating phone. *Sell* HuntCom? Where the hell did that idea come from?

"The New Delhi facility will be history and I'll sell Hurricane Island," Harry warned, his voice edged with steel. The isle was J.T.'s treasured escape and the idea of losing it probably hit J.T. harder than the idea of losing the company.

Then Harry turned his painfully serious gaze on Justin. "I'll sell HuntCom's interest in the Idaho ranch if you don't marry and have a child." Without waiting for a response, he looked at Alex. "I'll shut down the foundation if you refuse to cooperate."

The weight of the brothers' fury filled the room.

Then Harry finally looked at Gray, delivering the only possible remaining blow. "HuntCom won't need a president because there will no longer be a company for you to run."

He was Harry's second in command. Harry had started HuntCom, but Gray *was* HuntCom.

Selling the company itself—the very root of everything they had—was a fine threat. One that Gray wasn't about to let himself believe. He had only to look at Harry's behavior since the heart attack. He'd scaled back only some of his workload since then. To Gray, that looked like plenty of proof that even Harry couldn't part ways all that easily with the company he'd built. He'd never sell.

"But that's insane," Alex said, clearly trying to sound reasonable and not quite making the mark. "What do you hope to accomplish by doing this, Harry?"

"I mean to see you all settled, with a family started before I die. With a decent woman who'll make a good wife and mother."

Gray swallowed an oath. That was rich. In the four marriages that had resulted in the four Hunt brothers, Harry had *never* managed to make one with a decent woman.

"The women you marry have to win Cornelia's approval," their father concluded.

"Does Aunt Cornelia know about this?" Justin demanded. Cornelia Fairchild was the widow of Harry's best friend. Like Gray, Justin obviously found it hard to believe that she was a willing accomplice to Harry's fit of madness.

"Not yet," Harry allowed.

Justin looked relieved. Gray understood why, but he couldn't say that he was as confident that their honorary aunt would have any sway in derailing Harry from his plan. She was more a mother figure to them than their own mothers had been, but that didn't mean her allegiance wouldn't stick with the old man. Cornelia and Harry went *way* back. She, along with her husband, George, and Harry had been friends since childhood.

Harry lifted his hand. "She's a shrewd woman. She'll know if any of the women aren't good wife material."

Too bad she hadn't chosen Harry's wives, Gray thought. Their lives would have been considerably different.

Unaware of Gray's dark thoughts, Harry went on, making the situation even more surreal. "You can't tell the women you're rich, nor that you're my sons. I don't want any fortune hunters in the family. God knows I married enough of them myself. I don't want any of my sons making the mistakes I made."

Then none of them should be courting real disaster by walking down an aisle, Gray thought. Much less trying to pro-create.

Justin was still trying to pin down Harry. "So Aunt Cornelia has to approve our prospective brides *and* they can't know who we are. Is *that* all?"

Harry hesitated long enough to make every nerve at the back of Gray's neck stand at suspicious attention. "That's all. I'll give you some time to think about this," he added into the thick silence.

Not likely, Gray thought, reading his brothers' faces.

"You have until 8:00 p.m., Pacific daylight time, three days from now," Harry continued with an infuriating confidence. "If I don't hear from you to the contrary before then, I'll tell my lawyer to start looking for a buyer for HuntCom."

And with that, he left the library.

J.T.'s lips twisted derisively. "I don't see it happening. He'll never sell HuntCom."

"He can't possibly be serious," Justin concluded.

Gray shrugged into his jacket. Enough time had been wasted at the shack. He hadn't known what to expect when Harry'd called him, but he damn sure hadn't expected this. "We're in the middle of a buyout. There's no way he'd consider selling the company until it's finished and that might be months away. He's bluffing."

"How can you be sure?" Alex asked. He freely eschewed the wealth and privilege that came with being a Hunt, but Gray knew that he tolerated the Hunt duty because it allowed him to satisfy his mile-deep humanitarian streak. He would be happy never to have a Hunt dime—only that would mean he couldn't give it away to someone who did need it. "What if you're wrong? Do you want to take that chance? Lose everything you've worked for over the past eighteen years? I know I sure as hell don't want to see the foundation shut down…or run by someone else."

"The only baby Harry's ever cared about *is* HuntCom," Gray said. "There's no way he won't do what's ultimately best for the company. He always does."

"I sure as hell hope you're right," Justin muttered. "Where did he get the idea it was time we all went hunting for brides?"

J.T. made a face, shaking his head. "Just so we're all agreed. None of us are caving in to his crazy ultimatum?"

"Not in this lifetime," Gray muttered.

For him, it was the end of the discussion.

Chapter One

Ten months later

Find. Wife. Find. Wife. Find. Wife.

Every time the soles of Gray's running shoes bounced against the narrow tree-lined path, the words seemed to echo in his head.

He picked up speed, pushing harder as the path rose sharply beneath his feet.

"Shut. Up. Shut. Up," he muttered under his breath.

Find. Wife. Find. Wife. His footsteps answered.

He made it to the peak of the hillside and looked out over the horizon that would have been nearly obscured if not for the footpath cut through the trees. He propped his hands on his hips, hauling in long breaths, feeling his heartbeat charging in his chest. The sweat soaking his shirt felt cold.

He spent precious time driving most mornings to this particular park because it was far enough away from his digs near the waterfront that he'd never once run into someone he knew.

The park wasn't a fancy place. It didn't have paved paths. It didn't have riding stables, or formal picnic areas or art displays. And often, he seemed to have the hilly tree-congested expanse to himself, but even when he didn't, it was rare to encounter more than one or two other runners.

Pretty much the way he liked it since his time was generally used up dealing with others. That was just one of the prices he paid for being president of a major corporation. A price he'd gladly pay many times over since—according to those who knew him—he'd been aiming for the helm of HuntCom since he was in the womb.

Until lately, Gray had never doubted that he would someday succeed his father as chairman of the board.

Until lately.

He set off down the hillside, oblivious of the slim rim of golden sunshine working its way into a sky that was unusually clear.

Find. Wife. Find. Wife.

He muttered an oath, and picked up speed.

Nearly a year had gone by since Harry called him and his brothers into his library and issued his damn marriage decree. Nearly a year since his brothers—and he, he admitted reluctantly—came to the consensus that they *had* to fall in line with their father's wishes or lose everything that mattered.

Everything. Not that giving in had been easy. Hell, no. In fact, Gray'd had his attorney come up with the flipping contract he and his brothers had all signed—as well as Harry, after some serious arm-twisting of their own—that detailed everything from marital deadlines and requirements of intent to procreate on one side to transfers of HuntCom voting shares on the other. But he'd only done it when it had become clear that Harry was *not* going to come to his senses.

Harry was a literal-minded soul. Not good with relationships of any sort, pretty much. He was more like the early computers he'd once programmed. Want results of X? Then do A. Then do B. Then do C.

He hadn't been successful in his marriages and family life and didn't want his sons ending up like him. So the answer?

Do what Harry hadn't done.

Marry the right woman. Resulting in the right kids. Resulting in an existence unlike Harry's.

Find. Wife. Find. Wife.

Gray gritted his teeth, moving even faster down the sharply curving trail, muscles warm and fluid from years of running, even though his brain felt uncommonly cold and tight. He'd thought that Harry would realize the error of his ways before it came down to the crunch.

But Harry was immovable. And he'd started talking to those in the industry who *could* possibly buy out portions of HuntCom.

Find. Wife. Find. Wife.

Everything that Gray had ever wanted to accomplish in life, he had. He was successful in every endeavor, because that was who he was. What was the point of wasting his time if he *didn't* plan to succeed?

But in this one…damned…thing…he was—

Barreling straight for a runner squatting square in his path.

Cursing a blue streak, he tried slowing up, but momentum had him in its grip. "On the left," he barked, hoping the girl—oh, yeah, definitely a girl—would heed his warning and move to the side. But the path was too narrow and Gray's speed was too fast and maybe if she hadn't decided to straighten from her crouch, he could have hurdled over her—

Instead, he got a glimpse of pale skin, wide dark eyes and flying dark hair as she rose and took the impact with a gasping "oomph!"

He cursed again, reaching to catch her in the same moment that he'd been trying to avoid her, and managed to miss the mark as completely as he'd managed to plow over her.

His shoes skidded on the dirt as he finally succeeded in slowing enough to turn around and run back to her.

She was flat down, sprawled across the rocks that lined the edge of the path.

"I didn't see you."

"Obviously." Her voice was muffled as she gingerly pushed herself to her hands and knees. The gray sweatpants she wore were as utilitarian as the ones he had on, but she'd rolled the waist over a few times and as her rear pushed off the ground, the skin between the nearly threadbare sweats and the hem of the thin T-shirt she wore gleamed smooth and pale in the dawn.

His lips tightened, as much from noticing that band of skin below the white shirt as from her husky sarcasm. "I tried to warn you," he reminded.

She tossed back her head, giving him a severe look that not even the half-light could dim. "If you'd given me more than a microsecond, it might have helped." She drew her knees up farther beneath her, which only caused that shapely derriere to round even more.

He grimaced again, well aware that she was right. "Let me help you up." He closed his hand around her arm and felt her instantaneous recoil. He let go, backing up a step. "Relax. Just trying to help."

"Well…don't. I can do it myself." She ducked her chin, and her hair slid over her shoulder. Muttering under her breath, she finally pushed herself to her feet and faced him, only to sway unsteadily.

His hands shot out and caught her shoulders. "Easy there."

She hitched her shoulder, clearly wanting him to let go again.

Which he did.

She leaned over, plucking at the knees of her sweatpants and he realized they were both torn right through.

"You're hurt."

She gave him a quick "you think?" look that made him grimace all over again. This time at himself.

A preoccupied bastard is what he was.

Just like Harry.

He shoved his fingers through his hair. "Are you parked in the lot?"

"No."

Which could mean anything, he knew, but most likely that she lived within close proximity. "Can you make it to the bottom of the hill?" His cell phone was in his car. It would be a simple matter to call for assistance whether or not she could make it there under her own steam. He'd get her bandaged up, make sure there were no lasting effects that would come back to bite him or HuntCom in the butt, and on their way they'd go.

She nodded and started to move past him, only to gasp again, hitching forward to grab her left knee.

He caught her around the shoulders. "Don't put any weight on it." She'd stiffened again, but this time he ignored it. "If you want to sit, I'll go down and call for help."

"No."

"Then you can let me help you walk down. Your choice." He realized her hands were scraped, as well, when she pressed them gingerly against her thighs, leaving behind a smear of blood. "Something tells me you're not going to let me just carry you down."

Her head ducked again. "That won't be necessary," she assured stiffly.

He eyed the top of her head. The brightening sunlight picked out glints of gold among the soft brown strands. She was a bitty thing next to him, even with the shapely curves that pushed against her running clothes. And he was not bitty at all. "I *am* sorry," he said quietly.

She hesitated, then looked up at him. He couldn't quite tell the color of her eyes. Just that they were dark and rimmed with long, curling lashes.

She pressed her lips together for a moment. "I am, too," she finally said. "I, um, I stopped to tie my shoe." She wiggled her left foot, drawing his attention.

The lacing of her shoe—definitely not custom-made as his own were—lay untied and bedraggled against the dirt path.

"Hold on." He cautiously let go of her shoulders and, once certain that she wasn't going to tip over, crouched down at her feet.

She made a soft sound and he glanced up as he tied the shoelace. "Something wrong?"

She shook her head slightly. "No. It's just…I…it's been a long time since I've had my shoelaces tied for me."

His head was on a level with her thighs. He made himself keep his eyes on her scraped knees and lower. To his chagrin it was harder than he'd have thought.

He tugged the bow tight, then double looped it. "Next time, use a double knot," he suggested wryly.

He rose and caught the twitch at the corner of her lips. But the second she took a step, the barely there smile was replaced by a definite wince of pain.

"We need to get you to the hospital."

Her eyes widened. "No. Really, that's not necessary."

"You might have a sprain. A fracture."

She shook her head emphatically. "Just bumps, I promise."

"Bumps and gravel and blood," he pointed out. "At the very least I need to make sure you get cleaned up, and clearly, you can't walk on that ankle."

She gave him a look he couldn't interpret. "I don't need medical care."

And sad to say, he didn't need a nuisance suit for personal injury, either. Not to say that she'd instigate anything of the kind, but he hadn't gotten to where he was without learning a thing or two about human nature.

People were greedy beings. And though Gray knew he wasn't any particular exception to that trait, he also knew painfully well that the Hunt family and HuntCom made a particularly enticing target even to people who would ordinarily never think such things.

That was reality.

But so was the sight of her bleeding knees that made him wince inside. She *was* hurt and he *was* responsible. She hadn't untied her fraying shoelace on purpose, after all.

"I insist," he told her.

Her eyebrows rose, nearly disappearing into the tendrils of hair clinging to her sweaty forehead. "Is that so?" She seemed about to say more, only to press her lips together again.

"We can work it out when we get you off this path," he suggested. He'd simply call Loretta. She'd arrange everything with her usual minimum of fuss. Gray could be assured that this girl wouldn't suffer any ill effects from their collision and he could get back to the matters at hand.

"You mean you think you'll get your way," the girl murmured. "Once we're off the trail."

He almost smiled. Fact was, Gray nearly always got his way, as she put it. "Do you have something against doctors?"

"Only their bills," she assured, looking a little too solemn for her wry tone. She lifted her shoulder. "I'm in the insurance void and, well, to be honest, I can't afford yet another bill."

"Void?"

"I, um, just started a new job here. My health insurance won't kick in for another few weeks."

All new employees of HuntCom had to wait out their probationary period of ninety days before receiving insurance benefits. Simple business practice, he knew, yet this was the first time he'd ever personally encountered someone in the "void" as she called it. "Where do you work?"

He could feel her withdrawal again like a physical thing. Who'd she think he was, anyway?

The thought had him looking more sharply at her smooth, oval face. There was no question that she was pretty. But she had a wide-eyed earnestness about her that was disconcertingly disarming. "Are you new to the area, too?"

"Pretty much." She swiped her hand over her forehead, leaving her bangs in disheveled spikes, and another smear of blood in its wake.

"Then as a Seattle lifer, I can't have you thinking we're

hogs on the running trails." He put his arm around her again, and this time she didn't protest. He took part of her weight as they laboriously stepped along the path. It would have been much more expedient for him just to tote her entirely, but this time he kept his mouth shut on the reasoning.

"On the left."

He looked over his shoulder at the runner bearing down on them and moved the girl out of the way with plenty of time as the young guy trotted past.

"Worked for him," Gray pointed out.

She gave a soft half laugh, as if she couldn't quite prevent it, even though she wanted to. "He also wasn't going eighty in a thirty-mile zone."

He knew he'd been putting on the speed. Trying to outrun the problem hanging over him. "You should visit the hospital," he said again. "The bill won't be a problem," he assured somewhat drily.

"I suppose you're another one of those guys who made a fortune in the dot-coms or something." She flicked him a glance from beneath those long, soft lashes.

"Or something," he murmured, giving her another measuring look. It wasn't arrogant of him to say that he was somewhat well-known, particularly in the Seattle area. Either she was a master of understatement, or she hadn't recognized him. Once he told her his name, though, she undoubtedly would. "Where'd you say you moved from?"

Her eyebrow arched. "I didn't."

They rounded another curve in the path. It was beginning to level out. Another quarter mile, he knew, and they'd be back at the lot where his BMW was parked. "If you won't let me take you to the hospital, at least let me get you to a clinic. You need some first aid, here. Even you must admit that."

She stopped her laborious limp of a walk and gave him a searching look. "Why are you doing this?"

"That's an odd question."

"Why?"

"I plowed over you."

"Well—" she looked slightly discomfited "—I'm a big girl. I can take care of myself."

"*Big* is a relative term," he countered. "I could fit you in my pocket."

"Or your trunk."

He frowned at the flat statement. "Believe me, honey, you're safe with me."

She looked away again.

"And if you're so wary of strangers, why do you run at this hour of the morning? It's just now getting light and there are hardly *any* people here."

"I fit it in before work." She still sounded stiff. "Why are *you* here at this hour?"

"I fit it in before work," he returned.

Her lips compressed. "Well, there you go, then." She began limping along again, faster this time, but no less awkwardly. "Look, I don't mean to be rude, but I really... well, I really don't need your coddling. And I have things to do before I go to work."

He could see the parking lot. There was only one car.

His.

"You plan to walk back home, then, do you?"

"That's how I got here."

There was no question that she'd decline if he suggested he drive her there. It was an odd position for him. There were people who liked him for who he was, and who didn't for the very same reason. But he'd never once been looked at with such wary distrust by another person.

He didn't know whether to laugh at himself for his own surprise at that, or whether to applaud her caution.

He had a million things on his schedule that day, not least of which was a meeting with Harry about the upcoming release of their latest operating platform. But he couldn't deny his reluctance at letting the girl just walk away.

And not only because of the whispering inside his head that hadn't ceased even when he'd stopped running.

Why else would he have noticed that this woman who didn't seem to know him wore no rings on her slender fingers; showed no evidence of having recently taken any off?

It was expedience that motivated him.

Not the way those wide eyes beckoned. Soft. Deep.

"Can I call someone for you? Your husband? Boyfriend?"

"Don't have one."

He let that settle inside him.

"Since you won't go the doctor route, will you at least let me stock you up with antiseptic and bandages?"

She looked torn, confirming his suspicion that she hadn't been exaggerating about wanting to avoid another bill. Even one so minor as first aid supplies. "It's the least I can do—"

He lifted his brows, waiting.

"Amelia," she provided after a moment. "Amelia White."

Brown, he determined, now that the sunlight was breaking over them in earnest. Her eyes were brown with a mix of golden flecks. "Nice to meet you, Amelia. I'm—" He barely even hesitated, which just proved he was as manipulative as people said. "Matthew. Gray," he tacked on.

"I suppose that's yours." She nodded toward the BMW. "Matthew Gray."

There was denying, and there was denying. "Company car." Could it really be so easy to meet a woman who didn't know who he was?

Thankfully oblivious to the devil inside his head that laughed uproariously at his piqued ego, she made a soft humming sound. "What kind of company?"

"Sales," he improvised.

"Sales must be good." She said it so mildly and seriously he wasn't certain whether he imagined the sarcasm or not.

"They're not bad. Are you going to make me call a cab for you? Never mind. I can see by your expression that I am."

She shrugged a little. "Just yesterday I told my niece, Molly, not to talk to strangers, even when they seem friendly. What kind of example would I be setting if I don't follow my own advice?"

Niece. Not daughter.

"When you put it that way, how can I argue?" He helped her across the lot and she waited, shapely seat propped against the hood of his car while he retrieved his cell phone and called for a cab. It was a salve to his conscience that he actually called information himself to get the number, spoke with the cab company himself. Ordinarily, he would simply have made one call to Loretta and let her deal with the details.

Task accomplished, he joined her at the front of his car. He crossed his arms over his chest and leaned back against the hood. "How old is your niece?"

"Ten." She peered at her scraped palms, slowly picking out small pieces of gravel. "Do you have kids?"

"No." He'd made sure of that. Now it was just one more complication.

Her eyebrows rose, but she said nothing.

"You look surprised."

She shrugged and pressed her palms carefully together. "No. Just most men your age—" She broke off, flushing, when he couldn't contain a snort of laughter.

"You're hell on my ego, Amelia. I don't quite have one foot in the grave yet."

Her cheeks went even pinker, which just made him wonder how long it had been since he'd encountered a female who could still blush. Nobody that he'd dated in the last twenty years, that was for damn sure.

"I didn't mean that," she said, patently lying.

"That I'm old enough to have kids as grown as you?"

She shook her head. "Hardly. Not unless you were *very* precocious."

"How old are you?"

"Old enough." She shot him a look from the corner of her eyes as if realizing how her comment might—just might— come across to a man.

"What's it going to take before you decide I'm not such a stranger?"

She turned her head when they heard a car.

It was the cab, inconveniently and firmly disproving the theory that they took forever to arrive.

"I don't know. I'll have to let you know." She straightened from the car and limped toward the distinctive, yellow taxi.

Gray easily beat her to the cab's door, opening the rear one for her. While she settled herself inside, he leaned in the driver's open window and settled enough cash on the driver to take Amelia to the nearest drugstore and then home— wherever that might be. Then he begged a business card off the guy and wrote his personal cell phone number on the back of it. The only people who had the number were his family, his attorney and Loretta.

He went around to Amelia's side again and handed her the card. "Call me if you need anything. *Anything.*"

She took the card from him, being careful not to brush his fingers.

More stranger-danger, or was it caution of a different nature?

"The driver said he'll stop at the drugstore for you." He handed her the smallest bills he'd had left in his money clip—two fifties. "If this doesn't cover what you need, you call me."

She waved away the cash, looking annoyed. "This *isn't* necessary."

He folded the bills in half and leaned in over her.

She clamped her lips shut, pressing herself solidly back against the seat.

He smiled faintly and deliberately tucked the bills at her hip, right beneath that rolled-over waistband. He ignored the way her skin felt—cool and warm all at once.

And silky.

Definitely silky.

"Believe me, Amelia," he told her softly. "It's *very* necessary."

Then he straightened and closed the cab door, taking her wide-eyed expression with him as he headed toward his own car.

Find. Wife. Find. Wife.

"Maybe," he murmured under his breath and watched the cab slowly turn out of the lot, carrying the blushing Amelia White away.

Of course in his case, finding a wife was only part of his problem. He also needed a child.

Chapter Two

The moment the parking lot was out of sight through the cab's windows, Amelia's shoulders collapsed with relief.

Dumb, dumb, dumb, Amelia, she thought silently. *You had your chance to confront the man in person!*

And what had she done?

Gotten into the cab, alone.

Matthew. She shook her head at the name he'd given her, looking blindly out at the park where she'd been running now for the past several weeks.

What a liar.

Not that she'd expected anything else of the man given his treatment of Daphne.

"Miss, I don't mind driving around until the meter hits the roll your fella gave me—" the gray-haired cabbie shot her a grin over his shoulder "—but it might be easier if you'd just give me your address."

"He's not my fella," she assured, suppressing a shiver. It appalled her that it *was* a shiver, though, and not a shudder.

In the flesh, Grayson Hunt, aka, Matthew Gray, hadn't been quite what she'd expected.

He was supposed to be the devil incarnate. He'd toyed with her sister, only to toss Daphne aside when she'd needed him. To this day he continued to deny the child he and Daphne had created together. Amelia had expected to feel nothing but revulsion for the man who wielded his power like some despot over the lesser beings he used as playthings.

But what she had felt was not so easily defined.

She pressed her hands to her hot cheeks, but winced at even that mild contact against her abraded palms. She lowered them to her lap only to snatch at the money he'd slid beneath her waistband.

How easily he'd dropped the cash on her, even when she'd tried to avoid it.

Too bad he didn't take his other, far more important responsibilities so seriously.

She rolled the bills into a tight cylinder. If she'd ever hoped to make an impression on the great Grayson Hunt that she was a serious adversary, she'd definitely shot that right down into the dust.

Typical, typical Amelia.

She never had been any good at confrontations. Why should she be, when it was ever so much easier to be the world's doormat?

"Miss?" the driver prompted.

She jerked, feeling foolish for letting Grayson Hunt distract her so deeply, and gave the driver the address of Daphne's apartment. She'd moved into it to be with the children when it had become apparent that Daphne would not be returning to her home anytime soon.

"There a pharmacy close by?"

"I'm sorry," she admitted. "I just don't know." The only pharmacy she'd been in was the one at the hospital where Timmy had been born. "There's a corner grocery, though. That ought to do." She didn't often shop at Heller's, because she'd realized right off that the prices were higher than the larger shopping center that took two buses to get to.

The cabbie grunted, whether in agreement or not she didn't know, nor did she particularly care. He was taking her home, and her aching knees were glad of it.

Of course, she ought to know more about the businesses surrounding the apartment, considering she'd been living in Seattle for three months now. But her time had been spent dealing with the disaster of Daphne's life. Disaster caused by none other than Grayson Hunt.

Medical bills. Doctors. Hospitals. Lawyers. The red tape of being named the children's guardian and more red tape. And of course, there were the children to care for.

Jack was twelve and alarmingly self-sufficient given the situation with his mother. Two years younger was Molly, who only spoke in whispers these days. Finally, there was Timmy. Three months old and as sweet and warm as a ray of sunshine, and never once held in the arms of his mother, Daphne.

Amelia stared out the window, weeks beyond tears now. She'd shed plenty in the past few months. First, when she'd stood in the hospital emergency room to hear that her sister had suffered a stroke during labor. Next during the three weeks it had taken before Daphne regained consciousness. It soon became clear that she didn't recognize her own children, much less her only sister. Amelia had cried at night when she knew the children were asleep because for as long as she could remember it had just been her and Daphne against the world.

She ought to have been able to protect Daphne against what had happened.

She should have come to Seattle earlier when Daphne had admitted she'd gotten pregnant during her ill-fated and not-brief-enough affair with Grayson Hunt. Particularly once he'd made it clear to Daphne that he was not going to acknowledge their child.

Amelia had wanted Daphne to take the matter to court, but Daphne wouldn't do so then—and couldn't now.

She could hardly blame her, though, considering the way *they'd* grown up. Their father had only grudgingly acknowledged them because the courts had forced him to pay child support to their mother, not because he'd loved them.

Daphne had grown up always searching for love and the kind of family she'd wished they'd been.

Amelia, on the other hand, had resisted those very same things. Oh, she'd had a marriage planned, certainly. To a man who'd seemed to be on the same career-oriented, nonbaby track that she'd chosen.

"This the grocery store you meant?"

She realized the cab had stopped at the curb alongside the small neighborhood store. "Yes, it is. Thanks. You really will wait?"

"Told your fella I would."

"He's not—" She shook her head, dropping that battle just as she dropped most battles. "I appreciate it."

She reached for the door and laboriously climbed out. Much as she'd have preferred to head straight to the apartment, she knew there wasn't much there in the way of first aid supplies, except plastic bandage strips decorated with Molly's favorite cartoon character and the baby Tylenol that had come home from the hospital with Timmy. And whether or not she wanted to admit it, the only cash she had to her name was tucked in her purse back at the apartment and it had Food for the Children written all over it.

Grayson Hunt had given her more than enough to cover her needs for now and her pride would just have to suffer using it.

Her pride had taken quite a few lumps since she'd moved to Seattle. Priorities in her life had been dramatically reordered to focus on the children. On Daphne's care.

Inside the shop, there was one miserly shelf filled with bandages and ointments. Mindful of the prices that were as ridiculously high as she'd remembered, she selected the bare minimum, and added a loaf of fortified bread and an enormous jar of peanut butter—Jack never seemed to get enough of the stuff. She left the store with her bag and change that would be better used at her usual shopping center.

The cabbie was still waiting, and she must have made a pretty pathetic sight, for he actually met her on the sidewalk to take her purchases from her.

He helped her into the backseat of the cab again, tsking under his breath. "Girls these days," he said. "Taking all kinds of treatment."

Amelia flushed. "I fell while I was running."

He looked skeptical as he closed the door on her and got back behind the wheel. "Your fella rich?"

"He's not my…yes. I guess he's rich." She held the bulging sack on her lap.

The cabbie shrugged. "Lotta rich guys here. You can do better. Find yourself a nice young man that does an honest day's work."

Despite herself, Amelia felt a sharp pang. She'd had a nice young man who did an honest day's work.

He just hadn't wanted to keep *her*. Not when her coworker Pamela had offered more tempting treats.

Passion.

Kids.

She pushed aside the thoughts. John had fallen way down the list of things she needed to be worrying about.

She left the cab a short time later when the driver stopped in front of her building, and she figured there was one bright side to the events of the morning. She obviously didn't have to worry about the cabbie having recognized Grayson Hunt's face. The man would probably have said something if he had.

She pushed through the squeaking door of the building, only to come face-to-face with the Out of Order placard affixed to the center of the dented elevator doors. She'd gotten so used to seeing it that she'd stopped noticing it.

But now, with her entire body feeling like one big, scraped-up bruise, she looked from the inoperable elevator to the narrow staircase on the opposite side of the small vestibule. Sighing, she put her foot on the first step.

Only six more flights to go.

By the time she made it to her floor, her stomach was pitching with nausea and the thin plastic loops of the grocery bag were cutting into her wrist. Three doors down, she stopped and leaned her forehead wearily against the doorjamb. Jack would be waiting inside, she knew. Capably in charge of Molly and the baby, even though Amelia always had her neighbor, Paula, on alert to watch out for the children, too. Not that Jack appreciated that. He considered himself too old for such supervision. She finally lifted her free hand and tapped her knuckles against the woefully thin wood.

Sure enough, Jack must have been waiting and watching through the peephole, because she immediately heard the slide of locks and he yanked the door open almost before she'd stopped knocking.

His eyes, as dark a brown as his mother's and already on a level with Amelia's, took in her disheveled appearance without expression. "What happened?" He didn't comment on the lateness of her return. She was ordinarily back an hour earlier.

"I tripped. I'm fine." It was easier than explaining what had really happened. He just believed that she was an avid runner. Not that she'd been staking out that park, hoping for an opportunity to run into Grayson Hunt.

He stepped back and took the bag when she handed it to him. He looked inside. "Bread's kinda squashed."

"I'll make bread pudding out of the worst of it," she told him. The dessert would be a treat, for once.

Now that she was inside the apartment, she realized how cold she'd gotten outside, and she pulled an aging cardigan off the coatrack by the door and swung it around her shoulders. "Timmy?"

"He's still asleep."

It was a small miracle. The baby had only recently begun sleeping through the night, though she'd have to get him up quickly enough when she went to work. "And Molly? Is she ready for school yet?" Jack was already dressed in his uniform of tan chinos and navy-blue sweater, though his feet were bare.

He shrugged, poking through the items in the bag. "She's still in the bathroom."

Amelia took the gauze pads and antiseptic cream from Jack and headed into the kitchen that opened off to the left of the door.

Her niece and nephew had obviously eaten breakfast, because there were two cereal bowls and spoons sitting in the sink basin, already rinsed. A tall tin of baby formula was on the counter, too, and when she opened the refrigerator door, she saw several prepared bottles stacked neatly inside.

One less task to do. She closed the refrigerator door, eyeing her nephew. "You didn't have to do that. But thanks."

He shrugged again, and hitched his hip onto one of the simple wooden stools that were lined up at the breakfast counter opposite the tiny kitchen. "If you're fine, why're you limping?" He opened the peanut butter and peeled back the protective seal, then lifted the jar, sniffing at it slightly.

"I just scraped my knees. Don't worry about it. Here." She pulled out a spoon and handed it to him. He almost smiled as he took it and dipped it into the pristine contents. With the spoon full, he tucked it in his mouth and fit the lid back on the jar.

Another thing he'd gotten from his mother. The kid loved peanut butter.

"Are you ready for your math test today?" She ran her hands under the faucet, wincing as the warm water hit her scraped palms.

He pulled the spoon out of his mouth. "Gonna fail it, anyway." He leaned over the width of the counter and dropped the silverware into the sink with a clatter.

"Jack—"

"I'll get Mol." He headed through the short hallway that broke off into the hall bathroom and the two bedrooms the apartment possessed before she could deliver the pep talk forming on her lips.

He was back in minutes, Molly trailing in his wake. She wore her school uniform, too, a navy skirt and matching cardigan over her tan blouse. Her long blond hair was brushed and shiny and her eyes—as dark as her brother's—widened when she saw Amelia's appearance.

"I'm fine," Amelia assured hurriedly. Not unnaturally, Molly worried so easily these days. "I tripped over my shoelace." She waggled her foot with the lace that Grayson Hunt had securely tied. "Just like you did the other day in the park."

Molly nibbled her lip for a moment, absorbing that. When she wordlessly held out two bands and a comb, Amelia was relieved. She managed not to wince as she wrapped her fingers around the comb and deftly parted her niece's silky hair. "Ponytails today instead of braids, okay?"

"Okay," Molly whispered.

Amelia finished the simple hairstyle and dropped a kiss on the child's head. "All set."

"Will we visit Mommy today?" Molly's voice never raised above the whisper.

Amelia's heart ached. "After school," she promised. She took the kids at least twice a week to the convalescent center. Daphne, unfortunately, didn't react to their presence when they did visit. She was alert, but her own children might as well be strangers. Amelia looked over Molly's head at Jack. "You two can't wait for me to go to school this morning or you'll be late. You'll be all right catching the bus by yourselves?"

The corner of Jack's lips turned down. "We always did before."

She couldn't help herself. She reached forward and brushed her fingers through the reddish-blond hair falling across his forehead. *Before* meant before Timmy was born, she knew. Before his mother had become incapacitated and the aunt he'd barely known had come to take over. "I know, sweetheart." She smoothed her hand down his cheek even as he was stepping away, too grown at twelve years old to suffer such displays of affection. "And you'll do fine on your math test. Just take your time, Jack."

He made a face. Math was the only subject in which he really struggled. "Get your pack, Mol."

But Molly didn't go for her backpack. Instead, she slipped her hands around Amelia's waist, hugging her tightly. "Are you staying home today?"

Amelia had counted herself fortunate that she'd found a librarian position with the very school that Jack and Molly attended on scholarship. It didn't pay as well as her old job at the university library in Oregon, but her schedule was in sync with the children's. "I'll just be a little late," she assured, and hoped Mr. Nguyen, the headmaster, didn't quibble over the matter. In addition to insurance benefits, she wasn't yet entitled to sick leave, either. "You have your lunch money?"

Molly's head bobbed and she finally let Amelia loose to take the backpack that Jack held out for her. She slid her arms through the loops and followed her brother out the door.

Amelia stood there in the silent apartment for a moment. The furnishings were simple but cheerful, seeming to carry Daphne's personality even after all these weeks without her presence. The beige walls were covered with an eclectic collection of travel posters. Places that Daphne had always dreamed of visiting, but hadn't. The woven blanket tucked over the couch carried the same brilliance, as did the pillows scattered among the two threadbare armchairs.

No, the apartment wasn't fancy. It was an aeon away from the type of digs that Grayson Hunt occupied. The research she'd done about the man over the last three months had told her just how great an aeon. Not only did he have his place at the family home on Lake Washington, but he occupied a stunningly modern penthouse near the waterfront that, according to the spread done in an architectural journal, included a rooftop garden that rivaled a forested park.

Unlike the Hunt's mansion, Daphne's apartment did not possess walls of windows that afforded its occupants the finest views that money could buy. Nor were Daphne's furnishings custom-made by the world's greatest designers, but her sister's apartment *was* a home because Daphne had made it so.

Now, Amelia's sister languished in a facility that provided only the medical care for which she could qualify. Adequate, but definitely basic.

Amelia's knees ached as she crossed the tidy beige carpet and flipped the locks back into place.

If only she'd been able to convince Daphne to bring the kids and go stay with her in Oregon where they'd both grown up.

Everything would be different.

She put Molly's comb away and called the school and her neighbor Paula, who minded Timmy during the day, to let them know she'd be late, then carried the first aid supplies into the bedroom that she shared with the baby and his crib.

Timmy was still sound asleep, his soft lips pursed together, his fists curled. Three months now, Amelia couldn't help but marvel. Three months that had passed in a blink.

She'd cared for the baby since she'd brought him home from the hospital. Without his mother. Three months focusing on everything she'd ever convinced herself she didn't want in this life. Not after the way she and Daphne had grown up.

How quickly a lifetime of belief had spun on its ear. Just because of this tiny, small being.

She chewed the inside of her lip, resisting the urge to touch the sweet boy. Just because she wanted the comfort of cuddling Daphne's baby was no reason to disturb his sound sleep.

If Daphne hadn't left Oregon at all, this beautiful baby wouldn't even exist and there would have been no reason whatsoever for Amelia to take on Grayson Hunt.

Less than an hour later, bandages on her knees hidden beneath her gray slacks, Amelia was handing Timmy and his diaper bag and extra bottles over to Paula Browning. The woman wasn't only their neighbor; she was about the only person Amelia considered a friend in Seattle. She was ten years Amelia's senior, widowed, and her only child was already away at college. If it weren't for Paula, Amelia wasn't quite certain how she would have managed. It was Paula who'd volunteered to watch the children. To mind Timmy during the day, and Amelia had been so far out of her depth, that she'd gratefully accepted. Not only was Paula unfailingly reliable, but she was a font of practical advice about babies.

And on that subject, Amelia had needed all the advice she could get.

Paula's green eyes were nothing if not sharp, though, and there was no hope of her failing to notice the bandages Amelia had taped to her palms as she transferred Timmy to the woman's arms. Timmy's fingers twined around her hair and she worked the strands free, kissing his soft little fist as the other woman took him.

"I figured there must be something wrong for you to be running late," Paula said now, smiling into Timmy's bright eyes. "What happened?"

"I tripped when I was running. Nothing major."

Paula looked knowing. "That's what happens when you run before the sun even comes up." She shook her artfully blond head. "Not like you need the exercise, either. You're even thinner now than when you arrived in Seattle."

Amelia frowned down at herself. She supposed it was true that her clothes hung a little more loosely on her frame these days.

"Any luck spotting the great one, himself?"

Amelia flushed. Before she'd gone into labor, Daphne had confided in Paula about the identity of her child's father. She knew that Amelia's choice of running trails had far more to do with *him* than anything else. "He was there, actually," she admitted. "I couldn't believe it, at first. I've never even spotted him before. And—" She broke off.

Paula's eyebrows rose. "And?"

"And…nothing." Amelia was still kicking herself. "I mean, I *did* nothing." Except get run over by the man, and that truly had been unintentional. Until it had happened, she wasn't even aware that Grayson Hunt was on the trail at all.

And then when he was there—helping her, even—she hadn't told him who she was, hadn't told him that if he didn't come to some terms over his responsibilities, she was going straight to the media.

She had done absolutely nothing.

"Well, at least you know all the interviews you've been poring over for the past month haven't been wasted," Paula consoled.

Grayson hadn't announced to the news outlets that he chose to run in a small, hilly park over an hour away from his waterfront home. That comment had been strictly off-the-cuff, captured only in a live feed moments before he'd addressed the graduating class at MIT over a year earlier. But the close proximity of the park to the restaurant where Daphne had waitressed and met Grayson had been enough reason for Amelia to try her chances there.

Goodness knows her efforts at obtaining a meeting with the man in person had been utterly futile. *Regular* people just couldn't get in to see him without good reason, and she knew the second she mentioned her sister and paternity, she'd be shuffled off to his attorneys. As it was, then, the closest she'd been able to get was an appointment with some underling of his—and that was set for six months down the road.

Amelia didn't have six months.

More importantly, *Daphne* didn't have six months. If her sister's condition was going to improve, it would take a miracle. A miracle by God, or a miracle by money.

Amelia wasn't taking her chances, either way. She went to bed at night praying, and she started her day running in the park on the off chance that she just might encounter him.

And when she had, what had she done besides end up with her nose in the dirt?

Paula watched her. "So what are you going to do now?"

Amelia curled her fingers, feeling the bandages on her palms. It was fine to envision herself tackling Goliath head-on. But she'd never before been good at confrontations, never been good at fighting battles.

That had been Daphne's strong suit, and even *she* had chosen not to fight for her child's rights. If it hadn't been for the way she and Amelia had been raised, that fact would have had Amelia wondering if Daphne could somehow be mistaken. Her sister had never lacked for male company, even though she'd kept her companions away from her children and her home.

But Amelia did remember how it had been for them as children. Both she and Daphne knew what it felt like to be acknowledged by a father *only* because the law had forced it, so it wasn't surprising that Daphne had shied away from forcing that issue herself.

"The only answer I can still think of is to go to the media if he does threaten me with a lawsuit like he threatened Daphne," Amelia admitted.

Paula looked uncertain. "It's pretty rare for anything unflattering about the Hunts to make it into the news."

Which left the gossip rags, they both knew, who'd lap up anything salacious about the wealthy man. "I *hate* the idea. I don't want the world looking at Daphne. Or the children. But I have to do something, Paula. He's my last hope where my sister is concerned. Even the attorney I hired has told me that Daphne's case is at a standstill. She has no health insurance and unless it's privately financed, there is no hope of her receiving the kind of care and therapy that could improve her condition."

"Honey, I hate to say it, but even if you find a way to get her into that rehabilitation institute you found, Daphne might *not* improve. I know it's tragic, but she did have a major stroke the likes of which many people don't even survive."

The doctors—all but one—had claimed the same thing. "She's my sister," Amelia said quietly. "She and the kids are all I have. I have to try."

"Even if it means going against Grayson Hunt? Once that lawyer of his threatened Daphne with that lawsuit when she notified him of her pregnancy, she vowed never to acknowledge his existence again."

How well Amelia knew that. Daphne was a fighter, but she'd had her pride, as well.

"I have to try," she said again.

It was the only thing she could do.

Chapter Three

It wasn't all that easy tracking down Miss Amelia White, Gray learned later that day. Not even for him. It would have been much easier if he'd delegated the task to someone else, but something kept him from doing so.

Stubborn pride, probably.

Hell. His brothers had managed to find wives without calling out the HuntCom dogs to help. The fact that Gray had to force himself *not* to do just that seemed to point out the difference between him and Harry's other sons. They'd all been prepared to sacrifice their HuntCom ties for the women that they'd chosen. Women that they'd—amazingly enough—convinced themselves they'd fallen in love with.

Gray was happy enough for his brothers, even though he figured it was just a matter of time before the happy fog cleared from their heads.

They *were* Harry's sons, after all.

What did any of them know about making a marriage work?

But what Gray did know was that he wouldn't—couldn't—sacrifice HuntCom for anything. He might as well stop breathing. So he'd tackled the task of finding Amelia, himself.

Even though he'd given her his private number, he wasn't going to wait around on the chance that she might phone him. Not when he considered her wariness where he was concerned. It would take a miracle for her to use that number.

And Gray wasn't a big believer in miracles.

Fortunately, the cab company had a record of the address where that particular fare had been dropped. And when money hadn't provided the impetus to release the data, some computer hacking *had*.

Now he sat at his desk in his downtown apartment that evening, his earpiece tucked in his ear, and worked his way down the list of phone numbers assigned to every apartment inside Amelia's building.

Unfortunately, none of the phone numbers belonged to an Amelia White, so it was a matter of calling every number.

Call, after call, after call. "Amelia White, please. Wrong number? Pardon me. Sorry for the interruption."

Most times, he didn't even get to the "pardon me" part.

He recited the next number. "Amelia White, please," he said automatically when the call was answered.

"She's busy right now. Who is this?"

He almost missed it, so accustomed was he to failure. He sat up straighter, eyeing the display on the desk unit of his voice-activated telephone.

The voice that had answered was male. Young. Maybe on the verge of puberty considering the way it seemed to crack.

"This is Gray." He rubbed the bridge of his nose again, stifling an oath. "Matthew Gray," he corrected. "Who is *this?*"

"Jack. What do you want?"

The kid didn't lack nerve, that's for certain. "I want to talk to Amelia."

"What for?"

"Do you always give her callers the third degree?"

"My aunt doesn't *have* callers," the boy returned.

Aunt. The nugget of information made Gray smile. So Amelia had a niece *and* a nephew. "I'm calling to see how she's feeling after her tumble in the park this morning."

"How do you know about that?"

"I was there."

The boy sighed a little. "She's in the bathtub," he supplied grudgingly.

Every nerve inside of Gray tightened at the image that immediately jumped into his head of Amelia's curves glistening with water.

Was she a bubble bath kind of girl?

Or was she strictly in it for the Epsom salts route, given the way he'd plowed into her?

He pinched his eyes shut. What the hell was wrong with him? He'd never lacked for feminine company when he wanted it, but his reaction was more like a man who'd gone hungry for it for about a decade too long.

"Could you tell her I'm on the phone?" Decency should have had him leaving a message with the boy, but Gray didn't have time to pussyfoot around with the good manners his all-about-appearances mother had tried to drill into him during their infrequent visits. Besides, he didn't expect that Amelia would return his call.

"Yeah. I guess. Hold on." A clatter blasted through Gray's earpiece and he winced, pulling it off even as he hit the speaker on the desk unit and waited.

"H-hello?"

For some reason, she sounded even younger when she finally came on the phone line. "How're the knees?"

She exhaled softly. In his mind's eye, he saw the soft purse of her lips, the sweep of her lashes hiding her brown eyes from him. "Sore. I was, um, soaking them."

And everything else. "Epsom salts?"

"I...what? Oh. No, I don't have any of that."

"Should have picked some up when you stocked up on bandages. Good for taking the pain out of sore muscles and stuff."

"I have heard of it," she said, sounding slightly affronted. "And you seem awfully certain that I did stock up on bandages. Maybe I used your money for—oh, I don't know—a manicure."

He was reasonably confident that she hadn't. Her slender fingers had been entirely natural, the nails trimmed short and neat. The women he knew paid ridiculous sums to keep their hands looking unnaturally natural. "Did you?"

She sighed a little. "Not exactly. How did you find this number, anyway?" Her voice was suspicious.

He glanced at the list. The phone number belonged to some woman named Mason. The mother of the niece and nephew? "I've called nearly every number listed for your building."

"And you knew which building, because—"

"Because the cab company said that's where you were dropped."

She was silent for a moment as if she were trying to figure him out. "Why would you go to such trouble, Mr. Gray?"

"Matt."

"Fine." Her voice sounded suddenly tight. "Matt."

"Because I'm that kind of guy."

Her silence was loud.

He tried again. "Because I've thought about you all day." There was more truth than he liked in the admission.

"I can't imagine why."

"There is the small matter of your bloodied knees and hands," he reminded. "How old is your nephew?"

"Jack?" Her soft voice lifted again with suspicion. "Why?"

"Because I'm curious. You mentioned your niece. Didn't mention a nephew."

"He's twelve," she supplied. "Look, I really have to be going."

"Bathwater getting cold?" Evidently he was developing a masochistic streak. Why else punish himself with the vision of her delicately placing one foot into the tub, followed by the other. Steamy water lapping at her calves, then her thighs as she lowered herself. Sank back against the side, water climbing higher, tickling the base of her throat, the point of her slightly triangular chin.

"If you must know, yes, it *is* getting cold."

He eyed the speakerphone, as if he could see her face, instead. "Did you think about me today?"

Silence reigned again, broken only by the background noise of that tinny television. "You have no idea," she finally answered.

"Don't sound so solemn."

She made a soft sound. He couldn't tell if it was annoyance or something else. "Look, Mr. Gray. Matt. I…I appreciate your efforts in making certain that I'm okay, but I think it's best if we just—"

A sound broke out that made the hair on Gray's nape stand on end.

A baby's cry.

"That's a baby." He stated the obvious. Another nephew? Or hers? She'd said she wasn't married. But women had babies all the time these days without benefit of marriage.

"My nephew," she said. "Timmy. And I have to see to him, as you can plainly hear."

"Are you playing babysitter or something?" he asked, speaking a little more loudly to be heard above the wail that was drawing closer to the telephone.

Either she'd gone to pick up the baby, or someone had brought the baby to her. Jack, maybe. Or the other one. Molly.

"Or something." Her voice was short. "I'm watching them for my sister. This is their place." She neatly satisfied Gray's speculation. "He's three months old," she said suddenly.

What he knew about babies would fit on the head of a pin and his ignorance hadn't been without design. "Sounds like he's got a healthy set of lungs."

"He's hungry."

"What about you? Have dinner with me tomorrow."

She made a strangled sound that not even the baby's crying could disguise. "I'm sorry, Mr....Matt. I have to go now."

The crying was cut off midwail to be replaced by the soft buzz of the dial tone.

Dammit.

He jabbed the phone with his finger and the dial tone went silent. He pushed at his desk, his chair swiveling around to face the windows behind him. But he didn't see beyond his own frustrated reflection, glaring back at him.

Smooth, Gray. Really smooth. He hadn't been turned down so flatly, so abruptly, in well…ever.

His phone buzzed softly and he glanced at the caller ID. He grimaced and jabbed the speaker. "What's up, Marissa?"

"Hello to you, too," his attorney drawled, sounding amused. "You're sounding rather tense, darling. Anything I can do to help?"

If only it were that simple. Marissa Matthews was a beautiful, leggy redhead who'd make the perfect wife for him. Independent, never demanding, perfectly accustomed to the requirements of being a Hunt. If he could have made a bargain with her to become his wife, he would have. Only she already knew who he was; and had made it plain all the way back when they were in school together that she'd be happy to marry *only* money.

"Not this time," Gray told her. "You get the paperwork from Birchman signed?"

"Not yet. But don't worry. I will. He's got no choice. He either sells his little operation to HuntCom at a very tidy sum, or he goes under. It's a slam dunk. You made sure of that, remember?"

He had. Tying up every possible venue for Edward Birchman to market his so far barely noticed software.

It was something Gray was good at. HuntCom hired the best developers in the world as a general rule, but Gray still kept his eye on what was going on outside of HuntCom walls. And when he spotted something that was going to be good, going to be big, he usually managed one way or another to bring it into the fold.

To everyone's profit, except HuntCom competitors.

"That's not why I called, though," Marissa said. "Unless you went out and purchased a yacht this afternoon—when I know you were supposed to be meeting with your father—I'm afraid that Gerry's up to his tricks again."

Gray grimaced. Gerry Dunleavy was Gray's half brother on his mother's side. Christina had married two more times after she'd been given the boot by Harry when Gray was still a tot. She'd only produced one other child, though, Gerry, from husband number three. And considering old Dunleavy was a contemporary of Moses when he'd married Christina, that was pretty much a medical miracle.

Gerry was ten years younger than Gray, and a royal pain in his backside given his proclivity for using Gray's name whenever it suited his purposes. And one of Marissa's tasks in life for Gray—for which he paid her handsomely—was to keep on top of Gerry's activities *and* keep him out of the news.

Personally, Gray avoided dealing with Gerry himself. Not hard, since they detested one another. He simply didn't want Gerry's behavior to reflect poorly on HuntCom.

"What the hell does Gerry need with a yacht? Christina's already got one courtesy of Daddy Dunleavy. He left it to her in his will." And Lord knew there was nothing that Christina ever denied Gerry.

Of course she conveniently left it to Gray to clean up whatever messes resulted from that particular habit.

"I guess a three-year-old yacht isn't good enough for Gerry. How do you want me to handle it?"

He'd like to launch Gerry off the nearest pier and never see his hide again.

There was no affection lost between them. As it was, Gray saw their mother only when he absolutely couldn't avoid it. But Gerry was fully aware that Gray didn't want their family laundry aired in public, despite the distance between them.

Not when there was already enough Hunt family business bandied about. "How much did he spend?"

Marissa told him.

Gray winced. "If I'm buying it, find out where he's planning to dock it, and make damn sure it's insured." The last time Gerry had acquired something in Gray's name, it had been a sports car that he'd totaled within hours of driving it off the lot, and they hadn't been so quick.

The only miracle was that Gerry hadn't hurt anyone. Not even himself.

The roadside diner down near Portland that he'd slammed into, however, had gotten itself rebuilt, bigger and better than ever, courtesy of a quiet meeting that Marissa had arranged with the owners within hours of the accident. Gray had been out of the country, but Marissa had acted promptly. Gerry hadn't even turned a hair when Gray had later laid into him for his carelessness. The expense of it all was covered from Gray's personal account, and Gerry had been happy to remind Gray that he'd never even miss the chunk.

It was true, but that had hardly been the point.

"Look at the bright side," Marissa said. "It's been an entire year since Gerry pulled a stunt like this."

"Yeah. A year when I'd stupidly let myself think he'd outgrown being jealous of me."

"Darling, I hate to tell you, but that is never going to happen. Gerry had the misfortune of being born well after Christina ceased being your father's wife. Old Dunleavy left her perfectly well-off, but it was peanuts compared to what you've got as a Hunt."

What he would keep as a Hunt only if he solved his wife and child dilemma, Gray amended silently.

Justin, J.T. and Alex had all held up their ends of the bargain. But if Gray failed now, they'd *all* lose. His brothers, his new sisters-in-law and scores of HuntCom employees who depended on the company for their livelihood. "Thanks for keeping on top of it, Marissa."

"It's what you pay me for," she said smoothly. "I'm having breakfast with Birchman tomorrow. I should have the papers on your desk by nine." She rang off without fanfare.

Despite that positive assurance, the results of the evening had definitely left a sour taste in his mouth.

He still had several reports to read in preparation for the following morning, but he had no patience for them just then.

He dragged the list of telephone numbers in front of him and studied the name that he'd circled.

Daphne Mason. The name on the phone listing.

One call to Marissa and he knew she could have a dossier on his desk within twenty-four hours that would tell him everything he ever wanted—and didn't want—to know about Amelia White and her sister, presumably Daphne Mason.

He drummed his fingers on the desktop. Turned to his computer and ran a search on both women's names, coming up with a plethora of useless matches from nuns to rock singers.

He pulled out his cell phone and hit J.T.'s number, only receiving his brother's voice mail in response. He disconnected without leaving a message.

What would he have said?

He'd put off toeing Harry's line for so damn long, that he had them all in danger of losing everything they'd ever worked for.

The phone vibrated in his palm. "Figured you were playing newlywed with your bride," he answered.

"I beg your pardon?"

The voice was female. Smooth. Lilting.

Definitely *not* J.T.

"Amelia." There was no baby crying in the background this time. No television that he could hear. No other voices at all—childish or adult. "Sorry about that. I thought you were my brother."

"Oh. Well, I—"

"I didn't mean to scare you off earlier. About dinner."

"You didn't."

She was a poor liar. He could hear it in her voice. And now that she'd called, he was going to make darn sure not to take another misstep. "Okay. What can I do for you?"

She hesitated so long he wasn't sure she was going to answer. And then, when she did answer, it was in one heck of a rush. "Wecouldmeetforcoffee."

Fortunately, he was a native Seattleite. Coffee flowed in his veins, and he understood any sentence containing that magic word just fine. "Sure. Sounds good." Better than good, if his lightening mood was any indication. "You said you're new to the area. Do you have a place in mind?" He'd prefer to name the place so that he could pick the setting and be assured that nobody would blow his cover. But he was treading carefully—an act that did not come naturally to him.

She named a coffeehouse that he'd never heard of, though, taking the decision out of his hands. "It's near the running park," she told him, "The, um, the day after tomorrow? Around seven? In the morning, I mean," she added hurriedly.

He didn't have to guess hard to tell that she was not in the habit of asking men to meet her. Not when she was practically tripping over her words in the process. "Perfect."

She hesitated again. "Really? You won't be running at that hour or something?"

He didn't bother reminding her that it had been well before 7:00 a.m. when he'd tripped over her on the running path. Nor did he have to look at his calendar to know that two days from now, he had a breakfast meeting at five, followed by departmental meetings starting at exactly seven. "Really," he assured her. "Seven is ideal."

In this instance, everyone else would have to work their schedules around his.

"Okay then. I'll…I'll see you then. Matt."

He looked out the window again, seeing his reflection and the faint smile playing around his lips. "I'm looking forward to it. Amelia."

The fact that the words were true wasn't something he was going to delve into too deeply.

Chapter Four

By the time she was to meet Grayson Hunt at Between the Bean, Amelia had worked out in her head a dozen times over exactly what she would say to the man.

The first, being that she knew just exactly who he was.

The second, that she was Daphne's sister and well aware of his threatened lawsuit against her if she hadn't dropped her claims about Timmy.

There were many things that Amelia wasn't good at, and lying topped every list, so it was definitely time to stop it.

Unfortunately, second runner-up to things that Amelia was not good at were confrontations.

If only Jack hadn't been within earshot. She could have gotten everything out within the safety of a non-face-to-face telephone call.

And would probably have had the man hang up on her the second she'd done so.

Face-to-face was definitely a better option, no matter how uncomfortable it made her.

She'd failed plenty of times in her thirty years, but not this time.

"Not this time," she repeated under her breath as she paid for two tall coffees and two oversize cranberry muffins.

Armed in her favorite iron-gray suit with her hair smoothed back in a sleek knot, at least she felt far more herself than she had wearing the running togs of Daphne's that she'd been borrowing. On top of that, she'd arrived a full twenty minutes early only to find herself too nervous to sit still at the little round corner table that she'd procured in the bustling shop. There were a few umbrella-topped tables on the sidewalk outside the coffeehouse, but rain or shine, Amelia had yet to see them ever empty.

So she'd waited in the line that waxed and waned, sometimes snaking out the door, and gone ahead and ordered for them both.

The purple-haired girl at the counter made no comment as Amelia counted out change to pay for her order. After several visits of Amelia's since she'd discovered the place, the clerk—Suki—had gotten used to Amelia's coin method. "You extra hungry today?" Suki dropped the change in the aging cash register and added several napkins to the thin cardboard box containing the muffins.

"I'm meeting someone."

"A man?"

Amelia carefully balanced the cups and the cardboard container. "Yes."

Suki's brows shot up, disappearing beneath her spiky bangs. "Well, you go, girl."

Not knowing whether to laugh or be insulted, Amelia started to head back to the table. Only her feet stopped dead still at the sight of Grayson Hunt turning his wide shoulders slightly as he entered the narrow doorway.

His sharp gaze spotted her immediately—not hard considering the miniscule dimensions of the shop—and she swallowed past the hard knot that formed in her throat.

She'd come armed in a suit, while he'd donned a loud crimson-and-lime Hawaiian-print shirt that hung loose over well-worn blue jeans. A Seahawks ball cap was pulled close over his forehead.

To shield his looks? Or protect that thick brownish-blond hair of his from the rain?

All the things she'd heard and read about the man told her that last was pretty unlikely.

But then, so were the jeans. In all the articles she'd seen about him, all the photos she'd amassed, all the arcane video sound bites she'd unearthed, she'd never once seen the man photographed wearing such casual attire.

Pity, a devilish brain cell noted.

The man, devil or not, looked seriously good in jeans.

He reached her in two steps, and his hands—seeming as long and lanky as the rest of him—took the coffees from her. "Morning. You look different."

"I don't wear sweats to work," she pointed out and nearly winced at the way her voice sounded breathless. She cleared her throat. "I saved that table over there. The one with the satchel on top."

He looked over his shoulder and nodded, setting off ahead

of her and cutting a swath for her to pass through the line that had stretched out the doorway all over again. She followed and with her hand freed, wrapped it around the cardboard container.

It had to be nerves causing the tingling from where his fingers had grazed hers. It *had* to be.

Not even her fiancé had caused sensations like that when he'd touched her. Not that there had been a whole lot of touching going on between John and Amelia. He'd been more interested in touching Pamela.

She'd seen that with her own eyes.

She moistened her lips and set the muffins on the table, pulling her briefcase off the chair and setting it on the floor. She realized with a start that Grayson wasn't taking the chair closest to the window—he was standing there, holding it out for her.

That knot was back in her throat again, threatening to choke her. She managed a smile and slipped into the seat, painfully aware of their proximity as she did so.

Even above the pervasively aromatic scent of coffee, she could smell him. Not piney. Definitely not flowery. Indefinable, almost. But fresh. Clean.

Memorable.

She ducked her chin, busying herself with separating the napkins as he brushed past her to take the other seat.

Devils weren't supposed to smell as good as he did.

"Are you on your way to work?" she asked, striving for a calm tone.

"I have some meetings later on." He slid the molded plastic lid from the top of his cup and lifted it, heedless of the steam. His eyes narrowed a little as he took a steady sip, which only seemed to make their blue-green color more pronounced between his black, spiky lashes.

"I, um, I should have waited until you got here to order. I just know what the lines are like, here. Pretty crazy sometimes. But you might have preferred something other than regular coffee."

His lips twisted slightly. "Like one of those?" He nodded toward a bearded guy departing with a cup overflowing with whipped topping. "I'm more of a purist." He set down his cup and took the enormous muffin she held out for him, looking slightly surprised as he broke it open. "Cranberry?"

She nodded, tearing her own muffin in half, then quarters. "It's a nice change from blueberry or bran." And she'd automatically ordered it, never thinking about the fact that she'd learned of his penchant for the things in a sound bite he'd given during a breast cancer run.

Just tell him, Amelia. Get it all out, so the threatening can begin.

She pulled off the cover of her own coffee and took too hasty a sip. She gasped as the heat singed her tongue and she exhaled. "Oh. Wow. I ought to know better."

He made a soft sound, was gone from the table and back again with a cup of water before she'd stopped blinking back the tears that stung her eyes. "Here." He folded her fingers around the cup.

She wanted to stick her tongue out and let it soak in the cool water, but since she was no longer three years old, that hardly seemed appropriate.

She drank slowly, letting the stinging in her tongue abate as she eyed him across the table. How could a man be as solicitous as he'd seemed to be—not just now, but when he'd nearly run over her—and be so callous where his own child was concerned?

She finally lowered the cup. "You probably think I'm accident prone or something."

He grinned, looking suddenly younger and even more approachable, and the sight made her catch her breath just as surely as the hot coffee had. "Maybe I like rescuing you," he drawled.

She smiled weakly. Picked at her muffin, doing more spreading of crumbs than anything.

"Not that you let me do much in the way of rescuing," he went on. He caught one of her hands in his, startling her, and made a deep sound low in his throat as he turned her palm upward, gently spreading her fingers flat. He touched the scrapes that had begun healing over. "Such soft skin to be collecting scrapes." He didn't release her hand as his gaze lifted to hers. "And your knees? Probably still sore, I'll bet."

She curled her fingers, as if to protect her palms from the warmth of his hand on hers, but only succeeded in folding them over his.

As if they were holding hands.

She yanked her hand away, tucking it in her lap. She cleared her throat. She'd always believed that running really wasn't her particular cup of tea. She was more a swimming kind of person. But the activity *had* been growing on her. "I'll admit that I haven't been out running just yet."

"I can believe that." He picked up the remaining portion of his muffin and polished off half of it in a single bite. "Do I make you nervous, Amelia?" His voice was low. Surprisingly gentle.

She flushed. "Of course not."

"You're doing more shredding than eating of that muffin."

There was no denying the truth of that particular observation. She'd spread crumbs well beyond the borders of the napkin that she'd opened out like a plate.

She delicately brushed her fingertips together, giving up the pretense of eating. "I'm not as hungry as I thought I'd be. Would you, um, like another muffin?" The man easily topped six feet, and though he had a lean body, his shoulders were still massively wide.

He didn't look away from her. "I'm good, thanks."

Good?

Anxiety oozed through her bloodstream.

Now, Amelia. Tell him, now.

She could feel perspiration sprouting from her temples. Words jammed beneath her lips.

"What kind of work do you do, Amelia?" His deep voice was still easy. Probably meant to be soothing. He reached across the table for the portion of muffin she hadn't mutilated. "Do you mind?"

"I know who you are," she blurted.

He merely plucked the muffin from her napkin and began peeling off the paper wrapping still stuck to the side of it. "What about family? Other than your sister and her kids, I mean. Parents?"

Feeling utterly ineffectual in the face of his nonreaction, she sat there, staring at him. "Mr.—"

"Matt," he supplied smoothly. "Remember?"

Her lips tightened. He polished off the muffin. *Her* muffin. Even if she hadn't been eating it.

Oblivious to her squirming discomfort, or uncaring about it, he continued in that smooth, deep voice. "I don't have any sisters. Just brothers. Half brothers, to be accurate. I have an honorary aunt with four daughters. Probably around your age. They're the closest thing to cousins that I've got."

"It's just my sister and her children," she managed

faintly. She was completely out of her depth. "Did you hear what I said?"

"I don't believe I've suffered a hearing loss in the past ten minutes. So, work, Amelia. What do you do that has you covering yourself practically from head to toe in gray wool?"

"I'm a librarian." The words emerged despite her painfully clenched jaw.

"Where?"

"Brandlebury Academy." And time was ticking, and she had to be there to start her day. Two instances of tardiness in one week were more than the headmaster would like.

"The librarians I remember from my school days were all middle-aged battle-axes with fierce tempers. If they'd been more like you, I might have spent more time reading. Brandlebury has a good reputation."

"So that means I shouldn't be working there?"

A whiff of surprise flitted over his carved features. "Did I say anything remotely like that?"

"No." There'd been plenty of parents at Brandlebury who hadn't been thrilled that the children of a cocktail waitress had been admitted there. But that's what scholarships were for, and Daphne had worked hard with Jack and Molly to earn them. She'd wanted the best for her children.

Amelia's sister just hadn't been willing to beard Grayson Hunt in his den to get that for Timmy. Not when she'd been determined and able to raise him without interference from the baby's uncaring father.

"Will you have lunch with me?"

Amelia's lips parted. The man had the gall of a hundred. Or maybe it was just sheer arrogance. "Why are you doing this? Is this some sort of game for you?"

"Chasing a pretty girl isn't that strange a game. How old are you?"

Never before had she felt any sympathy for Alice falling down the rabbit hole, but she did now.

She was thoroughly unnerved. Thoroughly confused. Which only annoyed her more.

The man was being deliberately obtuse. He *had* to be.

"I'm almost thirty-one. And *no*, I most certainly won't have lunch with you." She snatched up her coffee cup, only to set it down again without drinking. "Don't you have anything to say?"

"Thirty. I wouldn't have guessed. You look younger."

If that was supposed to be a compliment, it didn't feel like one. She wasn't sad to be thirty. But she'd thought by the time she reached that age, her life might be somewhat different.

For one thing, she and John should have been married for nearly a year.

"I suppose you prefer them that way." Though Amelia was two years younger than Daphne, she'd always taken the "big sister" role to her lively, gregarious sister. Maybe Daphne's age had had something to do with Grayson Hunt dumping her long before she'd learned he'd left her pregnant.

His lashes narrowed slightly. "Prefer who? Women?"

"Unless you like men, as well."

"Only as opponents at the poker table." He looked amused. "Women tend to be a distraction."

She leaned closer to the table. "Is that what Daphne was, Mr. Hunt? A distraction?"

He didn't lean forward. If anything, he seemed to lounge even more comfortably in his chair, despite the fact that the back of it was undoubtedly cut too low and too narrow to be particularly accommodating for his size. "Why would your sister be a distraction?"

She practically vibrated off her seat, so deep was her agitation. "You can drop the pretense, *Matt*. Even if I hadn't done my research where you're concerned, I'd still know all about you. And *you* know Daphne."

His expression didn't really change. But the gentle demeanor he'd portrayed up until then went suddenly missing.

Unease sliced through her.

This was the man who could buy and sell small countries if he chose to.

What hope did she have of keeping Timmy out of his clutches if he snapped his fingers otherwise?

What hope did Daphne have of any sort of recovery if Amelia didn't do everything she could to gain his cooperation?

Gray watched the parade of expressions crossing Amelia's pale face. Anger. Fear. Distress.

He didn't have to search his memory banks for references to her sister, Daphne Mason. Not when the first time he'd ever seen the name had been on the telephone list he'd obtained for the building where he'd tracked Amelia.

Which left the question remaining of why she should think her sister would have meaning—as a distraction, no less—to him.

The smart thing would be to cut his losses and move on. She was off her bean.

He'd invested no more time in Amelia White of the golden-flecked eyes and shapely limbs that were thoroughly disguised in that ugly suit than those hours of phone calls.

He needed a wife. Not another woman bearing her own agenda.

Which didn't explain why Gray didn't simply bid her goodbye and leave the cramped coffeehouse, *and* Amelia, behind. "There's a reason for that. For Matt."

Her lips tightened. "I'm not interested in your reasons, Mr. Hunt."

He looked past her, catching the glances that turned their way at her emphatic statement. "Keep your voice down," he said mildly, looking back at Amelia.

She looked incensed.

"I don't know about you, but I don't want to draw attention." He kept his voice low, a half smile on his lips. "Last time I had dinner with a woman in public, a half-dozen people started snapping pictures of us with their cell phones." One photograph, even off center and blurry, had made the morning paper. And the dinner date—a perfectly nice woman with political aspirations—had refused to have dinner, much less dessert or anything else, with him.

He'd hardly been brokenhearted.

That would take more of a heart than he possessed.

But if the same thing happened now, with Amelia, any hope of convincing Harry—much less Cornelia—that she was unaware of his real identity would be irrevocably lost.

"You don't like your personal life in the news." Amelia's voice was low. Practically shaking.

"Most sane people don't. Fortunately, I have an entire staff at hand to ensure my privacy." One guy in line was busier watching them than the line that was moving well ahead of him. Gray pushed back his chair. "Let's take this outside."

He left her no choice but to follow him, since he walked out carrying her briefcase.

The rain was little more than a drizzle, and it seemed to

bother her no more than it did him, when he finally stopped, several yards away from the umbrella-covered tables clustered around the outside of the coffee place.

She snatched the briefcase from him, looping the long shoulder strap over her shoulder and hugging the slightly battered black leather case protectively against her stomach. Moisture began collecting on her severe hairstyle, little pinpoints of shine among the dark strands.

"Are you married?" he asked bluntly. "And don't bother prevaricating. I can find out the truth if I choose. *Research* is right up my attorney's alley."

Her lips parted. "What does my being married have to do with anything?"

"*Are* you?"

Atop the briefcase, she curled one hand over her other. "No, I already told you I'm not married." Her soft voice was emphatic.

"Ever?"

"Never," she returned evenly, obviously annoyed with the subject.

"Fiancé? Boyfriend?"

Rosy color flagged her cheeks and her brown eyes looked fit to snap. "No." Her lips barely moved as the word passed the pearly white teeth he could see clenched together.

"Good." He wanted as few entanglements as possible. "Then we have plenty to discuss."

"Yes, we do," she agreed. "Plenty. And I won't be put off like Daphne."

"What is the deal you've got with your sister?"

She glared at him. "I suppose you sleep with so many cocktail waitresses that you can't be bothered to remember their names."

He let out a laugh, so absurd was the idea. "What? *Cocktail* waitresses? Where the hell did you get that idea?"

"From Daphne," she enunciated carefully.

His amusement dried up. As usual, his judgment where women was concerned was about as good as Harry's.

He should have known that the world wasn't going to toss down a suitable wife for him just because he was against a wall.

"So. What scam are you two running? Or is there even a Daphne at all?" He ignored the cell phone vibrating in his pocket. "Make it good, babe, because I can promise you that you won't get another pass at it." He should have gone with his first instinct to have Marissa run a check on her. It would have saved him the trouble.

Amelia leaned closer, managing to look down her nose at him despite being close to a foot shorter. "You know perfectly well that there is no scam. You used Daphne while it suited you and dropped her when it didn't. A-and if you don't help her now, there's going to be more people wanting to catch your picture on their cell phones than you ever dreamed of. There won't be any peace for you. I promise you that."

"You know, I've encountered my share of crazies, but you take the cake. I actually thought you were the vulnerable type. Shy. Not too certain of herself. Do you practice that act in the mirror, or does it just come naturally to you?"

She was visibly shaking. "You…insufferable…pig."

"Maybe," he agreed, more angry than he ought to have been. He'd learned long ago that his family was a natural target for all manner of cheats. Since then he'd made damn sure not to fall into their traps again.

More importantly, he'd made damn sure not to let anyone come close enough to even set one.

"But I don't throw around useless threats based on fiction," he continued, his voice hard. "Until I met you I'd never even heard the name Daphne, much less slept with a cocktail waitress."

"There's nothing wrong with being a cocktail waitress," she defended hotly.

"Well, trust me on this, honey. It's not my style. I like women who are a challenge to my brain as much as a challenge to my bed, and I haven't met a cocktail waitress yet who'd fit that bill. Now, if you really want to bandy threats around, using the media isn't the way to go. Haven't you heard? When it comes to the Hunt family and HuntCom, there's no such thing as bad publicity."

There were tears in her eyes, turning the gold flecks to green. "Are you sure about that, Mr. Hunt? Maybe the good people of this city won't hold you so dear to their hearts when they learn how you've denied your own child."

Chapter Five

Gray's head snapped back as if she'd hit him in the face with her briefcase.

But he recovered fast.

His hand shot out, wrapping around her upper arm. Tight. "I don't like people threatening me with crap, Amelia."

She pulled at her arm, but he held her fast. "And I don't like people manhandling me." The words snapped back at him as if it were someone else issuing them. "Let me *go*."

"Not until I'm good and ready." His long legs ate up the distance as he hustled her along the sidewalk. "And don't even think about calling for help." He forestalled her just as she opened her mouth to yell. "Or I'll have you tied up in such legal restraints you'll wish you'd never had the brilliant idea of taking me on. I don't take kindly to threats of blackmail. Neither does our legal system."

"Fine with me," she assured, hating the tears that clogged her throat, thickened her voice. "Then it will all become public for certain. How the magnanimous president of HuntCom threatened to ruin a single mother when she dared to ask him to acknowledge the baby they'd conceived together." She winced when his hold on her arm tightened even more.

"The only conceptions I participate in are of the business variety." He finally stopped on the sidewalk, alongside the BMW she remembered so easily from the other morning. "Your research should have been more comprehensive, Amelia. Tests disprove paternity as often as they prove it. And my attorney is well practiced in the art of deflecting the inevitable claims that have come my way. So much so, in fact, that she doesn't even bother me with the details anymore."

He didn't have to elaborate. Was that the case where Daphne was concerned? So unimportant that his attorney didn't even consult him on the matter?

"I'll bet there are claims," she muttered. "From plenty of women."

"Am I supposed to be a monk?" His gaze raked contemptuously down her form. "I'm forty-two years old, honey. I don't have to apologize for not being one."

"You do when you ignore the consequences of your own behavior!"

He pulled his car key out, punching the security button and she heard the soft snick of the door locks disengaging. He leaned down and yanked open the passenger door. "Get in."

"I'm not going anywhere with you."

He pulled the strap of her briefcase from her shoulder and tossed the thing inside before she could scrabble for it. "Get *in*."

"It's no wonder Daphne gave up on you. No woman in her

right mind would put up with— Oh!" She gaped at him when he lifted her off her heels and pushed her into the seat. Her skirt rode up her knees as she scrambled, inelegantly, to right herself against the butter-soft leather seat. "This is…is kidnapping!"

He shut the door on her accusation and rounded the car, climbing behind the wheel before she could even find the interior door latch. The locks softly engaged the moment before her frantic hands found the handle.

She pounded the window, fear climbing inside her. What did she *really* know about Grayson Hunt, after all? The man was a callous excuse for a human being, but was he anything worse?

"Be quiet," he said evenly. He made no attempt to start the vehicle. Just sat there in the luxurious confines, his narrowed gaze on her face.

Her jaws hurt from clenching her teeth so tightly. How credible an adversary would she appear if he could see the way her teeth wanted to chatter together? "There are p-people expecting me. Who know that I was m-meeting you."

He let out a short, exasperated snort. "What are you afraid I'm going to do with you, Amelia? Put you in my *trunk?*" The reference to her words in the park the other morning was pointed. "I don't have to resort to violence to get rid of nuisances."

"And that's all Daphne was. A nuisance."

"That's what *you* are," he said flatly. "It was all planned, wasn't it? Somewhere your research turned up where I like to run. And it was just a matter of you staking out the park and waiting. Should have let me call an ambulance or take you to the hospital, honey. You'd at least be able to claim some personal injury and hope for a small settlement from me. Nothing significant, mind you." He looked her over again. "But at least enough to buy a suit that didn't resemble a nun's habit."

"I didn't expect you to run over me on that running trail and *I* don't want anything from you."

He gave a bark of laughter that was completely devoid of amusement. "No kidding. You're doing a helluva job expressing that fact."

She was mad to have thought she could somehow negotiate an agreement with the man, whether through reason or through threats of public exposure. Daphne had been absolutely right to back away from him. Lord only knew what sort of influence he would have had on Timmy.

She fumbled with the door latch again, but the door didn't budge. "I want out." In more ways than one. She'd find some other way to finance Daphne's medical treatment.

But the silent assurance rang false in her head when she'd already exhausted every other possibility.

Tears burned her eyes.

If only Daphne would have come to live with her in Oregon. If only.

A sob escaped and she clapped her hand over her mouth to stifle the ones that wanted to follow so hard on its heels. She'd be damned if she would cry in front of Grayson Hunt. "Open the door." She yanked on the latch.

There was no denying that the huge tears streaming from her eyes were real, though Gray didn't let himself be moved by them. Any decent con woman could summon tears at the drop of a hat.

Gwen had certainly been able to. She'd also had her timing down pat, knowing exactly when to turn them on or off for maximum impact.

But back then, they'd both been in college. And only the experience of hindsight allowed him to admit that he'd still been wet behind the ears when it came to manipulative women, despite being raised by Christina Hunt Devereaux Dunleavy, the queen of manipulators. He'd been sucked in by Gwen, all right, so deeply that he'd planned to marry her.

Marry Gwen, who hadn't been wet behind the ears about anything at all.

In the end, however, she'd been the one to pay the ultimate price. She hadn't survived to see the fruition of her faked kidnapping scheme. The child she'd been carrying—his—hadn't survived, either.

And he'd made certain no one could ever use him in such a manner again.

Now, watching Amelia seem to unravel right there beside him, he reminded himself of all that. "You *are* good," he murmured.

Her brown eyes, looking wounded and as vulnerable as a puppy, slanted his way. Her brows drew together, forming a fine line over the bridge of her nose. "And you are hateful."

"Hate to tell you, Amelia, but if you're looking for originality, you're missing the mark."

She let out a shuddering sob again, turning her face away and covering it with her shaking hand. Her misery was palpable and almost—*almost*—real.

"I s'pose this sister of yours, Daphne the cocktail slinger, is waiting with bated breath for you to return, triumphant with assurances from me that I'll pay off whatever amount you plan to demand."

She bent forward, her face nearly buried in her lap, as if she felt ill. "Stop," she pleaded, her voice muffled. "Just…stop."

"Bad game for you to start playing if you don't like the

sport." He started the car, feeling dark inside even before she jerked and gave him a wrenchingly fearful look. "Cool your jets. We're just going to go to your apartment. Have a chat with this sister of yours. If she even exists." He seriously doubted it.

But then Gwen had had her accomplice, too, so what did he know?

Beside him, Amelia was still hunched, as if holding back nausea. Her face was pale, her expression resolute despite the tears still dripping down her cheeks and the blotchiness of her reddening nose.

Unlike Christina and Gwen, she hadn't yet learned the art of crying prettily. Or maybe that was just more of her plan.

Adding realism.

"She's not there."

"Well, we will just have to find that out for certain, won't we." He moved out into traffic, glad that he'd taken the time to figure out for himself just where her building was located.

Of course he'd been thinking about Amelia as a prospective bride when he'd hunted down that information from the cab company.

"I have to go to work," she said.

He snorted. "Thought that's what you'd been doing since you sprawled on the path, waiting for me to trip over you."

"I told you! That was an accident."

"You weren't at the park at that hour because you hoped to run into me?" he asked sardonically.

She snapped her lips closed, looking away.

He shook his head. "Honey, you've gotta work on the lying. You're having a serious problem with consistency. In your words and your reactions."

"I knew you ran there," she admitted, sounding grudging. "The rest was an accident. My shoelace—"

"Yeah, yeah. I remember." And he'd even let himself think that the shoelace hadn't been part of the act.

That's what he got for letting himself be so preoccupied with his hunt for a wife. He hadn't noticed the snake in the grass even when he'd tripped over her.

"There's the academy." She pointed out the window to the ivy-walled private school on the left side of the road. "Stop."

"You don't have to pretend that you really work there, Amelia. The jig's up."

"I won't be working there if I lose my job for being late again," she said thickly. "Now *let* me out of this car!"

It was curiosity as much as anything, he told himself, that had him pulling out of traffic and stopping at the curb near the iron-gated entrance of the school. Watching her, he released the door locks.

She hitched her briefcase against her chest and practically tumbled out of the car so great was her rush. But instead of heading down the road and away from him and the school, she jogged, briefcase bouncing against her hip, to the pedestrian gate situated near the drive.

A moment later, the security guard there was letting her through and she dashed out of sight without a single backward glance.

Gray sat there at the curb, engine idling softly, and tapped his thumb against the steering wheel. He punched a button on his cell phone, and almost immediately, Loretta came on the line.

"Look up the staff listing for Brandlebury Academy."

A moment later, she was back on the line. "Got it. Are you

planning to make another endowment? Brandlebury just missed the cut last year."

His brother Alex ran the philanthropic arm of HuntCom. But he wasn't the only one engaged in such efforts. Only Gray's version of giving was considerably less altruistic in nature than Alex's. He did it for financial reasons. Not because he liked to "give until it felt good," as Alex was wont to say. "Maybe. Who's the librarian?"

If she was curious about his reasons for asking, she kept it to herself. "Beverly Osborne."

His mood darkened and the fact that it did pissed him off no end. "There's only one librarian position?"

"Hold on." He heard the tap of a keyboard. "I'm looking at their organization chart that was in the RFP they sent us a few months ago for this year's awards. Yup. One position."

"Thanks."

"You've got a conference call scheduled in ten minutes."

"I'm on the road. Put it through to my cell," he told her. "I'll be in the office later." He disconnected, but continued to sit there, watching the school.

Eventually the security guard came over to his car. "Mind moving along, sir?" He leaned down, looking in the window that Gray lowered. "Oh. Mr. Hunt. Didn't realize it was you." He looked uncomfortable. "I'm sorry, but buses will begin arriving, and they need this lane to turn into."

"No sweat." He took in the discreet name plate on the man's uniform, "Marcus. I'm on my way."

He looked relieved. "Thank you, sir." He began to straighten.

"Marcus—"

The security guard bent over, looked through the window once more. "Sir?"

"That young woman you let through the gate a while ago. Dark hair. Gray suit. You know her?"

Marcus's aged face looked vaguely insulted. "We only let staff and students through. They all have to have their badge. Visitors have to be on the list. She had her badge."

Badges, Gray knew, could be faked easily enough. HuntCom didn't use only ID badges, but biometric authentication, from fingerprints to iris recognition, depending on the level of security required for the work in question. "Thanks, Marcus."

The man nodded, and stepped back from the car as Gray drove away from the curb.

Thanks to the hour, he took the conference call sitting in a gridlock of rush hour traffic, and once he'd exchanged the "Matt" getup for his usual suit and made it to the office, there wasn't any time left for him to be thinking about Amelia White.

There shouldn't have been, anyway.

Yet the woman kept sliding into his thoughts, between meetings, between calls, between reports. As usual, the day had slid past before Gray realized it. But Loretta came in, putting a fat folder of correspondence requiring his signature in front of him. His gray-haired secretary already had her briefcase slung over her arm.

Gray sighed slightly and flipped open the folder, grabbing his pen. "Thanks."

"Here." Loretta slid another piece of paper onto his desk. "I got hold of a fresh staff roster from Brandlebury this afternoon."

He paused. "Why?"

Loretta shrugged. She'd been with him since before he was appointed president of the company. She was ten years his senior; looked like someone's middle-aged mother from her gray curls to her sturdy, flat shoes; and was the most organized soul he knew. "You seemed interested," she said. "So I figured I would follow up. The roster we had was dated two months ago."

"And?" He dropped his palm over the paper and drew it closer.

"And the librarian's name changed. Amelia White. I spoke with the headmaster. He told me she'd been with them about five weeks now. She also has a niece and nephew who are students there. Have been for three years."

Gray looked at the roster. Her name seemed to leap out at him. So Amelia hadn't lied about the job, after all. The ID badge had been authentic.

"On scholarship," Loretta added.

He looked at her and she shrugged again, looking innocent. "Just in case you were interested."

"I'm not," he lied. "Have a good weekend."

She smiled faintly and headed for the door. "You, too, Gray."

"Loretta. Get her name to Marissa before you leave, if you would. I want a report on her by morning. Employment, family. The works."

"Anything you say, boss."

"Don't look at me like that."

"Like what?"

He snorted impatiently and turned back to the letters he needed to sign. "Tell her it's for my eyes only." He should have had Marissa pull together the information the first time he got it into his head that Amelia might fill the wife slot. But no. Pride had kept him from doing so.

"Anything else?"

He snapped off the lid of his pen, ignoring the knowing note in her tone. "Don't let it get back to Harry," he muttered.

She chuckled softly and returned to her adjoining office. He could hear the murmur of her voice as she made the call to Marissa, and then she headed out, calling a last g'night as she went.

Gray finished signing the letters—a task that took longer than it should, given the way he kept pulling the Brandlebury roster on top of them.

She'd worked at the school for five weeks. That, in itself, was no proof that she wasn't scamming him. But the fact that her niece and nephew had been students at the academy for three years niggled at him.

Irritated with the way the woman kept plaguing his thoughts, he left his office. But he had no particular place to go, or reason to be there, and merely ended up pacing the executive floor hallways.

HuntCom ran shifts 24-7 in many departments. But not on the executive floor. Fortunately, the place had cleared out for the weekend, so there wasn't anyone around to witness his uncharacteristic activity.

He passed by the office that used to be occupied by J.T. before he'd decided to hang out his own architectural shingle. They hadn't yet made the announcement that he was resigning, but he was staying on only long enough to finish the projects he'd been working on when he'd met Amy. Before Amy, J.T. had been away on business as often as he'd been in town. Now, he and Amy were definitely stateside, but Gray realized that since their wedding he'd seen even less of J.T. than when he'd been traveling.

He was glad J.T. was happy. That he'd found a silver lining—Amy—inside Harry's marriage demands. Yet he found himself missing him.

He leaned his shoulder against the doorjamb, looking into the darkened interior. The last time he'd spent any time with J.T. was at a Sonics game. Not the suite that HuntCom held, either. They'd picked up a pair of cheap seats the way they sometimes did—Alex, too, when he was free—and had sat among the masses pretty much incognito, drinking their beer and watching their beloved team lose their shirts.

He sighed faintly and turned back for his own office.

When he got there, his cell phone was buzzing against the desktop where he'd left it. He looked at the display, smiling faintly as he answered. It wasn't the first time he and J.T. found themselves oddly on the same wavelength. "Hey, bro. I was just thinking about you. What's up?"

"You want the good or the bad?" J.T.'s voice was terse.

Gray's nerves prickled. "Bad?"

"Harry's been taken to the hospital again."

Gray was already striding out of the office. "His heart?"

"We're assuming. The doctors haven't come out to tell us squat, yet."

"Who notified you?"

"Nobody. Amy and I were having dinner at the shack."

The elevator doors slid open in front of Gray the second he punched the call button, but he hardly took any notice. "You two were having *dinner* with Harry." J.T. and Harry may have come to a better understanding of one another in the past several months, but that didn't mean they'd taken to having father-son get-togethers.

"We had news to tell him." Gray could hear the murmur of a soft, female voice in the background. "Amy's pregnant."

Something inside Gray pinched, hard. Justin and Lily had

Ava, nearly two years old already, though his baby brother hadn't found out about his daughter until he'd been reunited with Lily. Now the three of them were as happy as pups in clover.

And now, J.T. and Amy were having a baby, too.

At this rate, Gray would probably wake up in the morning and Alex and P.J. would be picking preschools, as well.

"Congratulations." The word seemed to dredge up from somewhere dark and hollow. "Have you told anyone else?"

"I know. Strange to tell the old man first," J.T. admitted, his voice rough. He knew what Gray meant without him having to elaborate. "Amy's doing. You know how she feels about family." Since Amy had only a stepsister and stepmother to her name, Gray supposed he understood that. Plus, his brother's wife—like all of the new Hunt brides—was ending up far more charmed by Harry than was at all reasonable.

"And you can't resist Amy," Gray concluded.

"What can I say?" J.T. didn't sound remotely apologetic.

It was still hard for Gray to believe that even J.T.—globe-trotting cynic—had been taken to his knees by the love of a good woman.

He finally stepped into the patiently yawning elevator. "So how'd it happen?"

"We told him the news over aperitifs. Had dinner. Old man's steak was practically tartar. Crème brûlée for dessert. All the things we all know he shouldn't be eating. Insisted on an after-dinner brandy, and the next thing we knew, he collapsed. Helicopter lifted him to Harborview, same as last time. No doubt it'll hit the newswires any minute."

"Call Justin at the ranch." Gray stepped off the elevator

when it hit the lobby and he nodded briefly to the security guards on duty as he headed toward the tunnel leading to the parking garage. "I'll get Alex. He can meet us at the hospital."

"He and P.J. are in D.C. wringing money out of wallets there. Remember?"

Gray swore. It wasn't like him to forget such things. Up until recently the Hunt Foundation had been funded strictly from the family. But Alex and his new wife, P.J.—born of wealth and just as philanthropically minded as Alex—had decided to up the ante, take their work to even higher levels. "Right. I'll track him down. I'll find Aunt Cornelia, too. Is Amy all right? Seeing Harry collapse and all—"

"I'm just fine, Gray." Amy's voice came on the line. "Don't you worry yourself about me. Now are you driving yourself to the hospital, or is Peter standing by?"

He frowned, stepping into the parking garage where his car waited in its well-monitored slot. "I am."

"Promise me you'll be careful. Don't run any lights or anything. Harry's not going anywhere."

"You're married to the speed demon in the family," Gray murmured as he climbed behind the wheel.

She wasn't deterred by the observation. "Gray," she prompted, her voice gently warning.

He let out a short breath. Aside from Cornelia and her girls, and maybe Loretta and Marissa, he wasn't used to feeling much affection for any woman. But lately his sisters-in-law had been messing with his status quo. "I promise. And I'll see you in a few. Now go, go put your feet up or something. That's my niece or nephew you're carrying." He dropped the phone on the passenger seat and gunned the engine perhaps slightly less than he ordinarily would have.

Amelia had a niece and nephew.

He pushed away the unwelcome thought and squealed out of the parking lot. By the time he arrived at the hospital, he'd reached Alex at his hotel room in Alexandria. He and P.J. would be returning immediately.

He found J.T. and Amy sitting together in the emergency room's waiting room. The second Amy spotted him, she hopped up and wrapped her arms around Gray, as if it were the most natural thing in the world.

Gray eyed his brother over the top of her brunette head and awkwardly patted her shoulder. J.T. just shrugged, as if to say, get used to it.

Unfortunately, Gray was beginning to realize that he *could* get used to it.

Then Amy moved away, sliding her arm around J.T.'s waist and leaning her head against his arm. They looked…right together, Gray realized. Perhaps for the first time.

He pulled at his tie, loosening it, but the sensation of envy wasn't so easily loosened. "So, what do we know? Have you seen Harry yet?"

J.T. shook his head. "Justin and Lily will be here as soon as the jet can land. Alex?"

"Same. They're on their way." Gray looked around them. The waiting room was crowded with people. Coughing, sneezing, bundled in blankets, holding compresses to every body part imaginable.

If he'd had his way, he'd have brought Amelia to this same hospital that early morning in the park.

He scrubbed his hand down his face. "I'm going to find the doctor."

Looking into his father's condition was a lot more productive than standing around allowing that woman to keep boring into his head.

Chapter Six

Gray stared at the file lying open on his lap.

Marissa had delivered Amelia's dossier to the hospital early that morning.

The item stacked on top of the thin contents was the most telling of all—Marissa's letter to Amelia's sister, one Daphne Mason, dated seven months earlier, warning the woman to discontinue her attempted communication with Gray or face legal repercussions.

As usual, Marissa had done exactly what she was paid to do. Protect him. Protect HuntCom, particularly against a claim she'd have known had no merit, since he'd been in Europe during the alleged "relationship" that produced Daphne's child. It had been so easily dismissed by Marissa that she hadn't even thought to discuss it with Gray.

In contrast, the rest of the file had been ordinary in the

extreme. Amelia White, second daughter of Victor White and Janice White née Townsend. Unmarried. Employed since graduating cum laude with the Oregon State University system. Small savings account recently closed. Same with checking. Only significant asset, a townhome near the university, recently sold for less than market value, indicating a rushed sale. No new mortgage on record, only credit card already charged to its very modest limit.

Mother died more than ten years ago. Father's whereabouts unknown. Sister, Daphne Mason, currently a patient at the Biggs-Tolley convalescent hospital—condition unavailable.

For now, Gray thought. He closed the folder and looked across the hospital bed where his father lay, still sleeping.

J.T. had insisted on taking Amy home around midnight when they'd learned that Harry hadn't had another heart attack.

Not that Harry's doctor was pleased with the cardiac episode. If anything, he was positively grim, warning Gray that unless Harry made serious changes to his lifestyle—and not just giving up the steaks and rich desserts that had been slowly creeping back into his world since last year—but changing his very lifestyle, he believed that Harry was leading up to another attack. Probably worse than the first one.

Which had nearly felled the old man.

Dr. Richardson was adamant. Harry *had* to retire. Not next year. Not when it was convenient. *Now.*

"How is he?" The hushed voice brought Gray's attention around to the door of the private room. Cornelia Fairchild stood there. She was a slender, tall woman who carried her age—just a few years Harry's junior—as elegantly as everything else in her life. Even now, despite the early hour, she wore pristine ivory slacks and a soft blue blouse that made her waving hair look even more fair. But now, her gaze on Harry, she didn't just look typically stylish and elegant.

She looked frail.

Gray rose, setting aside the file and went to her, taking her hands and kissing her softly lined cheek. "He's sleeping," Gray told her. "See for yourself."

She squeezed his hand and walked into the room, stopping only when her hip brushed the mattress. She seemed to sigh a little, then leaned over and kissed Harry's forehead. "Darned fool," she whispered.

Harry opened his eyes then, and spotted the slender woman hovering over him. He made a gruff sound. "Stop looking as if you're at my wake."

Cornelia huffed slightly and straightened. But Gray noticed the way her hand trembled, as she gave Harry his glasses, then closed it over Harry's, carefully avoiding the IV lead taped to the back of his hand. "Stop giving us all such a scare," she returned smoothly. "I've a good mind to fire your cook myself. He's already admitted to me the kinds of meals you've been taking. What were you thinking?"

"I'm thinking that I'm sick of fish and consommé," Harry retorted, though his voice lacked its usual steam. He looked past the woman Gray knew he counted as his oldest friend and slid his glasses into place as he peered at the manila file Gray had left sitting on the chair beside the bed. "What's that?"

Gray moved over to retrieve it and tucked it beneath his arm. "Few things Marissa is handling."

"Hmm." Harry began pushing against the mattress. "Sit me up."

"Be still," Cornelia chided. She reached for the panel on

the wall above his head and pushed a button that slowly raised the mattress several inches. Then she began plumping the pillows behind Harry's back.

"That Birchman deal? I warned you he'd hold out for more money."

"No business," Cornelia warned. "Not one word of it."

"You're getting awfully bossy, Corny."

"Maybe you need someone to boss you," she returned.

Harry just harrumphed again. He crossed his arms over the blue hospital gown covering his chest. "J.T.'s done his part," he said, eyeing Gray. "What're you holding out for?"

There was no question to what Harry referred. "Who says I've been holding out?"

"This entire agreement is ridiculous," Cornelia interrupted.

Harry shot her a look. "You saying that Justin and Alex and J.T. aren't finally happy?"

She tsked. "Of course I'm not saying that. They're lovely girls. I know that."

"Well then?" Harry squinted at Gray. "I don't have to remind you that even though *they've* stuck to the agreement, they'll still lose everything if you don't."

Gray had years of experience beneath his belt in the art of negotiating. Alex might be the family's most avowed poker fiend, but Gray knew how to bluff with the best of them. "I haven't defaulted," he assured mildly.

Harry pursed his lips. "You haven't left Seattle for more than three days at a stretch in the past three months. And that's always been on business. How are you finding a woman that doesn't know who you are if you're always in town? Hell, the last time you were in Europe was a year ago. You can't romance a woman long-distance, boy. They don't like it. They want you there. With them. Showing devotion and all that…stuff."

"Don't agitate yourself," Cornelia cautioned.

"Sorry if I'm not going to take romancing tips from you," Gray said flatly. "As it happens, I don't need to. I can manage fine on my own."

Harry pushed up on his elbows despite Cornelia's efforts at keeping him still. "There's a woman?"

Gray couldn't ignore the glint of hope in the old man's eyes and it felt like a stab to his gut. It was like being ten years old all over again, doing anything and everything he could just to get a speck of pride and satisfaction out of his father, who was more often buried in computer code than anything else. "Yes."

There *was* a woman, just not one that he was prepared to trust yet, despite the dossier that suggested her claims weren't entirely the scam he'd believed. Officially speaking, Amelia wasn't the one to attempt that absurd paternity suit. Her sister had.

The file folder tucked under his arm seemed to burn into his ribs.

Maybe he didn't have to trust her, though. Not when there seemed to be something they both needed.

"What's her name? Where'd you meet?"

"Amelia. Running."

Harry's eyes narrowed and Gray could practically see the wheels turning inside his father's formidable brain. "How long have you been seeing her?"

"Long enough," he lied smoothly.

"When do we meet her?"

"You don't. Not until we're married, remember?"

"She has to pass Cornelia's muster," Harry reminded.

His honorary aunt looked pained. "Harrison Hunt. Really. I don't know why you insist on not trusting your sons' judgment."

"I trust their judgment fine. Just not when it comes to women."

"Then you should have been more discerning in *your* own choice of wives," Cornelia said, her voice oddly tight. She stepped away from Harry's bedside, brushing her hands down her trim slacks. "I'm going to go find some tea. Gray? Can I bring you back something?"

"What about me," Harry asked.

"*You* can have whatever the doctor says you can have, *when* he says you can have it."

"You're getting pretty snippy in your old age, Cornelia."

She ignored him and lifted her eyebrows, looking at Gray. "Well?"

He shook his head. "Thanks. But I've got to get to the office soon."

"Workaholic," she chided and tsked. But she patted his arm as she slipped past him and left the room.

"Will she marry you? This Amelia girl?"

"You let me issue a release that you're stepping down as chairman of the board, effective immediately, and I promise you, I'll be married by the end of the week."

Harry snorted. "I know you, boy. You can't just go out and hire yourself a wife so you can step into my title as chairman. That isn't the agreement."

"Who else is going to succeed you? You've been training me for the day since you gave Christina the boot. And there *is* no hiring involved."

"I don't even want to hear your mother's name," Harry dismissed. "She loves you, then?"

Gray didn't make the mistake of thinking that Harry was referring to Christina. "Words can't describe," he assured.

"There was nothing in our agreement that said I had to step down as chairman."

There hadn't been. The content had been to retain their interests and increase their voting shares just enough that Harry no longer held controlling interest. Gray approached the bed, closing his hands over the high wooden footboard. "Resigning isn't about the agreement, Dad, and you know it."

Harry's sharp gaze slid away. "You never call me Dad."

"Your doc said you can't keep working like you do."

His father's hands curled into fists. "I've cut down on my hours," he defended. "It's my company."

"And it will live on whether you retire or not." The words were blunt. Painful. "Wouldn't you rather be around for a while longer to see it, or are you so stubborn that you'd rather be buried still bearing your precious title? Hell, Harry. Keep the title. I don't care. But *quit* the work."

"Don't try to kid me, boy. You want that title. You have for years."

"I've earned that title," Gray returned evenly. "HuntCom is my life as much as it is yours. I didn't give birth to it, but I've damn sure participated in helping it grow up."

"Whether I resign or not, you're still bound by our agreement."

"Yes. And if you don't step down, those grandkids you claim to want won't ever have a chance to bounce on your knee."

A muscle ticked in Harry's narrow jaw. "All right. Fine. You can make the announcement. *After* your wedding."

Gray exhaled, feeling tired and worn.

Now all he had to do was produce the aforementioned

bride. Considering the way they'd last parted, he figured it would not be one of his slam-dunk deals.

"Aunt Amelia, when will Mommy get to come home with us?"

The day following the debacle with Grayson Hunt, Amelia fit her key into the last door lock of their apartment and pushed it open. "I don't know, honey." She waited for Jack to go inside first, then nudged Molly through even as she began working Timmy out of his sling carrier. His diaper was wet and he was beginning to fuss, but changing him on the crowded bus ride back to the apartment from Daphne's convalescent center had been logistically impossible. All Amelia had managed to do was give him a bottle.

"Grow up," Jack muttered to his sister on his way to the bedroom.

The door closed with a slam behind him.

Molly looked fit to cry.

Amelia felt like crying, herself. Maybe she shouldn't continue taking the children to visit their mother so regularly when Daphne could hardly speak, much less recognize her children. Not when it left them all in such a state.

"You keep praying about your mom," Amelia told Molly. Prayer was their last best hope. Prayer for a miracle because every avenue that Amelia tried to take in order to get Daphne's rehabilitation amped up had failed miserably.

Particularly the avenue named Grayson Hunt.

Molly was only ten, but her expression clearly indicated that she didn't hold out much hope on the prayer thing.

Amelia leaned over and kissed Molly's head. She knew

exactly how the little girl felt. "Go put your jacket away and I'll start dinner as soon as I've taken care of Timmy."

If Amelia didn't find some way to pay for her sister's special care—and soon—Daphne would be transferred yet again to a long-term, state-funded facility where there would be *no* chance for the rehabilitation that had already been deemed unnecessary.

Molly nodded, looking dejected as she dragged her windbreaker behind her and headed for the bedroom door that Jack had emphatically closed. "Lemme in, Jack," Molly whispered loudly through the door.

What she wouldn't give to hear Molly give a real yell, Amelia thought, as she headed into the bedroom with Timmy. She'd realized quickly enough that keeping the baby supplied in disposable diapers was going to cost a small fortune, and used them only when she had to. The rest of the time, she went the old-fashioned route.

Cloth.

Fortunately, Paula had been an old hand at the art of folding and fastening cloth diapers, since that's what she'd used when her daughter was an infant. And now, after three months and more than a few painfully poked fingertips, Amelia was adept with the matter, too.

Dry again, Timmy stared up at her, mouth open in his angelic smile, legs kicking and hands reaching for her hair— his most recently mastered game.

Amelia leaned over her bed where she'd changed him— no changing table had been in the budget—and blew a kiss against his cheek.

Timmy gurgled and squealed and wriggled with delight.

He was dry, fed and loved. As far as he was concerned, his world was complete.

Molly and Jack were dry, fed and loved, too. Only they were old enough to know that without their mother, their world would never be the same again.

Amelia couldn't even dwell on the unbearable thought. She scooted the baby onto the middle of the bed and changed out of the lilac pantsuit she'd worn to see Daphne that day. She carefully hung it up next to the gray suit from the previous day.

The nun's habit. Grayson's cutting remark hung in her head.

She huffed, snapped the gray wool off the hanger and bundled it over the back of the straight chair she'd confiscated from the dining room to use at the narrow table that sufficed as a desk. There was no point leaving the garment in the Lilliputian closet, taking up precious space. The pieces needed to be dry-cleaned before they would be fit to wear again.

She yanked on a soft pair of sweats, gathered up Timmy and returned to the living room where she settled him in the infant seat she'd found in a secondhand store. He grinned back at her from his position of superiority smack dab in the center of their little round dining room table as she set about preparing dinner.

She'd never been much of a cook, but she'd been learning fast since she'd left Portland. And fortunately, the children weren't finicky eaters. Good thing, or they'd have starved, considering the results of her early efforts.

The meat was browning for simple tacos and she was shredding her way through a block of cheddar cheese when she heard the knock on the door. "Jack, can you get that? It's probably Paula."

He'd finally come out of his bedroom and had been sprawled on the floor in front of the television, laboriously doing homework. He pushed to his feet and went to the door, looking out the peephole. "It's not Paula."

She turned the cheese wedge on its side. "Who is it?"

"I dunno."

She set down the cheese, checked the heat under the ground beef and headed to the door. "Your homework almost finished?"

Jack shook his head but he didn't go back to the books spread on the floor. He stood alongside Amelia—almost protectively, she suspected—as she went on her tiptoes to look out the tiny viewer.

Her heart jumped into her throat at the fish-eye view of Grayson Hunt.

He knocked again. "Amelia. Open the door."

She went down on her heels, wanting nothing more than to pretend they weren't there.

They didn't have to answer the door, after all. There was no law that said they did. And just because he was an incredibly wealthy, influential man didn't mean he had any more rights then a stranger off the street to tell her what to do.

He'd already made it clear what he thought of her.

"Jack. Take Molly and the baby into the bedroom."

"But—"

"Please. Just do it."

Frowning mightily, he went to the table and scooped up Timmy, infant seat and all. "Come on, Mol."

"But I'm watching TV."

Grayson was knocking again, managing to express plenty of impatience in the act. "I can hear you through the door, Amelia."

"Molly," she said, more sharply than she ought to have. She didn't need to see her niece's crestfallen expression to know it. "Please," she said more calmly. "Just go with Jack for a few minutes. You can watch the television in my bedroom." It was all of nine inches and black-and-white, but it was the only one they had, other than the twenty-year-old model in the living room. "This won't take long."

"Who is he?" Jack asked, looking suspicious.

She swallowed. "Nobody you have to worry about."

"I heard that," Grayson said through the door.

She waited just until the children were safely closed behind her bedroom door. Then she fumbled with the locks and yanked open the door, standing squarely in the opening. "What are you doing here?"

He easily looked over her head through the slice of opening she'd left and she wished she were ten inches taller so she could block that view, as well. "We need to talk."

"No. We don't. You've said as much as I want to hear." And she still felt battered and bruised as a result. She started to close the door, but he stopped her simply by planting his very well-shod foot in its way. "Go away." She banged the door hard on his foot. But the woefully thin door was hardly a weapon.

"Not until we've talked."

Her shoulder leaning against the door, she glared at him. "Why? So you can assassinate my sister's character—and mine—just a little more? No thanks."

"I know about Daphne's stroke."

Her mouth dried. "Don't even speak her name to me." Her voice was low. Shaking.

He actually managed to look regretful.

Not that she believed it for a second.

"I want you to leave. You've made it clear that you have no business here and I agree with that. So just *go*."

"My father had a heart attack almost a year ago."

She'd seen that in the news, along with most of the rest of the civilized world. And if he thought to draw a comparison between the state of his father—who was still at the helm of HuntCom as far as she knew—and her sister, who couldn't qualify for anything beyond the most basic of care, he wasn't as intelligent as her information suggested.

"Move your foot. I don't want our dinner to burn."

"You sold your town house to pay down her hospital bills."

The small profit she'd made on the sale hadn't made a particularly significant dent in them, either.

The idea that he'd obviously done *his* research into her had her cheeks, as well as her blood, burning. "That's none of your business."

"Unlike you learning that I have a liking for cranberry muffins?"

"What I learned about you was already public knowledge. You…you poking into my life is pure invasiveness. What do you care, anyway? Unless you're planning to charge me with slander the way your attorney threatened Daphne."

"I don't want to argue with you about that." His voice was curt, his expression inflexible.

"Then we have nothing to say, argumentative or otherwise, to each other." She pushed again at the door, even harder, but his foot was as movable as a concrete block. "Do I have to call the police? Because, believe me, Mr. Hunt, I'm not afraid of doing so."

"I realize I was…hard on you," he allowed.

Her lips parted. "Hard on me? You accused me of, of—" She broke off, too angry for words. "Jack," she called loudly. "Bring me the telephone."

"Wait." Grayson withdrew his foot, only to press his palm against the door instead. He reached in his jacket and drew out a narrow envelope from his lapel. "Here."

She eyed the ivory-colored vellum as if it were a snake. "What is it?"

"An agreement. Maybe we can help each other."

She would have given anything to tell the man that under no circumstances would she ever require his help. But how could she? If she hadn't needed his help, she'd have never been in the park that early morning.

Jack came out, carrying their cordless phone to her. He eyed Grayson silently.

"Thank you." Amelia took the phone. "Go back with your sister."

"I can hear everything through the doors, too." He directed the comment at Grayson. Clearly warning.

Amelia held the phone to her chest, waiting until her nephew was once again behind the bedroom door, giving at least the illusion of protection. She looked up at Grayson. "There is *no* agreement I would ever make with you," she said evenly.

"That's not how it seemed to me yesterday."

"That was because I still possessed the ridiculous notion that there might be some decency in you despite the way you treated my sister."

His lips tightened. He extended the envelope again. "I never met your sister. Just take it. You might change your mind."

She studied him, suspicion and anger rampant in her cells. "There's no way I can help you. No way I would ever even *want* to help you."

His eyes cooled. "Fine. Read it anyway. Because despite my distaste for your methods, I actually had begun believing that you *did* want to help your sister. What's the name of that private facility you've been trying to get her into? Jackson-Whitney?"

Her hand reached out and snatched the envelope from his

fingers before she could stop it. She wanted, badly, to tear the thing into pieces, right in front of him.

But she didn't.

The man had done his research. "Sloan Jackson is the only doctor who doesn't believe Daphne's prognosis is hopeless."

"And you spent every dime on your only credit card to pay his consultation fee."

She was trembling. She managed to lift her chin, anyway. She didn't regret one dime of what she'd spent trying to find some hope for her sister. "He's not some kook out to take fools' money. His reputation is exemplary."

Surprisingly, Grayson nodded. "I agree. If you're sure you want him, read that." He removed his hand from the door.

Which Amelia didn't immediately slam shut in his face.

He gave a short nod, obviously satisfied with that particular fact. "You still have my number?"

She wanted to tell him that she'd burned that foul card on which he'd written his private number.

"Yes."

"Good. I'll expect to hear from you tomorrow." Then he turned around and walked away, leaving Amelia standing there in the opened doorway, clutching the envelope like a lifeline.

Chapter Seven

Amelia waited hours before she allowed herself to retrieve the card with his phone number. It was difficult, though, considering there wasn't a minute that passed that she wasn't thinking about the content of that agreement he'd left with her. Or to be more accurate, she'd been thinking about the content that had been left *out* of the agreement Grayson had left with her.

Specifically, whatever he was supposed to get from her in return for assuming—for a limited time the duration of which would be specified later—the medical costs for her sister's care. And at the termination of their agreement for these non-specified services, she'd receive a lump sum settlement of an amount that was so astronomical, Amelia didn't know whether to laugh or cry.

Interestingly, however, there had been absolutely no mention whatsoever about Timmy.

She didn't trust Gray enough to feel relieved about that omission. It probably meant absolutely nothing.

Both Jack and Molly had been mighty curious about her visit from the stranger, but Amelia hadn't satisfied them.

She wasn't surprised that Jack hadn't recognized Gray as the man who'd been involved with his mother. Since the death of her husband, Martin, when Molly was just two years old, Daphne had made it a strict practice never to bring her "friends" around her children. She'd told Amelia once that unless she had a diamond on her finger, there was no way a man was getting near her kids.

Another hangover from their childhood. After their parents divorced, their mother had brought home men at the drop of a hat. Daphne had hated it even more than Amelia. She'd been two years older, and miles prettier. Half the time, their mother's so-called boyfriends were just as interested in exploring Daphne's charms as they had been their mother's.

Even when Amelia pulled out the cabbie's business card with that distinctive, slashing handwriting on the back, though, She couldn't make herself pick up the telephone and dial the number written there.

So she slid the card back inside the pocket in her purse.

Whatever game Grayson Hunt had decided to play, she knew it was way out of her league. What matter could she possibly assist him with that would be worth him spending thousands and thousands on Daphne? A cocktail waitress he claimed was so beneath his standards he'd have never even looked at her?

Still, even twenty-four hours into pretending to ignore the agreement Gray had left, as Amelia fixed waffles for breakfast and braided Molly's hair and bathed Timmy and gave him his bottle, she couldn't help wondering. Couldn't help... hoping. Here was her chance, after all, to give her *sister* a chance.

Or was it just some trap, set by Grayson to rid himself of a nuisance?

She wasn't an uneducated woman. She knew enough to look before she leaped. Even as a child, she'd been the cautious one. The quiet one. The mostly invisible one. It had suited her just fine until John Czerny had noticed her. Convinced her that they were perfect for one another. Two quiet souls.

Only in the end, John preferred someone not so boring.

The morning passed without her dialing the number.

But there was no pretending she wasn't wondering whether or not she was making yet another mistake. Rather than torment herself until she was insane, she suggested a trip to the park since the weather outside was uncommonly clear.

Not the park she'd staked out to meet Grayson, but their nearest neighborhood park. Even Paula joined them and off they all went, trudging down their six flights of stairs with Jack's bicycle; the bulging diaper bag; stroller; picnic basket, which Paula had provided; and a tote bag full of things sure to keep the children active and happy on a sunny afternoon.

"I wish we could have swum," Molly said when, hours later, they all trooped back to their apartment.

"It was a nice day," Paula agreed, "but swimming is a ways away yet. You might have frozen your nose right off."

Molly wrinkled her nose, obviously pondering the matter as she skipped ahead of Paula and Amelia. Jack had already raced even farther ahead of them where his friend, Ty, was hanging around in front of the building, riding his bike off the concrete parking stops next to the building.

When Molly saw Jack's friend, though, she stopped trying to catch up to him.

Amelia saw the droop of Molly's shoulders and pulled out a small bottle of bubbles that she'd picked up at the dime store. "Here, Molly. See what kind of bubbles you can blow."

As a distraction, it worked admirably. Particularly when Molly figured out that she could just hold up the tiny plastic wand and run around on the sidewalk to send a wild stream of bubbles flying out behind her.

"So are you going to call him?" Paula asked, when Molly was out of earshot again.

Amelia had confided in her neighbor out of sheer desperation. "No," she finally said.

"You don't sound very certain."

Amelia sighed. "I wish I knew what to do."

"Molly says you've told her to pray that her mother gets to come home soon. So," she continued when Amelia gave her a what-else-could-I-say? look, "maybe your prayers haven't been ignored as much as you think."

"Paula, the man is—"

"—as rich as Midas. I'll admit that *I* am pretty curious about what he stands to gain. You have to be, as well."

Amelia hitched the diaper bag more firmly over the handle of Timmy's stroller as they crossed the street next to the building. The baby was kicking his legs, thoroughly delighted with the occasional bubble that drifted his way. "I don't trust him. And he's made it more than plain that he doesn't trust me."

"That doesn't explain the agreement he left."

Amelia chewed the inside of her lip. What if she *were* turning her back on her prayers' answer?

"Well." Paula murmured, as they drew even with the brick building. "Maybe you can get a better answer now."

Amelia caught her breath as Grayson exited the building not five yards away from her. He spotted her immediately, of course, and headed straight for her.

Paula nudged Amelia's hands away from the stroller. "I'll take the kids with me," she murmured and continued forward without waiting for Amelia's agreement.

He was wearing another suit. Charcoal-gray with a blinding white shirt and a muted tie, and he looked every inch the business magnate that he was.

Even though it was a Sunday and everyone around them was dressed in jeans and shorts, Amelia felt entirely under-dressed and unarmed in her velour sweatpants and T-shirt when Grayson stopped in her path.

"I've been expecting your call."

She managed to lift her shoulders in an uncaring shrug. "I'm not required to satisfy your expectations, Mr. Hunt."

"You read the agreement." There was complete certainty in his deep voice.

"Did I?" Through sheer will, she made her feet move, carrying her past him. His hand shot out, closing around her upper arm. She froze. "More manhandling, Mr. Hunt?" But his hold wasn't tight at all. Just immensely…disturbing.

He lowered his head closer to hers. "You read it," he repeated confidently. "Isn't that what you wanted from me? Why you brought up that ridiculous claim of your sister's? We both know I didn't father that baby of hers. But you want to get me to pay for her medical treatment so you're looking for whatever means you can find."

Ridiculous claim. Didn't father Timmy.

She exhaled. The man would never believe that he'd fathered Timmy. Not without physical proof, and *she* wasn't going to demand it. Not when it meant that his claim to the child would supersede hers.

"Yes." The word hissed from between her teeth. "But I notice that you didn't bother telling me what price I'd have to pay in return. Just that if I ever broke your condition of confidentiality over the matter, I'd be required to return every single dime, plus interest." She'd be in debt to the man for the rest of her life, and they both knew it. Not that she wouldn't jump on the opportunity if it meant Daphne's recovery.

If she believed his agreement was legitimate.

"I need a wife."

She blinked. "I...*excuse* me?"

For once, he looked pained. "You heard me."

"Not properly," she assured. "What am I supposed to do? Play matchmaker for you? I think you're more than capable of coercing some foolish woman into marrying you all on your own. Call directory assistance on that cell phone you're incessantly checking."

"Are you being deliberately obtuse, Amelia, or does it come naturally?"

Her cheeks heated. "Such charming words you always have for me."

"My father is in precarious health. He wants his sons married." His fingers tightened for a moment around her arm. "And if that particular tidbit ever hits the newswires, I'll know exactly who was responsible."

"That threat only works if I sign my name by the X."

His eyebrow lifted. "You think I need an agreement?"

A shiver danced down her spine as if clouds were rolling in.

But the sky overhead was still a brilliant, nearly painful shade of blue. "You're implying that you want *me* to be your wife."

"I want to satisfy an old man and in the process, you can get your sister whatever treatment you want."

"But…your *wife*." The notion was simply unfathomable.

His lips tightened. "I believe that's what I said."

She pushed her fingers through her hair, pulling it back from her face. "What's the catch? Why me? You could have women lining up around the city wanting to marry you."

"Marry Grayson Hunt," he agreed. "And all that the name implies. But not Matthew Gray."

"But you're *not* Matthew Gray." She shook her head. "This is too convoluted for words. You're right, Mr. Hunt. I'm too simple a woman to understand the kind of games you play." She pulled her arm free, only managing to brush the side of her breast against his fingers as she did so. She curled her hands into fists, resisting the strong urge to cross her arms protectively over her chest. "No. No thank you. You can take your weird desire for a wife elsewhere. I am *not* interested."

"Not even for your sister's sake."

He knew perfectly well that was the one hitch for her, because she'd revealed that fact to him herself. She looked away from his face. His turquoise eyes that saw far too much.

"Not even for her," she lied, and strode toward the apartment building, afraid that if she remained in his company, desperation might have her caving to the lunacy.

Gray watched Amelia hurry into the aging brick building as if the devil himself was nipping at her heels.

Maybe he was.

He stood there for a while, debating the merits of following her up those six flights of stairs.

Since Marissa's initial dossier, he'd learned much more about Amelia and her sister's current situation. Of course he still dismissed Daphne Mason's paternity claim where he was concerned, but that didn't mean he didn't recognize the real need that Amelia had now. It was his only leverage since he'd gone and told Harry what he had.

But continuing to drill away at Amelia's resistance held no appeal. Not because he was disinterested. But because every time he brought some pressure to bear, he felt as if he were doing something heinous. Kicking a puppy. Pulling the wings off a butterfly.

He yanked out his cell phone and dialed, grimacing a little as Amelia's words about it haunted him. "Loretta."

"It's Sunday evening, Gray," she reminded pointedly. "I'm on my way to church."

"I want to know who owns the building where Amelia White lives." The place was in miserable repair.

"Hold on." He could hear muffled sounds for a moment before she came back on the line. "So why do you want to know? Planning to add to your real estate holdings?"

In addition to HuntCom properties, he personally owned several buildings around the city. Not a one of them possessed an inoperable elevator or were constructed with interior walls that could have passed for tar paper. "Text me the information. I'll be at the shack for dinner."

"How is your father? I was surprised to hear he was released from the hospital this morning."

"I don't know if it was a release so much as him going AWOL," Gray admitted. "My aunt insists on having a nurse on duty, though, so he's not getting off quite so thoroughly."

"Give him my best."

"Will do." He pocketed his phone, continued watching the building for a moment longer, then returned to the limo two blocks away where he'd instructed Peter to wait. Without ceremony, he climbed in the rear.

The limo was attracting plenty of attention from the kids playing ball in the street. He should have come in something less conspicuous. But he'd come from a meeting with Edward Birchman, and had been laying on the trappings to soothe the man's lingering reluctance to sign on the dotted line.

"Where to, Gray?" Peter had been with them for so long there was no point in standing on ceremony.

Gray had two hours before dinner with Harry and Cornelia. He tugged at his tie. "Take me to Biggs-Tolley convalescent hospital. It's in Ballard somewhere." It was time he saw this Daphne Mason, face-to-face. He knew her child wasn't his. He also knew, in her condition, she wouldn't be relaying any information about who the father *was*. But he still wanted to see her.

Peter was looking back at him through the lowered panel separating the driver from the rear of the limo. "Everything all right, Gray?"

"It will be." Anything else was not an option.

By Monday afternoon, the elevator in Amelia's building was fixed. It caused quite a buzz of excitement, too, and Stan—the superintendent—was more than happy to accept all the accolades for finally accomplishing the task. Later, however, when Paula came over to share the batch of brownies she'd made with them, she told Amelia the scoop that she'd heard.

The building had a new owner.

Amelia finished rinsing their plates and began filling the sink to wash them. She looked over the narrow counter at

Paula, who was holding Timmy in the middle of the living room, swaying him in gentle circles. "As long as the rent doesn't go up, I don't care who the owner is."

"Are you sure about that?"

Amelia paused at the thought that leaped into her head. "No way."

Paula's eyebrows lifted, tellingly. "None other."

"Ty wants me to go down to the store with him," Jack announced, heading for the door.

"Wait a second."

He paused, looking oddly annoyed. "Mom used to let me go."

"Which store?"

"Heller's."

"Fine. Wait. Here." She dug in her purse for a few dollars. "We need a gallon of milk."

He pocketed the bills, grabbed his bike from behind the couch and was out the door in a flash.

"Wish I had that kind of energy," Paula said. "And I heard it from Tanisha Jones. You know she's been—" her gaze skipped over Molly's head where she was bent over a coloring paper from school "—keeping *company* with Stan for the past six months. That's why she's the only one who's gotten her heating fixed without having to wait two weeks."

"Why would he do that, though?" What would be the point of him acquiring the run-down building? He surely didn't want to add slumlord to his vitae. That went against his high-powered public image.

"There can only be one reason," Paula said, as if Amelia had gone dim-witted. "You," she mouthed silently.

"That's ridiculous," she dismissed. He couldn't have. Wouldn't have.

Would he?

She couldn't turn off the speculation running rampant inside her head as she finished the dishes and bathed Timmy after Paula headed back to her own place. She was quizzing Molly on her spelling when the phone rang, and nuzzling Timmy's sweet-smelling cheek, she went to answer it.

"This is Officer Luke Stonebraker. I'm looking for Amelia White."

Alarm shot through her. "Speaking."

"I understand that you're the guardian for Jack Mason. We have him down here at the station, ma'am."

"What happened?" Timmy let out a cry in response to her sharp voice.

"He's been arrested for shoplifting."

Her knees went watery. Jack? "But he was just going to Heller's Grocery. What could he possibly want to take from there?"

"He was at Rank Electronics, ma'am. They had over five hundred dollars worth of equipment on them."

She jiggled Timmy, who was crying in earnest now. "They?"

"He was with a couple other kids. Older. You're going to want to come on down to the station." He gave her the address, barely waiting for her to grab a pen and paper before reeling it off.

"Is he all right? What do I… Wait." But the officer, having given his notification, had already hung up.

Molly had left her list of spelling words on the couch and sidled next to Amelia, her arm slipping around her waist. Fear clouded her brown eyes as she stared up at Amelia, mute.

Stay calm. She ran her hand down Molly's head. "Don't be afraid. Everything's fine." Timmy was still wailing and she automatically felt his diaper. Dry. He'd already finished his bottle, too. "I...I just have to go down and pick up Jack."

"Where is he?"

Amelia's lips parted. She didn't know whether to lie or not. "He's at the police station," she finally admitted and wished she hadn't when Molly's eyes went wide as saucers and her mouth fell open.

"Is he going to jail?"

"Of course not." Jack was only twelve. They didn't put twelve-year-olds in jail.

Did they?

"I'm sure there is a mistake," she told Molly. There had to be. Jack had never gotten into any trouble before. "Here." She put Timmy in the girl's arms. "See if you can calm him down."

Molly took the baby to the couch and sat down with him. But her wide eyes followed Amelia as she called Paula and blurted out their latest disaster. The other woman arrived again in a flash. She calmly took Timmy and had him quieted by the time Amelia had pulled on shoes and headed out the door.

It took three different buses before Amelia finally arrived at the address the police officer had given her. Another hour went by before she made it past the gargoyle of a woman guarding the front desk, and then it was only to see the arresting officer

Of Jack there was no sign.

"I *want* to see my nephew," she insisted when the officer just put a sheaf of papers in front of her to read and sign.

"These things take time, ma'am." He didn't look unsympathetic, but he did seem swamped with interruptions. People stopping by his cubicle with questions or comments. Phone ringing almost nonstop.

Hating the feeling of being out of her depth, she read the papers—the listing of charges and her responsibilities if—*if*—Jack were released to her. She scribbled her name where she needed to and handed the forms back to the officer.

"Wait out in the lobby," he told her. "We'll call you soon."

More waiting? She nodded and made her way back through the labyrinth of cubicles to the gargoyle and the hard chairs lined up along the walls there.

She sat down, closing her eyes in an effort to block out the voices all around her. *Oh, Daphne. I'm just not good at this.*

"Miss White?"

Amelia opened her eyes again to see the gargoyle addressing her. Only there was a glint of kindness in the woman's eyes this time. "If you'd come with me?"

Her stomach in knots, she followed the uniformed woman back through the labyrinth. Only this time they didn't stop at the arresting officer's cubicle, but continued past to an elevator. Up two floors and when the doors opened, the gargoyle extended her hand. "They'll take care of you from here," she said.

Amelia stepped off the elevator into a corridor with thick carpet and paneled walls. Hardly the tile and modular cubes of the lower floor. She wrapped her hands more tightly around the leather strap of her purse and cautiously headed along the hall. It opened out after several yards into another lobby area, only this one didn't have a counter hidden behind safety glass and metal detectors. It had a wide desk with a pretty woman sitting behind it. Enormous planters filled with ficus trees were positioned around the upholstered chairs.

Amelia swallowed the alarm that kept growing inside her and headed toward the desk. She wanted to get Jack and get out of there. Period.

"Miss White?" The woman greeted her before Amelia moved two steps. "You can just go in that office there. To your right."

Afraid of what she might find, the first face she saw was her nephew's.

Relief swept through her, making her positively weak. She dashed forward, grabbing him by the shoulders and pulling him close. "What are you doing scaring me to death like this?"

He wriggled out of her arms, looking grim and avoiding her eyes. There were two others in the office. A man in uniform with about five pounds' worth of medals pinned to his breast, and a tall redhead wearing the kind of suit Amelia knew she'd never in her life be able to afford.

No nun's habit there.

The woman's striking appearance made Amelia painfully aware of her own faded jeans and washed-out blue T-shirt.

She focused on the uniform. "What is all this? Can I take my nephew home now?"

The man nodded. "I'm afraid Jack will have to appear for a hearing, but we'll notify Ms. Matthews here and it can be done as discreetly as possible."

Amelia's gaze darted to the woman. Ms. Matthews. She doubted that anyone dressed so expensively was court appointed. "Who sent you?" Suspicion raged rampant inside her, though it defied all logic as far as she was concerned.

The woman's demeanor was brisk but not curt as she confirmed for Amelia that the illogical sometimes won out.

"I'm Mr. *Gray's* attorney," she introduced herself. "Marissa Matthews."

Chapter Eight

The knots inside Amelia jerked even tighter. She recognized the woman's name perfectly well.

Grayson's watchdog whom he'd set on Daphne months earlier.

"How did he—"

Marissa cut her off smoothly. "Your friend Ms. Browning informed him what had happened." She looked back at the officer, extending her long, elegant hand. "Captain. Always a pleasure. Your discretion is most appreciated."

The man was still beaming when the attorney nudged Jack ahead of them and they returned to the elevator.

The moment the doors closed, Amelia whirled on the woman. "I suppose that police captain knows just who *Mr. Gray* is?"

"Naturally."

"Is he having us watched or something?"

"Of course not. I told you. Paula Browning—"

"How did *she* tell him? His number isn't exactly listed." It was a monumental understatement.

"He was phoning *you*, Amelia." Marissa's cultured voice was calm. "She informed him where you were. Of course he wanted to assist in any way he could, so he sent me. I don't ordinarily handle these types of things, but I'm not entirely without experience."

Did it matter?

In Amelia's experience, attorneys had never been a big success for her. But if Marissa had eased the way for Jack, she could swallow her pride and be grateful, despite the way the woman had once threatened Daphne in her letter.

Not that the bite went down very easily.

The elevator opened and the three of them left the building. Amelia couldn't even muster surprise at the distinctive BMW waiting for them.

Jack was saying nothing at all, of course. But his eyes widened slightly when the attorney stopped alongside the car and gestured for him to get in the backseat. Only Marissa stopped Amelia before she could follow him in. "Take the front. I have my own car."

Amelia reluctantly slid into the front seat and wished that she and Jack were anywhere else as Marissa leaned down and spoke across her to Gray, who didn't acknowledge Amelia's presence at all. "It's his first offense. He's a minor and the stolen equipment wasn't technically in his possession, but one of the older boys. With your involvement I can probably get the charges dropped before we even get to the hearing."

"Thanks."

Marissa smiled briefly. "Stay out of trouble, Jack," Marissa suggested as she straightened. "Amelia. I'm sure we'll be seeing more of each other before long."

Not if Amelia could help it, she thought mulishly.

She pulled the car door closed when the leggy attorney stepped away from the vehicle.

Gray's thumb tapped the steering wheel. "You okay?" The comment was directed at Jack.

"Yeah," Jack assured, his voice flat.

"Do you know who I am?"

"You're the guy who's hot for my aunt."

"Jack!" Amelia turned around, gaping at him, but her nephew looked unrepentant, his gaze firmly on Gray's.

"Anything else?" Gray pressed.

"What else is there to know?" Jack's lips twisted. "Cool car."

"Did you do it?"

"Did you?" She added her request to Gray's, because she truly needed to know.

"I didn't steal nothing."

"I didn't steal anything," she corrected.

"Neither did I," her nephew returned, full of sarcastic, wounded male pride.

"Jack—"

He looked away. A muscle flexed in his young jaw.

Oh, yes. She was doing a brilliant job of filling in for Daphne. Caring for Jack for just three short months and he'd taken to hanging out with shoplifters.

"We'll talk about this at home," she warned.

He didn't respond and with a sigh, Amelia turned around in her seat, silently fastening her seat belt.

She gave Gray a quick look. "Thank you. For trying to help

at the station." She barely succeeded in keeping her voice shy of grudging. "But I could have managed."

Particularly since, considering the situation, she was winning such great awards in child rearing.

"I have no doubt," he agreed. He drove away from the station, smoothly navigating the trip back to their apartment building.

Correction. *His* apartment building, if Tanisha Jones's gossip could be trusted.

He parked on the street, blatantly ignoring the no-parking zone and accompanied them inside. Amelia was suddenly so exhausted that she couldn't summon the will to argue.

They rode up in the elevator in silence and a portion of Amelia's mind wondered what Gray thought of the battered interior.

Paula greeted them at the apartment door when they arrived. Without a single word, Jack slouched across the living room, disappearing into his bedroom with a slammed door.

"Timmy's down and Molly's asleep in your bed," Paula told her. "She wanted to be near the baby."

"Thanks, Paula." Amelia hugged her friend, blinking back the weak tears that burned her eyes. "See you in the morning."

Paula patted her back comfortingly. "Kids do crazy things," she murmured. "It's not the end of the world. And don't be mad at me for spilling the beans to him."

"I'm not." Paula had only done what she thought would help.

Amelia moved away, going to the kitchen with no purpose other than to put as much distance between her and Grayson— who was showing Paula out the door with all the graciousness in the world—as she could.

But standing there hiding made her look as pathetic as she

felt, so she pulled open the refrigerator door and peered inside. "Can I, um, get you something to drink?"

"Hospitality, Amelia?"

She pushed the door and the bottles in the door shelves rattled noisily as it closed. "That attorney is the one you sicced on my sister."

"Marissa's been my counsel for years."

"She must have quite an opinion by now of me and my sister."

"If she does, she's paid well enough to keep it to herself."

"So why don't you marry *her?*"

He slid off his black suit jacket, looking around the modest apartment as if to find a suitable spot to place it.

"We don't have fleas," Amelia assured tartly.

His lips tightened. He dropped the jacket over the back of one of the table chairs. "If you're always going to believe the worst of me, the next few years are going to be pretty miserable."

"Years!" She crossed her arms. "Who said anything about *that?*"

"I figure at least two years ought to do it. Are all the apartments this size?"

Two years with the title of Grayson Hunt's wife? It hardly bore thinking about. "I'd have thought you'd have been curious enough to learn more about this building before you bought it."

He just looked at her.

She flopped her hands. "There isn't anything larger than a two-bedroom," she said. "Talk to Stan. Your building superintendent," she added when he clearly didn't recognize the name.

"I have people who manage my holdings," he said, as if doing anything else was unfathomable. "Would you prefer a judge or a minister?"

Her mouth parted, not just from the abrupt shift in topic,

but the topic to which he shifted. Only no words would escape, so she just stood there like a gaping fish.

"Minister," he decided for her. "You don't look like the civil wedding type."

She bristled. That was the kind of wedding that John had wanted and she'd gone along with him rather than cause dissension.

"We'll want the children at the ceremony, of course," Gray went on without pause. "Photographs would look odd if they weren't. Aside from this regrettable incident, Jack seems well behaved. What about Molly?"

"Well, she sings at the top of her lungs and turns cart-wheels whenever she feels like it," Amelia said tightly. "My niece and nephew have perfectly *fine* manners, thank you very much."

He lifted his eyebrows slightly. "I stand corrected. This Paula. She seems like a decent sort. Do you want her as your witness?" His gaze drifted over her. "I can arrange for someone else if you don't. We won't worry about guest lists and such. There's no time, first of all, and secondly, I prefer to keep it private." He glanced at her, as if waiting for her to argue.

When she didn't, he gave a brief, satisfied nod. "I'll warn you that there will be a formal reception. Maybe not immediately, but soon. It'll be expected. You can invite Paula to that if you prefer. You might want to, actually. Aside from my family, it'll be mostly social and business contacts who'll be there. Don't know whether it will be at the shack—the reception hall could certainly accommodate it, but it takes some time for security to run the guest list, and another venue might be easier. It'll be black tie, though. You'll have to resign at Brandlebury immediately."

That managed to loosen her tongue. "What? Absolutely not!"

He exhaled, portraying the very soul of patience with a not-very-bright student. "As my wife, you will have plenty of responsibilities *without* clocking in as a very poorly compensated librarian."

Her face felt hot. "What do you know about my compensation?"

"Honey, there is nothing much about you that I *don't* know, now."

It was bad enough to think that he'd investigated her to verify her sister's condition. Did he know every other failure in her life, too? "Please tell me there is something about me that you don't know."

He leaned his hip against one of the stools at the counter and leisurely unbuttoned his cuffs. "I suppose there are a few things," he allowed. "What *are* those?"

"What?" She realized he was looking at the stack of clean diapers that she'd folded and left sitting on the counter. "Surely you've seen diapers before. Don't worry. I've washed them," she assured acidly.

He grimaced and continued folding the white linen shirtsleeves over a few times, leaving most of his forearms—sinewy and tanned and dusted with dark hair—bare.

She dragged her gaze from the sight and reached for the refrigerator again. She pulled out a bottle of apple juice that she didn't really want and twisted it open. "What *kind* of responsibilities?"

"Keeping my father's suspicious nature from rearing will be one." He shrugged. "Social functions, mostly. Don't worry," he added when she paled at the idea, "it'll mostly be appearance only. Short. Brief. You'll be the beautiful brunette on my arm. That's all."

She pressed her lips together. Beautiful? Then she mentally shook sense back into her head. Getting her sidetracked was probably some tactic of his to keep her off balance. "You're assuming that I'll agree to this farce you've proposed."

His vivid eyes were steady on her face. "No farce, Amelia. A marriage."

"Marriage proposals are usually accompanied by a ring."

He went to his jacket, pulled out a small box and handed it to her.

She swallowed. "Oh."

"Open it." His voice was careless. "Don't worry. When we reach the end of our agreement, you can keep it, as well as any other…physical assets you acquire. In addition, you'll be well compensated for your time just as the terms of the agreement spelled out."

She couldn't help herself. Her shaking fingers flipped open the box.

The ring inside practically leaped out at her, the stones were so huge.

"Well?"

Maybe he wasn't as blasé about the ring as she'd thought. She set the box on the counter where it looked extremely odd sitting next to Daphne's bright red souvenir salt and pepper shakers. "It's…spectacular," she settled for.

In truth, it was the kind of ring she'd never ever have desired for herself. A wide white metal—she supposed it was platinum band that had dozens of stones working down the sides with a mammoth square rock set high in the center. It was beautiful, of that there was no doubt. But it wasn't at all *her.* It was too large. Too ostentatious. Too everything.

But then what did it matter? It wasn't as if the engagement

ring was proffered with undying love. The small solitaire that John had offered had been.

And look how well that had turned out.

She supposed it was the passage of time that made the pain of his defection less acute.

He'd told her she was too settled and boring and plain.

Grayson claimed she was beautiful.

The thought circled like an annoying little gnat.

She picked up the juice bottle again, spun it between her fingers. "Aren't you even the least bit embarrassed?" Her voice shook and she forcefully injected it with a healthy dose of aspersion. "Not about the ring. But, you know. That you of all people have to resort to hiring a wife."

His lips curled, but he didn't look amused. "Everything in life is business, Amelia. The sooner you learn that, the better off you'll be."

She paused, watching him. Sitting between them, the ring seemed to wink like a big caution sign. "You really believe that," she said after a moment. She could tell by his face that he did.

And it struck her as unbearably sad.

"It's gotten me where I am."

"Then I feel sorry for you, Mr. Hunt."

"Don't waste your pity," he assured. "Small ceremony or not, you'll have to have a proper dress. There's not really time to get a designer at this point for something original, but I can put Loretta on it. You never know what she'll pull out of her hat. Are there any particular labels that you prefer?"

She nearly choked on her sip of apple juice. Somehow she doubted he meant one that instructed Do Not Dry Clean.

She couldn't believe this conversation was transpiring. As if she'd already signed that paper of his, consigning herself to the next few years as his wife in exchange for a not insignificant ransom. "Who is Loretta?"

"My secretary."

"Marry *her.*"

"Her husband might have something to say about it." He reached over the counter and slid the bottle from her fingers, lifting it to his lips.

Amelia's mouth ran oddly dry.

She realized she was staring at his mouth and hurriedly flipped on the faucet, wet the dishcloth and needlessly began wiping down the spotless countertop, carefully giving the jewelry box a safe berth.

"It has to be you, Amelia."

The rag bunched in her hand. "*Why?* Certainly not because you feel compelled to help my sister's situation."

"That's your goal," he agreed. "And it's one that I'm not above taking advantage of. Like me or not for it, but we both need something that the other can provide. This is simple expedience."

"Please don't insult me by pretending that I'm your only hope where a wife is concerned." He'd probably been carrying around that ring ready for dropping it on some unwary soul whenever it suited him.

"You're the one I believe can convince my father and my aunt that you chose me without knowing who I really am," he said equably. "Untrue though it is, your acting skills are…formidable. And through no one's fault but my own, I find I'm up against a rather tight deadline."

She winced. The observation was *not* a compliment. "How tight?"

"The ceremony needs to be this weekend."

She absorbed that, managing not to choke. "Why do they need to think I didn't know who you were?"

He shoved his hands through his hair, the first sign that he might not be quite as confident as he appeared. "I told you my father is in poor health."

She chewed the inside of her lip. "I saw on the news that he'd been in the hospital again. I'm sorry."

He lifted his fingers, as if dismissing the sentiment. "He's home again, fortunately. But he's made it clear to my brothers and me that in the time he has left, he wants to see us happily married. To women…unlike our mothers. My brothers have all succeeded in that."

Harrison Hunt's health was that precarious? She hadn't seen that in the news at all. She recalled stories about the man's ex-wives, though. They'd all profited aplenty at the demise of the relationships. "Your brothers hired wives, too?"

He looked vaguely chagrined. "No. They went about things in the more usual way. They're besotted with their brides, believe me."

"And these brides didn't know they were marrying a Hunt." She couldn't keep the skepticism from her voice. Grayson was the president of HuntCom, but she knew that the other three sons of Harrison Hunt were involved in the family's holdings in one way or another, though photographs of them had been extremely scarce.

"Pretty much."

She had the feeling he was glossing over quite a lot with those two words. "What about the children?"

"You'll have to get rid of them." He let out a short laugh when she just stared in shock. "Good Lord, Amelia. You *do* have a low opinion where I'm concerned. You're their caretaker. That's not going to change. There's plenty of room for them at the shack."

"Shack?" Her voice was faint.

He just shook his head, dismissing it. "There are entire wings at the family house that aren't in use. You'll have a lot more space than you do here, that's for certain."

"The, um, the family house. Your father lives there."

"So do I, unless I'm staying at my place downtown. Once we're married, I'll have to show more inclination to be at the house, though. With you." He crossed his arms on the countertop, nudging the jewelry box toward her. "You should be happy about this, Amelia. As my wife, you'll be getting what you wanted without having to drag anyone's name through the mud."

"The only name that was going to be dragged anywhere was yours."

He shook his head, that discomfiting mask of gentleness that he seemed able to don at will crossing his face. "Those types of things never work that way. Surely you realize that, if you're thinking sensibly. Trying to tar and feather me would far more likely end up with people believing your sister was just out for what she could get. There's no lack of gold-digging women where my family is concerned. All that research you claimed to have done surely told you that. Even your sister's current condition wouldn't change what people would say about her."

"They wouldn't say anything because her claims are true."

He set the juice bottle down. "I was never with your sister, Amelia. Never."

How convincing he could be. So convincing that the niggle of doubt that she possessed wanted to break loose and run around free as a bird. She went over to the narrow bookshelf that stood beside the television and yanked down a framed photograph. "Are you saying *she's* not beautiful?" She thrust the frame into his hands.

He looked at the snapshot of Daphne that Amelia had taken herself one summer at the beach a few years earlier. Her sister, long legged and lithe, her deep red hair spinning around her head in the breeze grinned back at the camera, full of life and vitality.

"She's very beautiful. She still is." At her sudden stare, he set the frame on the countertop. "I visited her. And before we start arguing about it, I can assure you that it was the first time I'd ever been in her company. In *any* way."

"My sister wouldn't lie."

He sighed faintly. "I can arrange a DNA test, Amelia. Is that what you truly want?"

What she wanted was to keep Timmy. What she wanted was to know that Daphne had at least a fighting chance to regain *some* portion of her life.

Gray had no interest whatsoever in claiming Timmy as his own. Without proof that the baby was his, she could walk away from their so-called marriage knowing the baby would remain with her. Or with Daphne if, miracle of miracles, the rehabilitation program at Jackson-Whitney helped.

Without proof, they'd never have to wage a fight for the baby if Grayson ever decided he needed a ready-made heir, after all.

"No," she said huskily. "I don't want there to be a DNA test." She knew what he'd believe she was admitting.

That there was no chance Timmy was his, after all.

"Then we have an agreement?"

"What if I can't convince your father that I'm, um, you know—"

"In love with Matthew Gray?" His gaze dropped to her lips

for a brief, burning moment. "That you had no clue who I was when you agreed to be my wife?"

She moistened her lips. "Yes."

"As I've said, you're a convincing woman, Amelia."

And again, she felt certain that assessment wasn't a compliment. "You mean you think I'm a good liar."

He shrugged. "Let's say that you actually had me wondering—briefly—what I was doing and with whom I was doing it about a year ago. However, the British prime minister could never be mistaken for a pretty female redhead."

She squeezed the rag, controlling the anger that wanted to rise inside her. Whether at his seeming callousness, or at that niggling doubt, she didn't know. "D-don't you have to be in love with me?"

"There are some things that even Harry knows he can't force." He smiled faintly. "Don't take that personally, though."

Oh, sure. Right. Not personal at all.

They were only discussing *marriage* for profit.

"What if there is something I want changed in that agreement?"

"Where is it?"

She silently went to her bedroom and retrieved the envelope from its place where it was still buried deep inside her briefcase. Molly didn't stir, but as Amelia turned back to the doorway, she could see Timmy's wide eyes following her. He made a protesting sound and she stopped and picked him up so that he wouldn't wake Molly. Cradling him in her arm, she closed the door behind her as she returned to the living room.

Gray didn't exactly ignore Timmy, but he didn't gape with recognition, either, as he took the envelope from her, extracted the sheets and flattened them on the counter. Then he uncapped his pen and handed it to her. "Just mark your changes where appropriate."

Montblanc, she noticed. Too fine of a writing instrument to merely go by the name of *pen*. She took it, balanced Timmy against her shoulder and scratched through the clause specifying the settlement of money she would personally receive at the conclusion of the agreement's "term."

Quite a euphemism for what was really a divorce.

The thought gave her pause and she lifted the pen from the paper. Divorce implied more than the end of marriage; it implied that there was a *real* marriage.

Why not an annulment? She desperately wanted to ask, but like the ninny she was, couldn't push the words out. There was no way the man would want conjugal visits. Not with her. She was much too ordinary for a man like him.

"You want *more?*" His voice was sardonic.

She dragged her thoughts out of the gutter. Money. He was referring to money.

"Ironic, isn't it," she said softly. "Evidently your father is determined for you not to marry gold diggers, as he'd done. And here you are, thinking to enter a binding agreement with that very purpose in mind. Well. They say that many men want to marry women just like their mothers."

"You're not in my mother's league," he assured evenly. "You'd have to work a lifetime to get close. And the difference between me and Harry is that I'm not blind to what I'm getting into. So how much are we talking?"

"Zero." She smoothed her hand over Timmy's warm back. Just holding the baby gave her comfort. Strength.

"Zero," he repeated, looking disbelieving.

She squelched the screaming meemies thundering inside

her stomach. "The only thing I want is for Daphne to receive the best medical care that money can buy."

Eyes narrowed, he studied her face for an uncomfortable moment. "Quite the bargain." He took the pen from her, initialed the deleted portion and handed the pen back to her.

Before she could talk herself out of it, she scratched her name at the bottom, right next to where his signature already resided.

She carefully set down the pen, staring at the document. Against her, she felt Timmy's tiny body heave a huge sigh.

She rubbed her cheek against his little cue-ball-bald head.

"All right, then." Gray folded the papers and slid them back inside the envelope. He glanced at his phone. Pressed a few buttons on it before jamming it in his pocket. "So, about the dress?"

She rocked Timmy back and forth, feeling hot and cold all at once. "Whatever is easiest." Thinking too hard about what she was doing made her feel vaguely nauseated.

"I'll make arrangements." He grabbed his jacket and headed for the door. "Loretta will be in touch. Be available."

She smiled weakly. So this was what it was like to be engaged to Grayson Hunt. What would *marriage* be like? The person who should be wondering these things was her sister. And Amelia felt more wretched than ever. "Sure. Whatever."

He paused, hand on the door. His gaze drifted over the baby for only a moment. "It will be all right, Amelia."

She couldn't have responded to save her soul.

And then he was gone and the only thing that Amelia could think was that she might not have a soul to save.

Not if she'd just sold it to the devil.

Chapter Nine

If she'd thought it was surreal to bargain away the next few years of her life in exchange for Daphne's health, it was nothing compared to the days that followed.

First, even before she had a chance to take Timmy to Paula's before work the next morning, a courier was at her door, delivering the papers that would effectively transfer Daphne from her present convalescent hospital to the Jackson-Whitney Institute where she'd be under the direct care of Dr. Sloane Jackson.

Amelia wanted to hug the documents to her chest, sit down and cry because, no matter how it had been brought about, the transfer was a miracle.

But the courier was waiting. Not to mention Molly and Jack, who were sitting at the table finishing their cereal, and would have probably thought she'd lost her marbles. Particu-

larly since she had no idea what she was going to tell them—
even after a sleepless night worrying about it.

"I'm supposed to deliver the papers right away, ma'am," the
courier told her, glancing at his clipboard. "To Biggs-Tolley."

Her vision blurring, she quickly signed them.

"What was that?" Jack asked the second she'd closed the
door on the departing courier.

"Good news, actually." She'd simply focus on Daphne,
and let the rest of things land where they might. "Your mom
is being moved to that rehabilitation center I told you about."

"You mean the one that we can't pay for."

"I was able to work out something." Her nerves squirmed.

Jack's brown eyes narrowed. "Because of that guy, huh."

Trust his twelve-year-old self to be suspicious. And
accurate. "I'll tell you about it later. I *am* going to have to
ground you, you know. It's not like I'm going to forget the
stunt you pulled last evening."

"I told you. I didn't steal anything."

She badly wanted to believe him, but just as badly didn't
want to fail him by falling too easily for a lie. "You asked for
permission to go to Heller's. Not that electronics place. So
what am I supposed to think, Jack?"

His gaze dropped, his lips turning down.

Molly suddenly burst into tears.

Amelia crouched next to her niece. "Honey, what is it?"

"I don't want you and Jack to fight."

"Jeez, Mol." Jack looked disgusted. He bolted from the
table only to return after a few steps to get his empty cereal
bowl, which he carried into the kitchen and rinsed in the sink.

"We're not fighting," Amelia soothed, trying to staunch
Molly's tears without letting herself give way to them, too.

"I don't want you to go away like Mommy."

"Oh, Molly." Amelia hugged the girl even more tightly. "I am not going *anywhere.* I promise you."

"B-but Jack and her were fighting, too. Before she—"

The bowl Jack was rinsing clattered noisily in the sink. "Yeah," he yelled suddenly, "blame Mom's stroke all on me." He grabbed his backpack from the counter and darted out the door.

Amelia scrambled after him. "Jack!" His steps didn't slow an instant. "Jack! Wait."

He pushed the call button for the elevator and the doors slid open. They closed just before she reached them and she smacked the call button.

The elevator doors remained firmly closed. There was no hope that she'd beat it to the lobby by the stairs and she ran back to the apartment. "Hurry up, Molly. Get your backpack, right now." She grabbed the fabric carrier and went into the bedroom to get the baby. He was none too happy to be yanked from his sleep and bundled into the sling, but it couldn't be helped. But when she turned to hustle Molly along, because she wasn't about to let Jack race off like that, he was standing in the doorway again.

Amelia hesitated, her heart slowly climbing back down from her throat. "I'm glad you came back."

He didn't look at her. "Hurry up, Mol, or we'll miss the bus."

"Wait for me," Amelia added. "I just need to get my brief-case." She headed for her bedroom. "Molly, grab the bottles from the fridge and put them in the diaper bag, please." She'd already packed everything else for Timmy's day with Paula.

"I thought you were quitting."

Amelia froze. She slowly turned to face her nephew,

who was standing just inside the opened doorway, looking as tense as a tree in the face of a storm. "Why would you think that?"

"I heard you last night. You and that…that guy."

Of course he had. The walls were paper-thin. She pressed her fingertips to her forehead, running a mental transcript in her head to recall just exactly how bad her conversation—negotiation—with Grayson must have sounded to him. "Then you also heard that I told him I wouldn't resign from Brandlebury."

"And I made it clear why you'd need to." Grayson stepped up behind Jack, clapping a hand over his shoulder.

The jolt that shot through her at his unexpected arrival was only surprise, she told herself. It *couldn't* be pleasure. "What are you doing here?"

"You haven't seen the papers, obviously."

She realized he had a newspaper folded beneath his arm. This time, the jolt she felt was tainted with dread. "What about them?"

He reached down and picked up a parcel from the hallway and stepped past Jack. "Sit tight for a few minutes, Jack."

"But the bus—"

"I'll make sure you and your sister get there on time." Gray dropped the enormous parcel on the floor and flipped open the paper where he'd obviously folded it to one of the interior pages and extended it to her.

Ignoring her curiosity over the package, she warily took the newspaper, holding it out of Timmy's grasping hands, only to groan at the photograph of her climbing into his vehicle outside the police station. There was no accompanying article. Just a caption that pondered the identity of Grayson Hunt's jean-clad mystery lady.

"At least it's in the leisure section." The humor was weak, but she made the effort.

"It's problematic," Gray said. He shut the door behind him. "And not very brilliant of me to have used my own vehicle that evening. My father will, unquestionably, see the photo. I'd hoped to get through the wedding before springing him and Cornelia on you. But if the paper has already snagged a shot of us together, he'll know you can't be unaware of my identity for long. We'll have to make a preemptive strike."

"Wedding?" Molly's face was still tear streaked, but she'd stopped crying. She leaned against Amelia's side. "Are you getting a wedding, Aunt Amelia?"

So much for discussing "it" later when she'd had a chance to figure out just how she would explain "it" to the kids. "Yes."

"Great," Jack muttered. "That's just great." He glared at Gray. "I knew you would ruin everything."

Amelia winced. "Jack, please. If anything you should be…relieved. Grateful. Mr.—" She shot Grayson a look, realizing she didn't know how she was supposed to refer to him now.

"Gray," the man inserted.

"—*Gray*," she repeated, feeling more awkward than she could ever recall feeling, "has done nothing but help you. And your mother," she forced herself to add.

"So what about me and Mol and Tim?" His demand was slightly choked and Amelia's heart ached for him.

"You'll all come to live with me, along with your aunt," Gray said immediately.

"I don't wanna," Molly whispered to Amelia.

"Yeah," Jack challenged. "What if we don't want to?"

Amelia gently disengaged herself from Molly and went to her nephew, cupping his face in her hands, making him look right at her. Timmy's hand flopped out, latching onto his brother's shirt collar. "Remember the night at the hospital when I explained about your mom and what had happened to her?" She could feel the muscles in Jack's jaw flexing beneath her fingers. So young. Trying to be so grown-up. "I told you that the three of us would have to be a team, from there on out. We'd have to pull together. To stay strong for your mom. Remember?"

He barely nodded.

"We've made most of our decisions as a team," she went on. "But for this one I'm pulling rank. We're a family and you and Molly and Timmy go where I go. But until your mom gets well and can come home again, there are some things that I'm going to decide for all of us—" she swallowed "—because it's the best thing for everyone. And this is one of those things." Her voice went hoarse.

"Can I drive that car of his?"

Oh, she loved this kid. She wanted to just sit there and cry. Instead, she managed to lift an eyebrow. "You're twelve," she reminded, her voice thick, but dry. "What do you think?" She tapped his cheek gently and let him escape her and Timmy's curious fists.

"So it's settled," Gray said, reaching for the door. "Peter's downstairs with the car. He'll drop the kids at Brandlebury."

"Wait." She nodded toward the parcel. "What—"

"Diapers," he said, his tone short.

Her eyebrows rose. "Excuse me?"

"You know. Disposable ones. So you don't have to wash them. My secretary tells me that there are services we can hire to do that for you if you still insist on using the cloth things, but—" He shrugged, as if the details of that were unimportant.

Amelia was tearing open the opaque plastic bag. Sure

enough, inside was a supply of disposable diapers that would last her for weeks. "He, um, he can drop all of us at Brandlebury," she corrected absently. The man showed no interest in Timmy at all, but he brought *diapers?*

Turning from the thoroughly unexpected gift, she patted Timmy through the carrier and reached for the diaper bag, but Gray beat her to it. "I'm not resigning over the phone."

"But you will be resigning," he pressed.

She wanted to argue, but Jack and Molly were there. "Yes." She finally capitulated. She'd turn in her notice, at least. That would give her several weeks left of employment, during which time Gray would probably realize that having her around all the time wasn't as desirable as he seemed to think.

He gave her a sharp look, almost as if he were reading her mind. But he nodded, and ushered them out the door, even taking the keys from Amelia's hands to lock it behind them.

She stopped at Paula's door. She knew there would be plenty of questions to answer when her friend silently took the diaper bag that Gray handed over to her. Amelia transferred the baby to Paula. "We'll talk later," she murmured.

"You bet we will," Paula promised.

Amelia could feel her friend's gaze following them to the elevator.

The ride down was mercifully quick, and the sight of the long, black limousine parked at the curb in front of the building was more than enough to distract Molly and Jack from their reservations about the situation.

The moment they appeared, the tall gray-haired driver opened the rear door.

"Amelia, this is Peter," Gray introduced. "Peter, Amelia White and her niece and nephew, Molly and Jack."

If the elderly man was surprised by his passengers, he hid it well. "Pleasure to meet you, miss." He took Amelia's hand and helped her into the rear of the limousine as if she were dressed for the Academy Awards. He did the same with Molly, who produced a stunning giggle as she climbed in beside Amelia. Even Jack couldn't keep his blasé facade entirely in place when he joined them, his eyes wide.

Molly scrambled across to sit on the facing seat next to her brother and when Gray took the seat alongside Amelia, her niece leaned forward toward him. "I like this a *lot* more than the bus," she whispered.

Gray leaned forward slightly, too. "I'm glad," he said, just as softly.

The shy smile that lit Molly's face had been far too rare in the past three months. And now, it came courtesy of Grayson Hunt. Amelia twisted the strap of her briefcase, struggling with that fact. When Gray's gaze found hers, she couldn't make herself look away from those unreadable blue-green eyes.

"Peter will pick you up after school," he told her. "No more bus rides."

Every independent cell that Amelia possessed bristled at that, though it was plain that neither Molly nor Jack looked inclined to argue, since they were both obviously enamored with the luxurious vehicle. "That doesn't seem necessary."

"It is." Gray's voice was short.

Her nerves prickled again, but she kept quiet.

"You'll need to be available this evening for dinner with Harry. Can your friend watch the kids, or do you want me to arrange a nanny?"

"Nanny!" Jack leaned forward, looking alarmed. "I don't need some freaking nanny."

"Jack," Amelia scolded.

"Maybe a parole officer suits you better?" Gray asked smoothly.

Jack's lips tightened and he sat back in his seat again, arms crossed over his chest.

"That wasn't necessary, either," Amelia told Gray. Across from them, that rare, precious smile had already faded from Molly's solemn face. "There's no need for you to arrange anything. I'm sure Paula can help out for a few hours." She couldn't let herself think too closely about his plans for that evening or she'd be incapacitated with nervousness.

"Are you certain?"

She nodded. "Yes. Of course."

But the truth was, Amelia wasn't certain about anything at all.

Later that evening driving out to the Hunt mansion on Lake Washington, Amelia decided she was wrong. She was certain about one thing.

Her uncertainty.

It just grew and grew until she felt as if she would choke from it even before Gray ushered her into the soaring structure that was his family home. The fact that he'd grabbed her hand as they left the car he'd parked in a wide, circular drive wasn't helping any, either.

It was just a hand. Long fingered. Warm. Surprisingly callused.

Why was she noticing the calluses on his hands, when she ought to be thinking how heavy and cold that ornate ring he'd made certain she was wearing felt on her ring finger. "Wait." It was as much a plea to him as to her own sensibilities.

He paused, one foot on the last of the shallow steps that led to an entrance that looked out over the moon-dusted water. "What?"

They'd said very little on the long drive out to the house. What was there to say? It wasn't as if he had a need to fill her in on his family dynamics, when she wasn't supposed to know about them, anyway. "Stick as close to the truth as possible," had been his advice.

They'd met on the running trail. It was nobody's business but their own why she'd been on the trail in the first place.

She opened her mouth, but no words emerged.

"Amelia, I'm not anxious to go in there, either," he said, obviously recognizing her reluctance, when she continued to hang back. "But we can't stand out here on the steps all evening."

She looked from his face to the tall wide door behind him. "This just isn't going to work," she blurted. "Your father will never believe we are…that I—"

"That you what?" He gave her a sidelong look, the corner of his lips quirking. "Were so smitten with me that you let me sweep you right off your feet?"

Her mouth ran unaccountably dry. It was becoming too frequent an occurrence for her comfort.

He lifted her hand, and she nearly jumped out of her skin when he brushed his lips across her knuckles below the engagement ring. "Such things *can* happen, Amelia."

She didn't doubt it. And it pained her immensely that her immediate thought wasn't of her sister at all. "Not to me."

He smiled faintly. His thumb dragged slowly, distractingly, across the ridges of her knuckles. "You're going to want to watch where you drop challenges like that, honey. Might as well put out a sign begging to be proven wrong."

"It's not a challenge." She tried tugging her hand free, but his hold was steady. "It's a fact."

"Are you saying that you've never lost your head to a man?" His gaze dropped to her lips and his voice seemed to drop a notch, as well. "Not even that accountant nerd you were engaged to?"

"How do you know about him?"

"Honey, I know everything. Remember?"

Her lips tightened. "Then you know why we're no longer engaged. And that I'm not exaggerating about…about… losing my head where men are concerned."

His lashes narrowed, leaving a slit of glowing aqua. "He knocked up a girl you worked with at the university."

Her cheeks flushed. She truly didn't want to know how he'd come by his information. "Is there some point to even getting into this? You're just proving my point, anyway."

"Your point being that you don't lose your head, as you put it." He found her other hand, lifting it, too, tsking with no small amount of amusement at the fist she'd made of it. "Haven't you ever been carried away with desire, Amelia?"

"No." She yanked her hands free. "Just because I agreed to this…plot…of yours, doesn't mean that I'm going to let you make fun of me for the next few years, either."

He laughed softly and grabbed her hand again, pulling her up the last step.

"I don't see that there's anything funny about this."

He just shook his head and reached for the door. "Harry's gonna love you. God help us all."

Amelia had enough reservations about that to fill a reservoir. "Gray—"

He tugged her one last step over the threshold, right into

his arms. She barely had a chance to draw in a shocked breath when he covered her mouth with his.

Shock? Shock was nothing compared to the electricity that streaked through her when his lips touched hers. Her fingers clutched the lapels of his suit coat—whether to push him away or pull him closer she didn't know. Didn't have the brain cells to ponder, really, as they seemed to shrivel into nonexistence when he lifted his head, breaking the contact almost infinitesimally. Just enough to mutter a soft oath. His curse whispered over her lips, then he kissed her again.

"Gray—"

He swallowed the protest she tried to raise—at least she told herself it was a protest, but even her feeble brain cells knew that for the lie it was. His hand swept down her spine; she felt the warmth of his palm, his widespread fingers through the soft fabric of her dress. They were no less warm than the hard chest beneath her grasping fingers.

"Good grief, Gray. Give the girl a chance to breathe."

Mortified, Amelia wrenched out of Gray's arms, as far as he allowed her to go. Which wasn't far, since she could still feel the brush of him against her thighs. Her cheeks felt on fire as Gray's gaze met hers for a moment before his head turned slowly in the direction of the man who'd interrupted them.

"Just trying to convince my fiancée not to follow her better instincts and head for the hills now that she's seen the kind of shack she'll be expected to live in." Gray's hand slid down and caught hers again, drawing her more fully across the threshold. "Amelia, this is my father, Harrison Hunt."

No amount of media coverage of the tall, gangly man could have prepared her for the moment. His sheer height was intimidating, for one thing, though Gray—a few inches shorter—struck her as a more sizable man. But the blue gaze that peered at her through black-rimmed glasses seemed to hold as much wariness as she, herself, felt.

He also looked pale, and she couldn't help but be aware that he'd so recently been in the hospital again.

"Welcome, my dear," he said, holding out his hand toward her.

She didn't have to feign nervousness as she stepped toward the computer mogul. "I'm pleased to meet you, Mr. Hunt."

He took her hand in both of his. "You're trembling."

She flushed and shot Gray a desperate look.

He didn't help matters any when he merely closed his hand in a thoroughly proprietary fashion over the back of her neck, bared by her chignon. "That's my effect, Harry," he said, looking satisfied. "Not yours."

Her flush went hotter until it felt like a wildfire was burning her cheeks from the inside out.

"As it should be." A small smile touched Harry's lips and he squeezed her hand, almost reassuringly.

Which was probably just wishful thinking on her part. There was no guarantee, after all, that he would believe she'd agreed to marry his son without knowing who he really was. "I'm sorry," she said, truthfully. "This is all a little…overwhelming."

Most overwhelming of all was the tingling current passing from Gray's hand on her nape, straight down her spine.

"We put our pants on one leg at a time," Harry assured, patting her hand comfortably. He didn't let go as he drew her hand through his arm and turned away from the door.

She swallowed and hurried along with him as they passed through the enormous foyer. Couldn't help but stare at the furnishings as they went from one room to the next, finally ending in a lushly appointed salon complete with a fireplace, a small fountain and an unobstructed view of Lake Washington through an entire wall of glass.

"Aunt Cornelia." Gray left Amelia's side for the slender, elegant woman who was standing near the windows, adjusting the placement of a long-stemmed red rose amid an enormous bouquet of equally vivid buds. "As beautiful as ever." He dropped a kiss on her softly lined cheek.

The genuine affection on his face snagged at Amelia, and then she found herself face-to-face with the older woman, as Gray introduced them.

"Gray wasn't exaggerating when he told us how lovely you were," Cornelia greeted. Her smile was welcoming and much less intimidating than Harrison's. She stepped forward and kissed Amelia's cheeks. "I'm so delighted to meet you."

"Thank you."

Gray slid his arm around her shoulders, saving her from searching for something appropriate to say. "Cornelia is like a mother to me," he said. "She was married to Harry's best friend, George."

Amelia knew that George Fairchild had been Harry's partner from the beginning, but had died many, many years ago.

"And Gray and his brothers are as dear as sons to me," Cornelia returned, smiling. Her gaze shifted from Gray to Amelia. "Harry, pour this girl some wine. What do you prefer, Amelia?"

Amelia glanced at the stemware sitting alongside the rose display. Cornelia had obviously been drinking from it. "Whatever you're having is fine." She had no particular palate for wine. Most of it tasted like bitter grapes to her.

"There you are." Harry handed over a wineglass filled with a delicately hued white. "Gray? What's your pleasure tonight?"

Gray tilted his head slightly. "Other than Amelia? Wine'll do."

Harry returned to the granite-topped bar and poured another glass. "Corny, why don't you give Amelia a tour of the place?"

Wariness shot through Amelia's veins, which wasn't alleviated at all by Gray leaning down and kissing her cheek. "Don't let her bore you with tales of me growing up."

Cornelia tucked her arm through Amelia's. "Women in love always want to know about their man's background."

"This wasn't a background I ever expected," Amelia murmured, burying her nose in her wineglass. She was miles away from being in love with Grayson Hunt, but there was no denying her curiosity about him. She couldn't even use Timmy as an excuse for that.

Cornelia laughed softly. "Well, life throws surprises at us all the time, dear. I've been telling my daughters that all of their life. But you mustn't blame Gray for his small deception."

Amelia managed not to wince as Cornelia picked up her wineglass before drawing her out of the room. And even though she'd braced herself for some sort of inquisition from the woman, none was forthcoming.

The only thing Cornelia did was provide a disarmingly entertaining narration of the Hunt family complex, from its design and construction to its current state.

Amelia didn't have to pretend to be awestruck by its futuristic technological touches, contrasted by its wealth of stunning antique furnishings. There was even a grand reception hall—the one that Gray had mentioned—where, Cornelia told her, over the Christmas holidays an eighteen-foot Christmas tree took center place. Circling above the massive space was a balcony hung with black-and-white photographs chronicling HuntCom's rise to glory.

"I'll let Gray show you his wing," Cornelia said, once they left behind the reception hall and passed a soaring staircase and yet another foyer. "It's back along that way." It seemed to Amelia as if they'd been walking in a mile-wide circle. "It'll be your wing, too, of course, once you're married. And I understand that you're caring for your sister's children right now, as well?"

"Yes.

"Poor darlings. And you." Cornelia stopped, and Amelia realized they'd reached a dining room.

It was so large that she actually found herself counting chairs, just from curiosity alone.

Thirty-six.

Four of which were set with diamond-bright crystal and china at one end of the gleaming wood behemoth of a table.

"Your sister's condition must be very difficult for you, as well," Cornelia commented. "Are you two very close?"

Amelia nodded, looking away from the table and focusing on her nearly empty wineglass. "Daphne and the children are all I have."

"Not anymore, dear. You'll have all of us now, too."

Who needed an inquisition when the woman's gracious kindness was far more devastating? "Mrs. Fairchild   "

"Cornelia. Or Corny."

Amelia swallowed. "C-Cornelia. You're very welcom-ing, and I—"

The older woman's head tilted slightly, her soft blond hair waving against her cheek. "Yes?"

"I hope I don't disappoint you. Any of you," she finished. It was the truth, in more ways than one.

"Gray chose you for a reason, Amelia."

The guilt sweeping through her had her fingers tightening around the wineglass stem so forcefully it was a miracle the delicate crystal didn't snap in half. "I—"

"He admires you a great deal. I have no reason to doubt his judgment. But I would like to know one thing."

Amelia braced herself. The only thing Gray admired was her supposed ability in carrying off a lie. "Yes?"

"Do you have any doubts about marrying Gray?"

There was nothing alarming in Cornelia's expression. But Amelia still wondered just how much the older woman knew. How much she saw. Suspected. "Only about a hundred million," she admitted.

Cornelia gave a silent half laugh at Amelia's not so oblique reference to Gray's significant wealth. "Are those reasons enough to keep you from it?"

"No," she admitted huskily.

Footsteps fell softly behind them and Amelia turned to find Harrison and Gray standing behind her. Gray's gaze captured hers.

But it was Harry who spoke. "Everything all right here?"

Amelia swallowed. Moistened her lips. She should be worried about the impression she'd made on Gray's honorary aunt. But the only thing consuming her mind just then was the memory of the way Gray tasted. Of the feel of his lips—surprisingly soft—on hers.

"Everything is fine, Harrison," Cornelia answered without hesitation. "Absolutely perfect."

Chapter Ten

Exactly eleven days after meeting Grayson Hunt, Amelia stood in a quaintly furnished bride's room, staring at herself in the floor-length mirror.

"It's not quite perfect, is it?" Amy, one of Amelia's soon-to-be sisters-in-law stared at the wedding gown that had been chosen for Amelia, her mouth turning down in dismay. She was more petite than all of them, with soft brown hair and eyes. Her expression was mirrored also by P.J. and Lily. They, like Amy, had all been wed in the past year to one of Harrison Hunt's sons. Amy to J.T., who was the closest brother to Gray. Lily to Justin, the youngest of the brothers, and P.J. to Alex, the one that Amelia privately believed Gray most admired.

Unlike Amelia, however, all three of them were utterly adored by their equally adored spouses. She'd seen that for herself the previous evening when they'd all met in town for drinks and introductions in lieu of a wedding rehearsal.

"It's definitely not perfect on me," Amelia said miserably, looking down at herself. "I look like an idiot."

"No," Loretta assured hurriedly. She was the one who'd delivered the gown to the church where Amelia was dressing. "You just…well, the gown doesn't quite suit you."

P.J. was nodding her head, her red curls bouncing slightly. She was an heiress in her own right but, according to Gray, felt much the same as Alex about their wealth—which was pretty much to give it away until it felt good. "Being comfortable in the gown you're wearing matters and, well—"

"I'm not comfortable," Amelia finished, plucking out the sides of the unbearably heavy satin gown. "Once Gray sees me in this, he'll *know* there is no way I can ever appear with him in public. I'll be an embarrassment to him." And when, exactly, had she begun caring about that? She'd seen the man exactly three times since they'd met with his father and Cornelia and apparently passed their muster.

First, when he'd taken her and the children out to meet Harry, after which he'd left her in the hands of André, the French-accented man charged with handling all of the wedding details that were crammed into their excruciatingly short time frame. The second when they'd met just yesterday with Dr. Jackson to discuss Daphne's course of care. He'd left from the doctor's office after the meeting without showing any interest in accompanying Amelia to Daphne's room, claiming he needed to return to the office and he'd send Peter back to pick her up and drop her at Brandlebury, where she finally turned in her resignation.

So Amelia had sat beside her sister's bedside muddling her

way through an explanation of what was happening to their lives, while Daphne stared blindly into space.

When the car had arrived for Amelia, she'd spent the drive to Brandlebury wondering just how much Daphne had understood, and tormenting herself with guilt over having to work hard at remembering that the entire situation was merely a business transaction. Particularly when Gray had picked her up again that evening to meet his brothers and their wives.

It was that kiss that was causing the problem.

Since then, the only thing Amelia had concluded was that Gray kissing her had been as calculated as everything else he ever did. He'd probably known they'd be seen. Just as he'd probably known his accompanying her to Daphne's new care facility would be caught and cataloged for the public: Grayson Hunt's adoration for his unexpected fiancée was so great it naturally extended to her poor sister.

Everyone seemed to eat up the story. A fourth Cinderella Bride for one of the famed Hunt men.

Now, Amelia was ensconced in the bride's room of this century-old church, playing the blushing bride in just a few hours for an estimated guest list of one hundred of Gray's closest friends and relations. Later that evening, that guest list would swell to about five hundred, for the formal reception. It was a testament to Gray's status that so many people would even be available on a few days' notice.

On the other hand, Amelia's guest list had consisted of Paula and, of course, the children. Her friend was watching the children right now, in fact, back at her apartment until the car Gray had arranged brought them all to the church. If Amelia had plenty of reservations about what she was doing, Paula didn't seem to share them. She was the only one, other than

Gray and Amelia, who knew the truth behind the marriage, but Amelia implicitly trusted the other woman to keep the confidence.

Loretta was rolling her eyes, drawing Amelia's scattered panic back, front and center. "Of course he will be proud to have you on his arm. Why else would he be marrying you?"

The other three women were nodding their heads, clearly in agreement. Just as Gray had planned, they, like everyone else in his family, believed he'd swept Amelia right off her feet.

So Amelia swallowed down the reasons that answered exactly "why else."

"It's not that it doesn't fit you," Lily murmured, walking around Amelia, studying. She ought to know plenty about appropriate fit, since the lovely, green-eyed woman designed women's lingerie. "You've got the right curves in the right places, though personally I think you could use a few more pounds."

Amelia crossed her arms over her chest. The dress had straps of stone-encrusted lace that cupped the points of her shoulders, worked its way—barely—over her breasts, and ended in a deep V almost at her navel. It was beautiful lace, but there needed to be another yard of it on the bodice, rather than creeping up from the sweeping hem in heavy, ornate swirls that reached as high as her knees.

"I don't know if it would be better if I were flat chested or not." She tugged at the bodice, hoping to cover a little more cleavage. But it was useless. "I feel like I need to tape this stuff in place so that, well—"

"—things don't pop out when they shouldn't?" Lily quipped humorously.

"I feel naked!"

"A fact that doesn't bother most of the women Gray has dated, which is probably why the man picked the dress,"

Loretta said briskly. "Pure habit. What can I say? Gray's a good man, but he's still a man and sometimes they don't have a shred of fashion sense. Don't be ashamed of possessing some modesty."

"Well, there's no point wishing that there'd been a chance for Amelia to try on the gown before today. But what *are* our options?" P.J. asked sensibly.

"Well…" Loretta considered for a moment. "The gowns that were sent over for Gray to choose from last night are still at his apartment downtown. They're all Amelia's size."

"Wait a minute." Amelia reached out and caught Loretta's filmy blue sleeve. She, like the others were already dressed for the ceremony. "*Gray* chose my dress?" He'd led her to believe that someone from the design house that Loretta had consulted had done that.

Loretta tilted her salt-and-pepper curls. "Surprised me, too, I must say. Just an indication that the man is crazy about you." She smiled happily at the belief and patted Amelia's hand. "Anyway, I can send Peter for the dresses. There's got to be something you'll feel more comfortable wearing."

"Is there time?" Amy looked at the small clock sitting on the dressing table. "The hairdresser will be here soon."

Amelia looked at herself in the mirror. She was perfectly capable of fixing her own hair into a knot—she did it most every day. But evidently, when one was marrying into the Hunt family, certain proprieties had to be observed.

As Loretta went over options with Amy and the others, Amelia longed for the brief hours when she'd thought that they could get through this wedding with only her, Gray, the children and a couple of witnesses.

That was, of course, before Harry had stuck his thoroughly

interfering nose into things. Amelia couldn't deny the man's oddball charm; he had seemed to take a genuine interest in the children when they'd met. If Amelia let herself, his interest in them would be alarming.

But now, the wedding had become a well-orchestrated circus and she knew the only reason it was going as smoothly as it was—despite the gown—was because of the significant amounts of money that greased the wheels.

"She has plenty of time," Loretta was assuring. "Peter's a maniac behind the wheel. If everyone in Seattle has a tendency to drive like a bat out of hell, Peter drives five times worse. Or better, as the case may be. He'll be here with time to spare."

"So, the gown will probably be your *something new,*" Lily said, obviously satisfied with the solution. "What about borrowed and blue?"

"I hadn't thought about it," Amelia admitted.

The other women tsked. "Never fear," P.J. assured, practically. "We'll come up with something before the ceremony."

Amelia smiled, playing her part as best she could. The truth was, she instinctively liked all of Gray's sisters-in-law, and felt guilty for pretending to feel the kind of happiness they truly had experienced. "Thank you."

"We Hunt wives have to stick together," Amy told her, giving her a swift hug. P.J. and Lily followed suit, and then they headed out to deal with their tasks.

"There are still some things Gray needs me to go over with André," Loretta said after the others had departed. "Will you be all right here by yourself?"

"I'll be fine."

Loretta smiled, her eyes crinkling. She began gathering up the tissue that had been wrapped around the dress, shoes and lingerie that had been delivered to the church in several gilded boxes. "I never thought I'd see the day when Gray would let himself focus on his personal life again."

"Again?"

"Well, after Gwen died…" Loretta hesitated. Looked at Amelia. "Oh, dear. I assumed he told you about her." She crumpled the tissue into a ball. "They were engaged back when they were in college together."

Amelia pressed her lips together. None of her research about Gray had uncovered information about a fiancée. And he had no reason to tell her.

For some reason, the omission still stung, which was ridiculous. Emotions weren't supposed to be involved in this marriage of convenience. Only the *appearance* of emotion.

"It was a long time ago," Loretta dismissed quickly. "And certainly nothing to be thinking about on your wedding day." She pushed the crumpled tissue into the smallest box—the one that had contained the narrow, delicate strappy shoes lying on their sides in front of the cheval glass—as if she were pushing away the mention of Gray's fiancée along with the tissue.

Had he loved her? Did he still? The question hovered inside Amelia like some threatening plague. "What happened?"

But Loretta just shook her head and continued making her way for the door. "Gray will skin me if he thinks I've put more concerns into your head. It's all in the past. The distant past." She grabbed up her purse and pulled out a bound organizer, flipping it open. She'd already laughed with Amelia about her insistence on the paper method of tracking herself, considering she worked for the king of information technology. "Once your hair and makeup are done, the photographer will want a few shots. You'll want to be in the gown you prefer for them, so I'll put him off while we get that all worked out."

What did it matter that the gown was too much for Amelia? It wasn't as if any of this farce were *real*.

She needed to keep remembering that. Marrying Gray was for appearances only. That. Was. All.

"I don't want to cause any trouble." She plucked at the gown's sweeping skirt again. "Maybe I—"

"—should just get that look off your face," Loretta said firmly. "This is your wedding, honey. You don't want this thing—" she waved her hand, encompassing the ostentation that was The Gown "—and there is no earthly reason why you shouldn't wear one that you love." She smiled gently. "After all, you'll only be doing this once, right?"

Fortunately, Amelia was saved from answering by the arrival of Sondra, the hairdresser, and her partner, Mike, the makeup artist.

By the time Peter arrived with Loretta again in tow as they bore a half-dozen enormous garment bags between them, Amelia's hair had been curled and teased and combed and her face had been buffed and polished and painted until she hardly recognized her own reflection in the mirror.

She looked…like somebody who could actually *be* married to a man like Grayson Hunt. Too bad the butterflies inside her couldn't see the mirror.

"Okay, honey. We've got forty-five minutes to pick another gown." Loretta carefully began unloading her burden and Peter followed suit.

Amelia rose from the pretty, padded chair and tightened the sash of her robe. "I hope I didn't put you out, Peter."

He waved away the very notion of it. "I'm going off to pick

up your friend and the young 'uns." He grinned and winked. "Next time we talk, you'll be Mrs. Hunt."

The butterflies went into free fall.

"Go on, now." Loretta shooed him as she busily unzipped bags and began pulling out gowns, flipping them over the backs of the peach-and-white striped chairs that furnished the utterly feminine room. "Out."

With another wink, Peter closed the door behind him as he left.

"Take a look, hon. No time to waste now." Loretta turned to the next stack of garment bags.

The bride's room was beginning to look as if a bridal magazine had exploded inside it. She hesitantly approached one of the gowns. It was shocking how nervous she felt, touching the assortment of silks and satins and chiffons. Each gown seemed more elaborate than the last. "Loretta, maybe I should just stick with the one Gray picked." It seemed impossible, but perhaps he had picked the least inappropriate dress after all.

"Fiddle," Loretta said, shaking her head. "You've got all these to check out, too." She unzipped the final bag and drew out a bundle of floating off-white fabric. "Here." She shook out the gown, and long folds of finely pleated silk organza billowed to the floor, ending in a waterfall of lengths that floated with a ruffled look, without being ruffled at all. "What about this?"

There seemed yards and yards of fabric—no less than the first gown. Only the cut of this one was considerably simpler and much more modest, despite its strapless style. "Oh." Amelia sighed a little, looking at the beautiful, ethereal creation. The tightly smocked bodice had tiny crystals outlining the empire waist and she knew that the gown would suit her.

Loretta smiled triumphantly. "Ha! I knew there'd be at least one." She hurriedly began undoing the pearl buttons on the back of the dress. "Step into it, sweetie. Don't be shy."

Amelia shucked her robe. The merry widow she wore had been selected to go with the other gown, but it would do for this one, as well. She carefully maneuvered herself into the gown and faced the mirror while Loretta began doing up the back.

"You're beautiful."

Amelia gasped, grabbing the bodice against her nearly bare breasts.

"Gray," Loretta chided. "There will be plenty of time to catch Amelia half-dressed once the I do's are finished."

He looked unapologetic as he entered the room. He wore a severe black suit with a blinding white shirt that was unfastened at his tanned throat, and his hair was darker than usual—still damp and brushed back from the hard lines of his face.

He looked as though he'd stepped off the cover of a magazine, right down to the finely striped silvery tie that hung loose over his lapels.

Amelia sucked in her lower lip, aware that she was probably defiling the makeup artist's efforts, and forced herself to look away from his overwhelmingly masculine appeal. "You're bringing on bad luck."

"I make my own luck. Here, 'Retta. I'll do that." Gray nudged Loretta's hands aside and it took every speck of self-control that Amelia possessed not to jump out of her skin when she felt the brush of his warm fingers against the small of her back. "André is having kittens out there about something. Go calm him down, would you?"

Loretta gave him a knowing look. "You just want to get your hands on your intended." But she went, giving Amelia a quick wink on her way. "Give a shout if you need anything else, sweetie."

What she wanted to do was beg Loretta not to leave her, because once she did, Amelia knew this wedding would become even more dauntingly real. Instead, she nodded and ducked her chin slightly when she looked into the mirror and saw the picture she made in her half-fastened gown, Gray standing tall and close behind her. "I, um, I switched gowns."

"I noticed." His fingertips rose to the next button and shivers danced down Amelia's spine.

"I'm sorry."

"For having a mind of your own?"

"I didn't want to insult you or anything."

"Since when?" He reached another button, between her shoulder blades. "Neither one of us has been shy about trading insults up to now." He finished the last button and dropped his hands over her bare shoulders. "But maybe we can avoid doing so today."

Their reflection kept drawing her gaze. Sentimentality from Gray? It was as surreal as their wedding-topper appearance. "That sounds good to me," she said warily.

His thumb moved slowly—distractingly—against her skin. "It's been a busy week."

"Yes." Filled with the countless details involved in moving Daphne's family lock, stock and barrel into an elaborate house that could never really be their home.

"Harry likes you."

With no need to hold up her bodice any longer, her hands had nothing else to do. She pressed them together at her waist where they did nothing to calm the butterfly bevy. "That was the plan, right?"

His thumb moved again, brushing slowly back and forth. While the rest of her seemed shivering and cold that three-inch arc of skin beneath his caress felt glowing hot. "That was the plan."

"And now that it's coming to reality, you're troubled by it."

"I'm not troubled by anything," he assured smoothly.

But she knew he was lying.

She didn't know how. Or why. But she knew it right down in her bones. And it was considerably different than when he'd given her a false name that day in the park.

She turned to face him and found her hands lifting to the trailing ends of his tie. His eyes narrowed a little but he made no move to stop her as she reached up and flipped his collar to settle the tie more neatly. "Lift your chin a little."

He did and she fastened the top button of his shirt then began carefully winding the necktie into a very proper Windsor. "I'm sure this isn't how you expected to enter a marriage, either."

"I didn't expect to enter a marriage *ever*," he corrected.

That wasn't strictly accurate given what Loretta had revealed about his onetime fiancée. But though Amelia was floundering in curiosity over his past, she was loath to break the tenuous peace between them.

So she finished tying the knot and slid it into place, adjusted the dimple slightly and stepped back again to study her efforts.

Gray looked at his reflection over Amelia's gleaming head, which was crowned in a sexy cascade of curls that made his fingers itch with the desire to free them from their confining pins. "Where'd you learn to knot a tie?" Probably the geek she was better off without.

"My father." She sounded painfully matter-of-fact.

"He wore ties a lot?"

"He was a salesman. Whenever Daphne and I happened to see him, he was wearing one."

"*Happened* to see him?"

She lifted one shoulder and reached up to adjust the tie a centimeter. "He only came by a few times a year. For the sake of appearance. One year he had a sprained wrist and he needed help so he told me how to knot his tie."

Instead of a touching father-daughter tale, what she described sounded like the complete opposite. "Is he still alive?" Marissa hadn't been able to confirm that particular fact. But what father would ignore the needs of his daughters, considering Daphne's condition?

That was almost in the Harry realm of days long past.

"I have no idea." She looked toward the door when there was a soft knock on it. "Come in."

The photographer stuck his head into the room. "Mind if I interrupt long enough to snap off a few?"

Despite the flawless makeup, Amelia's cheeks looked pinched and pale. "Give us a minute," Gray requested.

"Sure thing, Mr. Hunt." The camera-laden man ducked his head back out of the doorway and softly closed it again.

No matter what he thought about Amelia—and his uncommon uncertainty about that was disturbing in itself—she was holding up her end of their agreement. "You're making Harry a happy man today." His father had been preening for days about how well he'd orchestrated the happiness of his sons, and practically gloated over the wedding details that had mushroomed out of Gray's control pretty much from the get-go.

She pressed her lips together for a moment. "Is that supposed to make it okay that we're living a lie? Never mind." She shook her head abruptly and turned to look at herself in the mirror, avoiding his gaze as she brushed needlessly at the gown that gave her an unexpectedly ethereal quality. "Don't answer that. We both know who's benefiting more out of this arrangement."

She wasn't referring to making an old man happy.

She was talking dollars and cents.

Despite her refusal of the settlement at the end of their marriage, her sister's medical costs weren't going to be insignificant. But those financial matters were merely sprinkles in the bucket compared to what stood in the balance if Harry had gone forward with his threat to dismantle HuntCom.

Not that Gray had any intention of sharing that particular nugget with her.

They were unlikely allies in this marital venture, but that didn't mean he intended to trust her any more than he ever trusted any woman.

Still, her pale cheeks nagged at him. Maybe just because he didn't want her standing alongside him in front of the minister and all those guests looking as if she were heading for the gallows rather than life as Mrs. Grayson Hunt. Maybe it was just his pride.

God knew he had more than his share of it.

He closed his hands over her shoulders, absorbing the fine quake that worked through her at the contact. He was almost getting used to those little explosive sensations whenever he touched her.

The lie was almost laughable.

The fact was, Gray knew he wanted Amelia. Hell. He'd

learned a long time ago that desire had little bearing on his liking for a person.

"Don't stare at me," she said huskily and he realized that he'd been doing just that.

He clamped down on his unruly thoughts and reached in his lapel to pull out a small cloth bag. "This is what I came in here for." He handed it to her. "Cornelia would have brought it in herself, but she's riding herd on Harry."

Amelia's soft lips sounded out a breathy "Oh," as she loosened the drawstring on the pink cloth and a thin, glittering necklace slid into her palm.

"Don't get excited," Gray warned. "She just figured you ought to have something borrowed. P.J. was about to send Alex back to their place so she could find something of her own when Cornelia announced that she'd already thought of it."

Amelia held up the delicate strand with three perfectly faceted diamonds hanging miraculously along the front. "It's beautiful."

"She wore it when she married her husband, George."

Amelia's lashes lifted, her gaze shocked. "Oh. My. I couldn't possibly."

"You couldn't possibly refuse," he assured drily. "Believe me. What Cornelia wants, she generally gets."

"She's like all of you Hunts, then."

"I suppose so. You need a necklace, anyway." Though the expanse of creamy skin stretching from the edge of her gown to the curves of her shoulders to the points of her collarbone and the hollow at the base of her long, lovely throat struck him as perfect in their unadorned state.

But she was marrying *him*. People would expect to see some jewels. Only the ones he'd initially arranged for her to wear had been relegated back to the safe once Cornelia had offered her necklace.

Even Gray couldn't refuse Cornelia.

"It's very kind of her to think of it." Her voice sounded thick. She unfastened the small clasp and after a brief hesitation, held up the slender white-gold chain. "Um, would you…?"

He could have said no. Her slender fingers were far more adept with tiny jewelry clasps than his fingers were.

He took the necklace in both hands and reached over her head, lowering the stones until they nestled against her flesh just above the edge of her gown. When he fit the clasp together at the back of her bared nape, the stones slowly climbed up that faint shadow of cleavage that—if he weren't towering over her from above—he wouldn't even see.

A swallow worked its way down her throat. The golden flecks in her eyes where they met his in the mirrored reflection seemed to multiply. Her fingertips fluttered to the stones at their final resting place in the seductive hollow of her throat. "Thank you."

Color had risen in her cheeks again.

He stuck his hand in his pocket and pulled out another item—a slender, flat box. "Lily said to give you this. Something blue, she said."

Amelia blinked hard as if she were trying to hold back tears. "Your brothers' wives are very thoughtful," she murmured. "If I were a proper bride—" She shook her head, breaking off and lifted the lid of the small box only to blink slightly at the tiny hank of lace and blue satin that lay nestled inside.

Gray looked at the contents, his lip quirking at the corner. "Well." He tucked a finger into the box and lifted the panties by one of their ribbon ties. "No wonder she was kind of laughing when she said it was more enjoyable than a blue garter." He didn't have to work hard at summoning an image of Amelia's derriere barely covered by the skimpy garment. He did, however, have to work hard at eradicating it again.

Amelia was flushed as she snatched the diminutive panties off his finger and slapped the lid over them in the box, turning away from him.

"So. I guess it's time to get this show on the road," he said slowly. He reached out and needlessly adjusted the lay of Cornelia's necklace against the back of Amelia's neck.

In the mirror, he could see her slick the tip of her tongue over the center of her lower lip. "I, um, yes. I guess it is."

His job was done.

He'd delivered the necklace and the surprising garter substitute. Would be able to assure those concerned that the "borrowed and blue" they were nattering about was duly taken care of. The photographer was waiting and after that, a small church full of guests expected to see a show.

He and Amelia had a marital contract that needed their signatures on a marriage license to ensure that Harry's threats could never be repeated.

But instead of moving his fingers away from her nape, he spread them wide, fanning them around her neck. Beneath his fingertips, he could feel the wild beat of her pulse.

Fear?

Her eyes were wide in the mirror.

He slid his fingers until they were beneath her chin. Slowly nudged it upward.

In the mirror, her amber-flecked gaze stayed glued to his. Her fingers looked white where they surrounded the small lingerie box.

"Are you afraid of me, Amelia?" His voice was low.

"Should I be?" Her voice was even lower. Almost a whisper.

"It might be safer if you were."

"Safer for who? You or me?"

The taut skin beneath her throat was almost translucent. Delicate.

Vulnerable.

"I don't know." The admission surprised him as much as it probably did her. He lowered his head over hers and brushed his mouth slowly across those softly parted lips.

She inhaled sharply and it felt as if he were being breathed in by her. Her hand lifted halfway, only there was nothing for her to touch but the unyielding mirror in front of her.

He closed his eyes against the sight they made and dragged his mouth away through sheer effort.

The silence surrounding them was deafening. Broken only by the whisper of their breaths. Finally, he opened his eyes again.

She was staring at him, her pulse beating visibly at the base of her throat. "Why did you do that?" Her voice was hushed.

He shoved his fisted hand into his pocket. He might feel manipulated into this situation, but nobody—not even Harry—was holding a gun to his head.

He'd kissed her because he hadn't been able to get the taste of her out of his head. If he thought she was afraid of him, maybe his feeble conscience would have drawn the line at touching her again.

But she wasn't afraid.

Not of *that*.

"Consider it practice," he said tersely and strode out the door as if the hounds of hell were on his heels.

No. She wasn't afraid. *He* was.

Chapter Eleven

Amelia wondered if the receiving line would ever end.

It was just her and Gray standing there, the center of attention for the guests milling around the historic ballroom of the Fairmont Olympic Hotel, as they greeted Gray's guests.

Their guests, if one were going to waste one's time on being strictly accurate.

The wedding ceremony itself was mostly a blur for Amelia. She assumed she must have made the appropriate responses, because nobody had pointed a finger and accused her of not being good enough to marry Grayson Hunt. And afterward, she'd managed to smile and pose where the photographer had indicated for the formal photographs that Harry had insisted were necessary.

But now, they'd been standing there in that stunningly appointed ballroom for what seemed hours while a live orchestra played—not too obtrusively, of course—and fancily dressed waiters passed trays of sumptuous hors d'oeuvres and heady cocktails to the throng of bejeweled, gowned and tuxedoed guests.

In her world, wedding receptions were usually a fairly brief affair of cake and punch, a toast or two, tossing the bouquet and garter and racing out as if the couple couldn't wait to start the wedding night. At least that's how it had been when Daphne married Martin.

How long were receptions supposed to last in Gray's world?

Her feet hurt from the sexy shoes strapped around her feet and the cloying scent of too many perfumes hung uncomfortably in her head. Even her cheeks hurt from keeping a smile on her face as Gray introduced her to the never-ending passage of guests.

A part of her was impressed that he really did know every single person present. Not just by name. That wasn't so difficult—connecting a name to a face. But he actually seemed to *know* them.

It was just another facet of this stranger she found herself wedded to that didn't fit her expectations.

He slid his palm down the back of her neck, stopping to rest between her shoulder blades and everything that pained her slid into the background, superseded yet again by something as simple as a touch. *His* touch.

She smiled blindly at the woman who appeared in front of them, automatically prepared for the double-handed squeezing handshake, the airbrush of a meaningless kiss on her cheeks.

"So this is the girl who has sneaked in and stolen my son away from me."

Amelia felt Gray's fingertips flex against her back.

Keeping the smile on her face seemed suddenly even more difficult as she hurriedly gathered her wits and focused on the tall, slender woman.

Christina Hunt Devereaux Dunleavy.

"Hello, Mother." Gray's voice was even. "And we all know one can't steal what was bartered off decades ago."

Amelia winced a little.

But Gray's mother didn't seem to turn a single one of her soft blond hairs that were swept up in a sophisticated knot atop her head, "Oh, Grayson. It's your wedding, darling. Don't be tiresome. And I understand there is more to congratulate than just your little marriage, here."

"Pull in the claws," Gray advised mildly. "And remember that you're here only because I'm allowing it."

Christina's pale blue eyes tightened. "Well. As usual, you're displaying your father's propensity for putting me in my place. You'll do an admirable job replacing him as chairman of the board for HuntCom. People won't even be able to tell that the mantle has been passed to you." She slanted her gaze to Amelia's face, then dropped to focus on the diamond necklace. "You and I have so much in common, Amelia. We'll have to do lunch soon. Somebody will have to take you in hand." She lifted Amelia's hand at that, studying the wedding ring that Gray had slid on her finger during the ceremony where it nestled against the enormous stones of the engagement ring. "That necklace looks like a schoolgirl chose it, but at least he's given you a decent ring. But someone will need to teach you what it means to be the wife of a Hunt."

Amelia's fingers curled. Cornelia's necklace couldn't be more beautiful. And while she didn't personally care for the ring, having this woman call it "decent" in that superior tone sent defensiveness shooting right through her.

Gray's hand moved away from her spine, only to settle around her shoulders, instead. "Amelia needs no lessons from you, Christina."

The woman tilted her chin, never losing her regal bearing. She wore three strands of enormous pearls and diamonds around her neck, and the soft gold strapless gown clinging to her figure from breast to toe could have come straight from a fashion runway. "One day when Gray takes your children from you, you might change your mind."

Amelia stiffened. She automatically looked over to the table not far from them where the children were sitting with Paula, looking somewhat shell-shocked, and Gray's brothers and wives.

Harry had Timmy in his arms and was making funny faces at the baby.

On one hand, she was relieved that the Hunts had so generously welcomed not just Timmy, but Molly and Jack, as well. On the other hand, it was a definite worry.

"Where's Gerry?" Gray's hand on her shoulder was clasping her a little more tightly against his side.

Christina lifted an indolent shoulder at his deliberate change of subject. "Around here somewhere. My *other* son may not hold the reins to a fortune like HuntCom, but at least he knows what it's like to honor his mother. Of course he wasn't raised by a boor like Harry." Oblivious to Amelia's reluctance, she caught Amelia's cold hands in hers again and leaned forward, brushing her lips over her cheek. "Congratulations, dear. Snagging Gray can't have been easy."

Cornelia appeared beside the other woman, almost like a fairy godmother sent to prevent Amelia from publicly embarrassing herself by wrenching away from the woman who'd borne her brand-new husband. "Christina," she hailed musically, "don't you look particularly beautiful tonight. You can't help outshining every female here."

Christina smiled coolly at Cornelia who, in Amelia's opinion, was far lovelier in her golden-colored gown than Christina's gilded perfection.

Seeing them standing there together, there was no denying the similarity between the two women.

Similar ages, though Christina's extraordinarily and undoubtedly surgically smooth face lacked the soft lines that gave Cornelia's features a wealth of mature beauty. Their hair was a similar shade. And given their color choice in gowns, their tastes had run along similar lines—at least for this occasion.

But Christina was cold in her gold dress.

Cornelia, on the other hand, glowed like a warm beacon.

"It figures that you'd be here, Cornelia. Never far from Harry's side, are you."

"Not when I can help it," Cornelia agreed, her tone still gracious. "Go on over and say hello. I'm sure he'd be delighted."

Christina lifted an eyebrow, as if the comment were unquestioned. She leaned up to brush a kiss over Gray's jaw, and swept away, heading toward the family's table.

Cornelia met Amelia's eyes the moment Christina was out of earshot. She magically produced a small, delicate hankie almost out of nowhere, and smudged it against the lipstick that Christina had left behind on Amelia's cheek.

"Two hundred other women here, and not a smudge of lipstick." She tsked under her breath, rolling her eyes humorously.

She obviously didn't let the other woman get under her skin.

"That's Christina," Gray muttered, taking his hand away from Amelia's shoulder finally, and dashing his own handkerchief over the smear on his chin. "One of a kind. Thank God."

"And I'd better make certain that she doesn't send Harry off the edge of reason or damage that sweet baby for life," Cornelia murmured as she headed off toward the family's table.

Gray sighed faintly. "I'm sorry. I should have warned you about her."

Amelia slipped the squarely folded handkerchief from his fingers. "You didn't quite get it all." She reached up and dabbed away the last little smear of coral then she turned the lipstick inside the folds. His fingers brushed hers as he took it again and tucked it back in his pocket. "Is what she said true? About replacing Harry?"

"Yes."

She didn't want to wonder if the timing had anything to do with their marriage, but she wondered anyway. And decided it didn't matter. Her motivation to help Daphne wouldn't be changed even if he'd achieved more than he'd implied. "Then you do deserve some congratulations. And you don't have to be sorry. Look at the bright side. Everyone who was still waiting to greet us disappeared the second they saw your mother."

It was true.

The line of guests waiting to greet them had miraculously dispersed.

"Small mercies," Gray muttered. "I'm starving." He tucked his hand beneath her bare elbow, the picture of a solicitous groom, even though there was a sudden, distinctive clink of metal against crystal.

Only she could hear his whispered oath. "We should have eloped."

The tinkling sound was repeated, joined by dozens more as it swelled to a noisy demand.

Gray smiled out at the crowd, lifting a hand in wry acknowledgment before turning to her.

"They're expecting us to kiss," he said for her ears.

Who else other than her saw the tension behind his apparent ease? She swallowed. Lifted her chin a little.

He brushed a chaste kiss over her lips that brought on a spate of heckling and laughter that seemed oddly out of place among all the formality.

"You can do better than that, Gray." One man in particular was louder than the rest as he strode closer. Amelia almost did a double take, for his resemblance to Gray was striking. "Or maybe you need me to step in for you. Hello, sweet thing. I'm Gerry. Younger and longer lasting than old Gray there. Whatcha say? Wanna give me a go? I'll be a lot more fun on the honeymoon, I'll bet." His gray-green eyes were mocking as he stopped in front of Amelia, seemingly prepared to take her right into his arms.

But there was no way he could, considering the way Gray had his arm around her. Almost protectively, it seemed.

But that was probably her imagination.

Still, her hand slid through his arm because, ironically, he seemed a whole lot safer than Gerry. And judging by these two members of Gray's family, it was almost no wonder he had to go out and hire himself a wife. "We're not going on a honeymoon but even if we were—"

"No honeymoon?" Gerry nearly spilled his drink when he gave a loud bark of laughter. "Damn, Gray. Nothing ever gets in the way of work for you, does it?"

"I didn't want to leave my niece and nephews," Amelia

cut in swiftly. It was true in its way. She wouldn't have wanted to leave them if Gray had ever suggested a honeymoon. Which he hadn't.

"Oh, right. The rug rats. Nice work, Gray. Doing the whole package deal and all. You're nothing if not expedient."

"How much have you drunk tonight, Gerry? Usually it takes you a while longer before you work up to this stage."

Gerry ignored Gray. "Sure you don't want to think on it a bit? Gray's got the dough, of course, but I—"

"—need to start living your own life and stop trying to live mine," Gray interrupted, his voice flat.

Gerry tossed back his head, laughing uproariously. "But yours is so much more fun, bro. I can't tell you all the sweet perks I get along the way."

Amelia saw Marissa Matthews making a beeline for them, seemingly unhampered by the svelte lines of her scarlet gown. "Tonight's perk is that you can be my dance partner," she said rather breathlessly, casting them a faintly apologetic look before sending a boldly challenging one at Gerry. "That is if you think you're up to the task."

The man's gaze had dropped to the wealth of smooth skin revealed by Marissa's down-to-there neckline. It was every bit as plunging as the gown that Amelia had chosen not to wear. But Marissa carried it off with enviable panache.

And fortunately, she carried off Gerry in her wake just as adeptly. "Sorry, sweet thing, but I guess you're stuck with old Gray after all," Gerry said, barely looking at Amelia again as he shifted his attention to the tall redhead. "A guy's gotta do what a guy's gotta do."

Marissa's smile didn't waver in the least as she tucked her hand through Gerry's arm and led him away.

"Did Marissa help you pick out that wedding gown you chose for me?" Amelia asked softly as they watched the woman guide an obviously inebriated Gerry back to a table situated on the opposite side of the room.

"Why would you think that?"

Amelia lifted her shoulder, wishing she'd kept her foolish mouth shut. "The gown would suit her perfectly."

"Yeah, if she were the one getting married. But I chose you. Why'd you tell Gerry that about a honeymoon? We never even talked about it."

"I didn't like the way he acted toward you."

His brows quirked together for a millisecond. "So you were, what? Protecting me?"

Certain that he was making fun of her, she ignored the question.

He smiled faintly, then. "What'd you do with Lily's gift?"

Shocked that he would dare to ask, and still annoyed, she gave him a sweet smile. "I'm wearing them."

His pupils seemed to reduce to pinpoints. He let out a rough breath. "Figures." Then he dragged her onto the toes of her expensively shod feet and covered her mouth with his.

Amelia knew it was for the benefit of the guests who immediately began cheering at the sight.

She *knew* it.

But that didn't stop the blood from rushing through her veins or her heart from feeling as if it would burst out of her chest. It didn't hinder one tendril of the kaleidoscope of sensation swirling through her and when he finally lifted his head, she barely managed to hold back the protest that nudged at her swollen lips.

Looking somewhat dazed, he grabbed her hand and drew

her toward the family's table. The smiles and laughing faces turned toward them barely penetrated the fog still clogging her senses as Gray pulled out a chair for her next to Harry.

Amy laughed softly as she hurried around the table to help situate the trail of floaty, pleated organza. "Molly was saying that she thinks you look like an angel in your gown. And I think she's right," she said. "Like you could float away on a breeze. You couldn't have chosen a more perfect gown. There. That's better. Don't want to catch anything under the chair legs." She moved back to her seat beside J.T. "Timmy's been such a doll. Not fussing at all despite the attention he's been getting."

"What's there to fuss about? Except, since Justin and Lily are off at the ranch so much with little Ava, Timmy here probably can't wait for some more playmates to come along." Harry lifted the baby until they were tiny-to not-so-tiny nose. "Isn't that right, Master Timothy?"

Amy blushed prettily, her gaze flying to her husband's face. Gray had told Amelia of their recent announcement of his sister-in-law's pregnancy. So far, there was no outward evidence of it, though.

Just a glow that Amelia found herself envying. What would it be like to be so adored?

Jack and Molly were sitting across from them, next to Paula. The suit Jack wore was a sized-down version of Gray's, and though Amelia had feared he'd be bored out of his mind at the reception, he was showing his male stripes by seeming thoroughly preoccupied by the wealth of beautiful young women present.

Gray leaned closer to her. "What's the sigh for?"

She hadn't even realized she *had* sighed. "He's growing up."

Alex grinned, obviously overhearing. "Boys'll do that.

How old were you, Gray, when you realized girls didn't have cooties after all?"

"Six months," J.T. inserted wryly to a round of chuckles.

"Twenty-one," Harry corrected. "When he decided to marry Gwen."

"Harry," Cornelia clucked softly as silence settled suddenly around the table.

"What?" The old man tucked the baby back in his arm as if he had been carting babies around all of his life and lifted his champagne flute.

Amelia cast a look toward Gray. She doubted that many could see past his impassive expression over Harry's apparent gaff. But, she realized, she was beginning to spot the subtleties.

And he *was* annoyed.

"The only girl I care about now," he said in a letter-perfect imitation of a besotted man that had her suspecting he'd been studying his Hunt brothers, "is this one." He picked up Amelia's hand and pressed his lips to her knuckles.

"Hear, hear." J.T. lifted his glass, too, which set off a round of toasts that quickly filled that brief, uncomfortable silence, and Amelia's head was swimming from alcohol by the time the toasts finished, despite the multitude of courses the waiters set before them. Molly's chin was practically drooping in her lobster bisque when Amelia agreed with Paula's suggestion that she take the children up to the hotel suite that had been arranged for them.

"I'm going with her for a moment," Amelia said, scooping Timmy from Harry's arms.

"Don't be long," P.J. warned. "People are beginning to eye that towering cake."

"You mean you are eyeing the cake," Alex added, looking indulgent.

P.J. grinned. "What can I say? Lately my sweet tooth has been definitely acting up."

Avoiding Gray's gaze, Amelia headed through the ballroom with Paula and the children. She didn't stop until they reached the elevators, and then, turning Timmy over to her friend seemed to take an incredible amount of willpower. But the baby was finally beginning to show some temper over the upheaval of the day, and she knew it was the best thing for Paula to get him settled for the night.

The elevator doors slid open and Jack nudged Molly inside while Paula hung back with Amelia. "Are you going to be all right?"

"Why wouldn't I be?"

Paula looked knowing. "Honey, I saw your face after he kissed you. And it *is* your wedding night."

Amelia flushed. The elevator doors began sliding shut. "Jack, hold the doors open." Her nephew reached for the button panel and the doors silently retreated. "Don't worry about me," she said softly to Paula, giving her friend a hug. "I can't tell you how much I appreciate everything you've done. Not just today, but—"

"Forget it." Paula patted her shoulder. "This was a once-in-a-lifetime event for me, too. My daughter will love hearing all the details when I talk with her."

"Aunt Amelia," Molly whispered. Her eyes were tired pools, but she still looked pretty as a picture in her floor-length salmon-colored dress. "Are we going home soon?"

Amelia leaned down to her niece. "Remember the big house we visited the other day? That's where we'll be going soon. All of our stuff will be moved over there from the apartment by tomorrow. But for tonight, Paula is going to stay with you and Jack and Timmy right here in this hotel."

"Where are *you* going to stay?"

Amelia avoided Paula's knowing gaze. "I'll be with Gray right here, too."

"With us?"

It was Jack who answered. "Not in the same room, Mol. They're married now."

Molly nodded. "They gotta kiss and stuff."

Amelia gulped. "Anyway, you can pretend you're a princess," she suggested hurriedly and fortunately the notion was an appealing distraction to Molly, who squeezed her neck in a tight hug and went inside the lift to lean her head against her brother's side. Amelia looked at the two of them. "I wish your mom could've seen how you all looked tonight."

"There will be pictures," Paula reminded as she stepped through the yawning doors. "Go on now. At least enjoy the party."

Amelia hugged her arms around herself as the doors slid shut.

That was the problem.

She should be hating every second of it all if only out of loyalty to her sister.

But she wasn't.

She returned to the ballroom only to hesitate at the threshold, a lifetime of reticence clawing at her to run and hide.

But she couldn't hide. Not anymore. In the eyes of the world, she was the wife of Grayson Hunt.

But it wasn't even that particular fact that had her chin lifting and her shoulders straightening as she stepped into the ballroom, her gown softly swishing around her legs as she passed the tables of guests, greeting them all again and hiding the fact that she couldn't remember a single name among them.

It wasn't even knowing that she was only there at all because of Daphne's situation that had Amelia battling down all of that shyness, all of that fear that had plagued her nearly all her life.

It was the man, himself, who drew her.

Chapter Twelve

"Of *course* I'm going to finish out the rest of my notice at Brandlebury." It was Monday morning. Their first Monday morning spent under the Hunt roof and Amelia stared at Gray across the breakfast table where Molly and Jack were working their way through eggs and bacon and fragrant blueberry muffins. She suspected there would be no more cold cereal once they discovered the joys of a chef seemingly devoted to pleasing their palates. "Why wouldn't I?"

"Because it's unnecessary."

"I have a responsibility—"

"To more than serving out two weeks in that library. The school's roof won't cave in if you don't."

"Thank you," she said quietly, "for pointing out how unimportant I am."

"That's not—" He broke off when they heard Timmy's wail

through the baby monitor that Amelia had brought down to the breakfast room.

She snatched up the monitor. "Excuse me. Jack, Molly, finish up and get your backpacks ready," she said as she hurried out of the room. They needed to leave soon so that she could drop off Timmy with Paula, who'd happily agreed to continue watching the baby as long as Amelia needed.

She'd barely made it halfway to the staircase leading to their unfamiliar quarters within the sprawling, complex house before Gray caught her shoulders, dragging her to a halt.

"Nobody said you were unimportant."

She'd turned down the volume on the monitor, but she could still hear Timmy crying. She felt like joining him and hated herself for it. If she were this sensitive after just a few days, how was she supposed to get through the next few *years?* "That was certainly the impression I got."

His brows drew together in a fierce frown. "Are you always crabby like this in the morning?"

She felt her face go hot. She opened her mouth to retort, but naturally, there was no retort ready at her beck and call. She twisted out from his hold and headed for the staircase once more.

"Dammit, Amelia—"

"—I have to see to Timmy." She started up the steps.

"That's what Bonny is there for."

She stopped midstair. "Bonny?" She looked back at him, her voice slowing warily. "*Who* is Bonny?"

"The nanny."

She tucked her tongue between her teeth and counted to ten. Twelve. Seventeen. "The nanny. You hired a nanny already." She couldn't pretend that she'd never considered that he might. Even Paula had warned her to expect it. "Without consulting me." *That,* she hadn't expected him to do. "Did you smuggle her into the nursery or something so that I wouldn't notice her?"

"She arrived over an hour ago, as I arranged," he said evenly. "You were in the shower or I would have introduced you already. If you don't like her, you can choose someone else."

"How magnanimous of you." Her voice was tight. Through the monitor, Timmy's crying suddenly ceased and she could hear, instead, a softly sung nursery song. "So what am I supposed to do about Paula? I've paid her through the week." Not that Paula had ever wanted money for minding Timmy. But back in the beginning, Amelia had insisted. Now, she mostly didn't like thinking she wouldn't see her friend every day.

"Then she can consider it a small bonus."

"So you want me to quit my job *and* have a nanny for the children. What on earth am I supposed to do with my time?"

"That's something for us to discuss. You're my wife. Naturally you'll have a nanny—*here*—for the children."

"Wife on paper only," she reminded under her breath.

His eyes narrowed, but not quickly enough to mask their sudden, sharp gleam. "Ah."

She flushed. "What's *that* supposed to mean?"

"Maybe you would have preferred that I spent our wedding night at the hotel suite in that canopied bed with you rather than on the couch."

Naturally, he'd had to keep up the appearance that they were a regular newly wedded couple. So they'd spent the night in an enormous suite at the hotel, replete with two bedrooms, two king-sized beds—one that was a canopied fantasy—and a living area into which she could have fit Daphne's entire apartment. He hadn't even used the second bedroom, though, sleeping instead on the couch in the living area. They might forgo a honeymoon with reasons that could pass a public validity test, but how would he have explained it if they'd seemed to have slept separately on their wedding night?

Then, when they returned to the shack the day before, Gray had ensured that she and the children were comfortably settled in their quarters where all of their belongings had been unpacked for them, and excused himself for the office. Sunday or not, he had work to do. She assumed he'd spent the night at his downtown apartment because he certainly hadn't been in the luxurious suite they were supposedly sharing now.

"Don't be ridiculous," she assured blithely. "I must say I'm a little surprised that you were absent last night, but maybe that's the kind of marital relationship your family is used to."

"The only *normal* marital relationships this family is used to are those my brothers are just now experiencing. And I wasn't absent. You went to sleep early."

Her eyebrows shot up. "Right." She hadn't climbed into the mammoth-size bed before eleven o'clock. And she knew that he hadn't climbed into that bed with her at any point after that. She would have heard him.

She was used to caring for Timmy. She hadn't slept that soundly in three months, despite the fact that the baby was now sleeping through the night.

"And you sleep on your stomach. With one foot sticking out from beneath the bedding. After I covered it up the first few times, and you worked it out again, I figured it was deliberate. I was right when I figured you for the flannel pj's type, though. *And* you're a pillow hog. What's the matter? Annoyed that I didn't…wake you?"

Her mouth snapped shut.

He smiled slightly and leaned closer, until she could feel the faint whisper of his warm breath against her ear. "If I didn't trust the maid service at the Olympic to keep their mouths shut, why do you think I would trust the cleaning staff here at the shack to refrain from gossiping over whether I'm sharing my bride's bed?"

Her mind couldn't wrap itself around the idea that she could have slept through him entering that bedroom suite at all, much less occupying for so much as a minute the other side of that sinfully comfortable bed.

She sidled up a step, wishing she still had on those flannel pants and cropped top beneath her robe. But all she wore beneath the aging terry cloth were the clean bra and panties she'd donned after her shower.

Next to his well-finished charcoal suit and red tie she felt alarmingly underdressed. "I'm going to check on Timmy." Though the baby was certainly not crying now. "Meet this…Bonny person." And if she *didn't* like the woman, she was going to do something about it, whether Gray expected her to take his comment about that seriously or not.

He didn't argue. Just watched her with that steady, all-seeing gaze of his, as if he knew what she was really doing.

Escaping.

She swallowed and backed her way up another step. "I— I'd appreciate it if you would urge Jack and Molly along before you leave."

"Who said I was leaving?"

"Why wouldn't you?"

"I'm a newlywed. Maybe I want to spend some extra time enjoying that state."

She flushed. "You didn't worry about that yesterday. What's wrong? Is somebody becoming too curious about how little time we spend together?"

"There were some things yesterday that couldn't wait." He reached in his pocket in that utterly familiar motion and pulled out his phone. Glanced at it. Pocketed it once more.

"Not important enough to bother answering?"

"It's Marissa, actually. But she'll wait."

Amelia swallowed her surprise. Gray prided himself on his availability to his closest associates. "Not on my account, I hope." She backed up another step. "Answer your cell phone all you want," she lied blithely. "Why would I care?"

"Most women would be flattered at being put first."

"I'm not most women."

"You can say that again."

Letting herself think that was a compliment would be folly. She dragged the sash of her robe tighter around her waist and lifted the monitor. "Excuse me."

"What did Dr. Jackson report yesterday?"

"How did you know he'd called me?" Her eyes narrowed. "Am I being *watched?*"

He let out a half laugh. "No more than I am, toots. Harry mentioned it."

The doctor had called late in the afternoon when Harry had insisted that she and the children join him lakeside to enjoy the fresh, warm day. Amazingly enough, he'd been teaching Jack and Molly how to fish. Or, to be more accurate, he'd been trying to teach them how to fish, since it had seemed to Amelia that Harry didn't exactly possess a wealth of knowledge or ability in that particular area.

Still, they'd all seemed to be having fun, and Timmy had

been an angel. When Harry hadn't been puzzling and muttering over the fancy lures he'd pulled out of a tackle box that looked as if it had come straight out of a sporting goods showroom, he'd been holding the baby.

She'd tormented herself wondering if the man suspected the child was his grandson. Tormented *herself* wondering if Timmy was his grandson.

"He was just giving me an update on the tests Daphne's had in the week she's been there."

"And?"

Amelia moistened her lips. "He wants to run more. She's not responding quite as quickly to the increase in her therapy sessions as he'd hoped."

"What about her long-term memory?"

"He doesn't know."

"When are you visiting her again?"

She tightened her belt robe again. "I don't know." She wasn't about to tell him that she was too cowardly after having married *him* to face her own sister just yet.

"I'll go out there with you and the kids today after school."

"More devoted husbandlike behavior?" she asked waspishly.

He didn't deny it. "About four? We'll grab an early supper somewhere for the kids afterward."

His apparent concern for them only bit at her more. It was a very slippery slope on which she perched, because the man *did* seem interested, and she couldn't afford to get used to it. To trust it.

She'd trusted John and look what happened.

Only lately, John's defection didn't hurt as badly as it once had.

"Fine." If only Daphne would recover her memory.

Maybe she'd recognize Gray and this whole situation could end, right now.

Except that Amelia had committed herself to Gray. Or rather she'd committed herself to helping him satisfy his father's wishes.

She realized that Gray was watching her. "What's going on inside that head of yours now?"

"Nothing."

"Which is why there is a parade of expressions crossing your face." He slowly ascended the stairs until he stood a riser below hers. He was still taller than she. "Things will be a lot easier for us if you just say what's on your mind, Amelia."

"Oh, and you do such an admirable job of that, yourself?"

The lines at the corners of his eyes crinkled ever so slightly. "What I'm thinking right now is that I *should* have joined you under that fancy canopy."

An odd sensation curled through her abdomen. Low. Warm. She wondered, somewhat desperately, how much longer Jack and Molly were going to dawdle over their breakfast, because their presence about now would go a long way toward keeping her from humiliating herself.

But there was no sign of her niece and nephew in the wide hallway that led to the breakfast room.

"I told you after the reception that I'd fit on the couch more easily than you would."

"That's not what I mean, and you know it."

"I don't sleep with men I don't love." She nearly winced at her prim tone.

He reached out and slid his fingers through her hair where it lay over the shoulder of her ancient terry cloth robe. "Sex doesn't have to have anything to do with love."

"It does for me." Which did an admirable job of not explaining the heat pooling inside her.

The corner of his lips tilted. "Sounding so certain like that makes a man want to test the theory."

"You don't even like me!"

"Actually, I don't think I ever said that."

She lifted her eyebrows in disbelief.

"Trust doesn't go hand in hand with liking, either," he murmured. "There are plenty of people that I like whom I trust even less than you."

"There you go, then," she said, feeling stung despite herself. "You don't trust me. Why would you want...want—"

"Want *you?*" he finished, looking vaguely amused. "You must not look in the mirror very often." His fingers drifted from her hair to the rolled lapel collar of her robe and slowly followed it downward.

She grabbed the banister with her free hand and swatted at his marauding fingertips with the baby monitor. "Stop it. Stop toying with me. I know I'm not the kind of woman you like."

His lashes dropped, until she could practically feel his gaze on her lips. "More of that infamous research of yours, I suppose?"

"Whatever works, Jack." She focused hard on her nephew's appearance. "There you are. Where's Molly?"

"Finishing her muffin."

"Tell her to do so more quickly if she wants me to braid her hair before school."

Gray's teeth flashed in silent laughter and he slowly retreated a step. "Saved by the boy," he murmured for her ears.

She gave him a stern glare that only had his smile widening. Thoroughly disconcerted, she yanked the lapels of her robe closer together at her throat and fled up the stairs. Behind her, she could hear the low murmur of Gray's and Jack's voices, but they faded as she continued along the corridor.

Gray's private rooms were more on the order of a spacious home within a home. Two stories of rooms guaranteed him plenty of privacy when he was in residence at the shack. She'd learned right away that there was little chance of running into anyone else unless you wanted to. When Gray had told her there would be plenty of space for the children, he hadn't been exaggerating. They had their own state-of-the-art kitchen, should they choose to use it, separate bedrooms and baths for the children—who thought they'd landed in heaven as a result—and a spacious living room that boasted the same spectacular lakeside view as the rest of the quarters. Every room was beautiful. And comfortable.

The nursery that had been prepared for Timmy with mind-boggling speed was one of Amelia's favorites, though. In her wildest dreams she couldn't have imagined a more perfect nursery. From the way the light through the many windows bathed the custom-painted nursery-rhyme murals in a dreamy glow each morning, to the mahogany sleigh crib and matching chests—which were so numerous, every item of clothing that Amelia and the children had possessed could have fit among the drawers—the room was completely wonderful.

Instead, only Timmy's belongings filled just a few of them, seeming to unnecessarily point out the significant difference between Gray's lifestyle and theirs.

Now, she stopped in the doorway, gathering her wits about her, and studied the woman who was standing at the changing table where Timmy lay, happily kicking up his heels as she changed his diaper.

His *cloth* diaper, thanks to the diaper service that Gray had arranged. What was left of the supply of disposables that he'd brought to the apartment that one day was currently housed in the built-in cabinet alongside the changing table. Everything had happened so quickly since then, she hadn't even had an opportunity to use them all.

Bonny had iron-gray hair, pulled back in a thick bun, a sensible-looking gray cotton dress belted at the waist and flat-soled shoes. She looked more like a warden than a nanny and Amelia was admittedly prepared to dislike the nanny on sight.

But the smile on the woman's face as she crooned a song to Timmy made it impossible to do so.

"Hello."

The woman looked over at her. "Mrs. Hunt. Good morning. I'd greet you more properly, but—" She lifted the soggy diaper, and laughed a little as she deftly exchanged it for a fresh one.

Amelia stifled her sigh. Darnit. She *was* going to like the woman. She joined her alongside the changing table and nudged Timmy's waving fist with her finger. He latched on, beaming beautifully up at her.

"He's a charming one, isn't he?" Bonny fit Timmy's rubber pants over the diaper and lifted him off the changing table, holding him toward Amelia. "Mr. Hunt warned me that he'd steal my heart right off the bat and I suspect he is right."

If it weren't for the way Bonny clearly expected Amelia to take the baby, she might have felt more uneasy. But Bonny just looked approving as Amelia took Timmy and he chortled happily, snagging his tiny little fingers in her hair. She distracted him with a small squishy turtle that Daphne had gotten for him before he was born. "He's a very good baby."

"He looks perfectly healthy and he's loved and well cared for," Bonny said comfortably. "You're clearly doing a wonderful job with him. He's happy."

"I've had a lot of help learning."

"Your friend, Ms. Browning?"

Amelia gave her a surprised look.

"Mr. Hunt told me what a good friend she's been to you all." Bonny finished wiping her hands with an antibacterial wipe and tossed it in the trash bin that was as cleverly disguised as beautiful wood furniture as the diaper pail. "Now, I'm here to care for the children—Timmy in particular, of course—but you and Mr. Hunt are the parents." She didn't blink at the term. "So you just tell me what you like and don't like and we'll take it from there."

A faint sound at the doorway alerted Amelia to Molly's presence. Her niece was eyeing Bonny with some alarm. Amelia handed Timmy back to the nanny and went to Molly, drawing her into the room. "Molly, this is Ms.—" She looked at Bonny questioningly.

"Just Bonny," the woman assured easily. "I'm here to help out your aunt and uncle." She held out her hand toward Molly. "And you are Molly. Mr. Hunt told me you were the prettiest little girl he'd ever seen, and I must say I'd have to agree."

Molly's eyes widened a little. "He said that?" she whispered.

"Cross my heart." Bonny suited words to action.

Even Amelia believed her.

She took the comb and bands that Molly was holding and swiftly braided her long hair, while Bonny asked a few questions about Timmy's typical schedule.

And then Jack was bolting down the hall, yelling at Molly to find her backpack and Amelia quickly excused herself, as well, kissing the top of Timmy's sweet-smelling head before reluctantly leaving.

Her clothes took up only a small space in the enormous closet that Gray's master suite possessed and she grabbed the first suit she came to. She pulled on the navy skirt, shoved her bare feet into matching pumps and buttoned the navy jacket over her bra. Tossing some hairpins and her brush into her briefcase, she made it out to the landing at the same time as the children.

There was no sign of Gray still about when they dashed down the stairs and headed out the private, side entrance. Peter was there with the car, waiting.

Amelia urged the children inside and followed, only to nearly bang her head on the roof of the vehicle.

Gray was already seated inside.

Feeling flushed and blaming it on her rush, she ignored the glint in his eyes and sat down as far from him as she could. They all fastened themselves in and Amelia grabbed her briefcase, dumping it on the wide seat between her and Gray. She fished out the hairpins, dropping them on her lap and stared blindly out the side window as she brushed her hair, gathering it at her nape.

"Leave it down. Or are you afraid it won't suit the librarian image you're trying to maintain?"

Her fingers were already shaking too much to work the pins into the chignon.

"I like it long, too," Molly added softly. Jack didn't give her a second look; his nose was buried in his handheld electronic game.

Gray had given one each to Jack and Molly when they'd moved from the apartment, and since then, Jack had only seemed to put his down when he'd been "fishing" with Harry.

Amelia gave up on her hair, contenting herself with the notion that she was doing so only to please her niece.

Though Brandlebury was still a fair distance from the Hunt mansion, the trip took considerably less time with Peter at the wheel. Using Gray's cell phone, she quickly called Paula with the latest update and mindful of the sets of ears listening in, promised to call later when they could chat. Then Peter pulled up in the turnout in front of the school, and they scrambled from the car, but Gray once more surprised her by getting out, too.

"What are you doing, now?"

The first bell was already ringing and children were running pell-mell toward the school building, their backpacks bouncing. In seconds, Molly and Jack were past the security guard and became just two more in the navy-and-tan throng who were snaking up the brick steps and disappearing through the wide, tall entrance.

"Going with you to talk to Mr. Nguyen," he answered as if it were obvious.

Her lips tightened. "I agreed to marry you," she said in a low voice. "That didn't mean I agreed for you to become my keeper."

He smiled slightly. "Sheathe your claws, tiger. This isn't about your resignation, though your stubbornness is almost admirable. It's about Jack and Molly's tuition."

Never in her life had she been likened to a tiger. "What about it? They're on scholarship."

"A *need*-based scholarship." Gray reminded. "Which should be redistributed to other students who have the need. That, dear wife, no longer applies in your case."

"I suppose you think that you're going to pay their tuition?"

"Of course."

"But they're *my* responsibility."

He wrapped his hand around her elbow and herded her through the security gate. "And you are mine. Don't pretend that you didn't expect this."

She clutched her briefcase more closely against her. Maybe she was proving to him what an idiot she was, but she didn't care just then. "I didn't think about it."

He gave her a studying look. "Oddly enough, I actually believe that."

She wasn't sure whether to be flattered or insulted. But if she were no longer earning her own wages, *she* couldn't afford to pay for the children's tuition, either. "Daphne worked hard to qualify them for that scholarship."

"Just because they no longer need it doesn't mean that her efforts didn't matter." He walked with her toward the brick steps that were now nearly vacant of students. The purple and yellow irises lining them were in full, glorious bloom. On any other day, Amelia would have appreciated their beauty.

"Letting you pay their tuition wasn't in that agreement we signed."

"Not everything can be covered in legalese." He grimaced. "Somewhere walls are probably crumbling down from me saying that. Look. This isn't charity, you know. Your situation has changed, Amelia. Yours *and* the kids. You need to start getting used to it."

"And when we do get used to it, what happens when it ends?" She looked up at him. "What happens then, Gray? You think it will be easy for Jack and Molly to leave that house? You laughingly call it a shack. They think they've found heaven on earth." She shook her head. "I don't know what I was thinking to get into this."

"You were thinking about your sister."

"Maybe I should have been thinking more about her children. Maybe Dr. Jackson overestimated things and the other doctors were right, after all. Maybe Daphne *won't* recover. And if she doesn't, what have I done to her children, Gray? Introduced them to a lifestyle that only seems real in fairy tales, that's what. *I* know nothing lasts forever. But they haven't learned that particularly painful lesson, yet."

"And here I thought I was the cynical one."

She flushed.

"Don't worry so much, Amelia. You don't have to have a plan for everything in your lives."

"I doubt you apply that thinking to your business. HuntCom wouldn't be what it is today if you did."

"Not everything is business."

She nearly gaped. "You're the one who told me that everything was!"

"And you're the one who said it wasn't. Maybe you were right, and I was wrong."

Somewhere, walls probably *were* crumbling.

"I don't understand you at all, sometimes."

He took her elbow in his hand and she absorbed the small shock wave from the contact. "Then that makes two of us. Now, do you *want* to keep working here at Brandlebury?"

She pressed her lips together for a moment. "If I said that I did?"

"I think you'd be making a mistake."

"Because of all these so-called duties that I'll be taking care of now that I'm married to you."

"There's that. Look, Alex would probably deck me for saying this, but there *are* different rules for people like me and—"

"People who can't buy and sell small countries?"

He looked pained. "You think you haven't changed as a result of our marriage, but I'm telling you that the world will look at you differently. I'm not saying it's right or that it's fair. Wealth has its privileges but it also has its dangers and you're going to have to be aware of that."

"What *kind* of dangers?"

He looked over his shoulder toward the street. "See that blue van parked across the street?"

She glanced past his wide shoulders. "What about it?"

"Reporters. See that black SUV parked two cars behind it?" He barely waited for her nod. "Security guards. They'll keep their distance unless the situation warrants otherwise."

"You don't have security guards following you around."

"You'd be surprised how often I *do*. Sometimes the best security is the nearly invisible kind. I wasn't just being autocratic when I told you no more buses for you and the kids. It's for your own safety. Particularly now."

"Why now?"

"The news release goes out today that I'm taking over HuntCom as chairman of the board. Harry's retirement is official. We'll have a public event marking it as soon as it can be arranged."

She swallowed down the unease curling through her.

"And every time something major happens at HuntCom— either in personnel or products—it seems to stir up some odd reactions from various sorts. But you don't have to worry," he added calmly. "That's what they're for." He gestured vaguely toward the vehicles.

"So everyone's gotten what they wanted. Me. Harry. You."

"One would think," he murmured. "But this means my position is even more visible. And so will be my wife." He reached in his pocket and pulled out a small brooch. "I want you to wear this from now on."

She slowly took the pin. "Why?" Tiny pearls were fashioned into a looping *A*.

"Because I'm asking you to." He waited a beat and when she didn't immediately pin it to her suit, he grimaced. "It's a security device. There's a button on the back." His fingers brushed hers as he turned the pin over to show her. "Push that and those guards will be on-site in seconds. It also has GPS tracking."

"So you can follow me?"

"So we can find you," he said gruffly. "It's just a precaution. There're similar devices in the gamers that I gave the kids. We'll come up with additional solutions for them, though. If there are times this pin doesn't suit your clothing, wear it underneath. But promise me you'll wear it."

Completely disconcerted, she pinned it to her collar. "All right."

"Good girl." He reached past her and plucked off a vivid yellow bloom from the numerous plants beside the steps, brushed the tip of the velvety petals over her chin then tucked the iris into her lapel pocket where it showed even more vividly against her navy suit. "Now, let's go see the headmaster."

Shaken, and not just because of the idea of her and the children requiring security, she didn't protest.

Chapter Thirteen

As promised, Gray was there with Peter and the long black car to pick up Amelia and the children after school, and drive them to Daphne's new care center. He didn't come only with Peter, though. Bonny and Timmy were with him, as well.

When they left Brandlebury, Amelia couldn't help but notice that the blue van and the black SUV both followed along behind.

When they arrived at the care facility, Amelia took the baby and was about to suggest Bonny wait for them in the courtyard's garden but Gray beat her to the punch.

With Molly's hand in hers and Jack trailing behind, still toying with his palm-sized gamer, she led the way to her sister's room. There was a knot in her stomach, though, that cinched tighter the closer they drew.

As if in tune to her tension, Timmy was fussier than usual

and standing outside Daphne's door, she joggled him gently. "Do the, um, the guys in the SUV know about my sister?"

Gray nodded and pushed open the door. Molly dropped Amelia's hand and darted inside. Jack followed, and when Amelia entered the room, Molly had already climbed up onto the hospital bed where Daphne reclined against the raised head and was chattering away about the big new castle where they lived and the pretty dress she'd gotten to wear to the wedding.

Daphne's eyes tracked Amelia's and Gray's entry and though Amelia was watching her sister's expression with painful anticipation, Daphne's smooth face didn't move a muscle. Her dark brown eyes showed no more recognition of Gray than they did of Amelia.

The knot eased a little.

Daphne's room here at the new center bore very little resemblance to the sterile environs of her previous facility. Here there were fresh flowers in the vase on the dresser, and there was music coming from the sound system sitting on one of the nightstands.

"Mom doesn't listen to that," Jack said as he picked up the remote and switched radio stations. Daphne's gaze shifted to her son when classic Motown replaced new country. "You gonna introduce him?"

Amelia realized Jack was talking to her. And "him" meant Gray, of course. Feeling thoroughly unnerved, she lifted Timmy against her shoulder, patting his back. "Daphne, this is Gray. Grayson." Timmy squirmed against her. "Hunt. Remember I told you about him last week."

Daphne didn't respond. Her gaze shifted slightly, seeming to focus on Timmy. Amelia moved next to Molly. "Here, sweetie. Hold your brother so your mom can see him, too."

Molly took the baby. "Look at Mommy, Timmy," Molly whispered. "Isn't she pretty?"

Daphne did look pretty, despite the lack of animation on her smooth face that before the stroke had imbued her with true beauty. Her long auburn hair was clean and shining and lay over the shoulders of her bright blue T-shirt. Timmy's crinkling expression turned sunny again as he reached out and batted his little hand through his mother's hair.

Daphne focused on her baby and Amelia bit her lip as a faint smile seemed to touch Daphne's lips.

Timmy waved his hand, yanking contentedly at his mother's hair and well aware just how hard a yank the baby could give, Amelia quickly reached out to work the red locks free of his grip.

"No," Daphne said clearly.

Molly's mouth dropped. "She spoke," she said in a perfectly normal tone of voice. Jack had bounced up from the bedside chair, his gamer forgotten at his mother's voice. Now, at Molly's, he looked even more dumbfounded.

Amelia laughed. She leaned over her sister and kissed the top of her head. "Yes, she did!" Her gaze shifted to Gray, who'd been entirely silent since they'd entered the room. He was studying Daphne, though the answering smile on his face was probably meant to mask that.

But Amelia saw beyond the mask.

He'd been adamant all along that he hadn't known Daphne before. Even after his solitary visit to see her before the wedding, was he trying to place her?

For a man who could recall the names of every person they'd greeted at their wedding reception, she now believed there was no way that Gray would have forgotten meeting

Daphne. And somewhere along the way, she'd stopped believing that he was lying.

Which meant that Daphne had. And that fact was still unfathomable.

Timmy was still bouncing his fistful of his mother's hair, but this time rather than trying to free Daphne's hair, Amelia rested her hip on the edge of the bed and just reached out to slow his yanking.

She knew she should be grateful that Daphne spoke even just that one word, but she couldn't help yearning with every fiber for another. And another. Her sister could say anything—even tell Amelia what she thought of her marrying Gray—if only she'd make her way back to living any portion of her life.

"Do you remember when Mom was alive, and she took us to that state park? She got her line caught on the back of her sweater and nearly cast herself into the lake. Well, you should have seen Molly and Jack this weekend, Daph. Harry—that's Gray's father—had them lakeside trying to show them how to fish. Since that time when you and I were kids, I don't think I've laughed so hard."

"I didn't like the worms." Molly wrinkled her nose. "But it was fun." She looked up at Amelia. "Can Mommy come to stay with us at our big house?" Her voice was once more a whisper.

"She can come anytime the doctor says she can," Gray promised.

Amelia didn't assume the assurance was a concession on Gray's part where Daphne was concerned. He probably believed the doctor would never say that Daphne would be well enough in the first place.

"Did you hear that, Mommy?" Molly's voice grew louder again and Amelia nearly sagged with relief. "I can't wait to show you my new room. I have a window seat and bookshelves with *all* the Harry Potter books, and even my own television. But Aunt Amelia says I can't watch it until I finish my homework."

"I'll go find a nurse," Gray said when Molly stopped, apparently to draw breath. "They'll want to know about this." He headed for the door and was surprised when Jack followed him out. "First time you've heard your mom speak in a while," he commented.

Jack shrugged, trying to look nonchalant, but it wasn't very convincing. "It's cool. She, um, wouldn't be real happy if she hears about me getting picked up by the cops."

"Ah. You're more afraid of your mom's punishment than your aunt's."

Jack lifted his shoulder. "Aunt Amelia's rules are stricter. But when Mom gets mad…" He shook his head dolefully.

"Didn't think about that too much when you were trying to lift those electronics."

"*I* wasn't. Ya think she'll get better?"

"Your aunt believes so." They stopped at a sleek desk located in an open area several doors away from Daphne's room. "Excuse me."

The young woman looked up from the paperwork spread before her. Her eyes widened a little. "Mr. Hunt. What can I do for you?"

"Send a doctor in for Mrs. Mason, would you please?"

She was already reaching for the phone. Satisfied, Gray looked back at Jack. "What do *you* think?"

"What's gonna happen with Mol and me when she's better?"

Gray closed his hand over the boy's shoulder and drew him away from the nurses' station. "What do you mean?"

"We'd go home with Mom, right?"

"You and your sister and Tim, you mean," Gray expanded cautiously. Was this what Amelia had been cautioning against? "You guys won't have to worry about money like you used to, if that's what you mean."

Jack flipped the gamer slowly between his hands.

"Jack?"

"It's not. Well, I mean, yeah. I don't want to go back to the apartment again."

"Then what *do* you mean?"

The kid's expression only grew more miserable. "Your dad wants Tim to stay with you if we ever have t' go home again."

Down the corridor, a white-jacketed woman was entering Daphne's room. "Did Harry tell you that?"

Jack hesitated. Sighed mightily. "While we were fishing."

Gray managed not to swear. He should have known his father wouldn't suddenly cease his interference just because Gray had said his "I do's." From the beginning he'd said he expected grandchildren.

"Does your aunt know this?"

"Nah. I think she'd be pissed."

That was putting it mildly. Gray was feeling plenty of that emotion himself. "Do you know why Harry would think that Tim wouldn't go back with your mom if—once—she gets better?" Amelia had been adamant that neither Jack nor Molly knew about Daphne's paternity claims.

"'Cause he's yours."

Gray kept a lid on his annoyance. "Harry said that? Or your aunt said it?" He should have known better than to start letting himself believe she'd dropped that nonsense. What was the point of pursuing the claim when she was already getting everything she wanted from him?

Gwen hadn't ceased *her* plot. Gray had fallen for her, hook, line and sinker, and she'd used that to her advantage. Thinking that he—that his family—would pay any amount of money to see her safely returned to them.

It was only after she and the baby she carried were dead—accidentally killed by her own accomplice when Harry had refused to pay a dime—that the truth about her had come to light.

"My aunt never talks about that stuff around me and Mol," Jack was saying. "Harry just said that Tim looks like you, right down to the birthmark on his arm. So. Is he?"

Gray went still. He did have a small mark on his shoulder, shaped almost like a diamond. Coincidence? He wasn't a big believer in it.

"Mom told us Tim's dad was a mistake." Jack spoke faster. "That he didn't want nothing to do with her or Tim."

"*If* Tim were mine—which he is not—I wouldn't turn away from him. I'm not going to turn away from him now. Or you or Molly or your aunt. Or—" he made himself say it "—your mom. The only thing you need to worry about is doing your math homework. None of you kids are going anywhere. And when the time comes for your mom to leave here, she can come stay with us, too."

The relief that crossed Jack's face was almost comical. "Then I really don't gotta go back to the apartment."

"You really don't have to," Gray corrected.

"It wasn't a bad place," Jack said suddenly, as if he felt the need to correct the impression. "My mom wouldn't have us living in a bad place."

"I know."

"It's just. You know. Ty lives there."

"Ty, one of the guys you were with when you were picked up."

Jack nodded. "It wasn't my idea, you know."

"So you weren't the mastermind. Just the hired help."

"Dincha ever do stuff you didn't want to have to do?"

Gray shoved his hands in his pockets. If the kid only knew. "What exactly did you *have* to do?"

"Ty told me to watch out for the store manager. Make sure he wasn't watching."

"A brilliant assignment from him, given the security cameras all over the store."

"I know. I told him—"

"But you still went along with him. Come on, Jack. Did you ever have something stolen from you?"

"My bike a few years ago. It took us a year before I could get another one."

"How'd you feel?" He nodded at the boy's grimace. "Why would you want to make someone else feel like that?"

"I *didn't*."

"Then why did you try?"

"'Cause it was the only way I could get Ty to shut up about Molly. He makes her feel even more stupid 'cause of her whispering."

Gray rubbed his hand down his face. He never thought he'd feel some sympathy for Harry's uninvolved parenting methods, but now he did. "If today's any indication, it sounds like she's over that for now. You couldn't have found a better way to deal with it?"

Jack grimaced. "Next time I'll just punch him in the face."

Gray let out a half laugh. "Yeah, kid. That's a good alternative."

"Well…what *was* I supposed to do? Molly's kind of a pain sometimes, but she's my sister. Mom expects me to protect her."

"Protect her by helping her learn it doesn't matter what people say about you. What matters is what *you* do and what you know is true."

"Figures you'd say something like that. Aunt Amelia says stuff like that, too."

"Says stuff like *what?*" Eyes still dancing, Amelia fairly floated to a stop behind them. She'd strapped Timmy again into his sling and looked so happy, so right, that Gray felt a jolt inside that went deeper than usual.

"Was that one of the doctors who went in there?"

Amelia nodded. She put her arm around Jack's shoulders and squeezed. "Dr. Coats. She thinks your mom speaking even one word is a *very* good sign. Molly's in there reciting her spelling words from school." She brushed Jack's bangs off his forehead. "Do you want to go on back and sit with her for a few more minutes? Dr. Coats doesn't want your mom getting too tired, but said the more interaction she has right now, the better."

"You don't want to be in there, too?" Gray asked when Jack—after a quick look toward Gray—headed back to his mother's room.

"I'll have plenty of time to come sit with her when the kids are in school, and I am *not,*" she said pointedly. But, for once, she didn't sound heated about it.

"Thought you were determined to serve out your full notice."

"Mr. Nguyen brought around my replacement this afternoon. She can start immediately."

"Why wait until now to mention it?"

"You don't have the corner on pride, Gray. You'll never know what it feels like to know how easily you can be replaced."

"It's a job they're filling. Nobody can replace *you*."

"Very tactfully put," she said. Her smile said that nothing was going to ruin her enthusiasm just then.

Gray found himself wishing that he knew how to make sure nothing ever did.

"I forgot to ask earlier. Did the news release go out? Usually, there's a radio going in the teachers's lounge, but there wasn't today."

"It's probably going out right now. Our media department wants to hold a press conference tomorrow. You'll need to be there."

Her eyes widened. "What for?"

"To stand beside your man," he drawled, watching the interesting flush rise and fall in her cheeks. "Think you can do that without looking like you'd just as soon stick a fork in me?"

"I imagine I can suffer through," she returned, deadpan.

He couldn't help smiling. She *did* have an ironic sense of humor that he could appreciate. "It'll be at the shack. Harry won't do it elsewhere. Says that now he's out of HuntCom's daily operations, he doesn't want to go to the offices again."

"You're kidding!"

"He's ornery. He's doing what he has to do, but he's damn sure going to make it as inconvenient on the rest of us as he can while he's about it."

She pressed her lips together.

"What?"

"Just…well—" a dimple came and went in her cheek "—kind of sounds like your apple didn't fall far from his tree."

"I don't need any reminders of how much like Harry I am."

"Can't be such a bad thing. Look what you were willing to do to make him happy."

"It wasn't selfless."

She was swaying slightly, a human rocking chair for her nephew. "Because you got the chairmanship, as well." She lifted her shoulder. "Did you think I'd miss that not-so-small detail? The timing is too coincidental."

"You're not going to give me hell for not disclosing that fact?"

There was a flicker in that happy expression of hers. "We're little more than strangers to each other, Gray. What do you think?"

"I think we stopped being strangers two weeks ago."

"We met two weeks ago."

"Yes."

Tension suddenly hung in the air and Gray couldn't tell if it was stemming from him, or from her. Or from both of them.

He wasn't used to being unable to read situations. People. Himself. And he wasn't certain how he felt about it. Annoyed. Disconcerted. Relieved.

Her lashes had lowered. She moistened her lips. "So, um, what were you and Jack discussing so seriously?"

"Guy stuff."

She made a soft *mmm* sound. Her hand had gone from patting Timmy's back to moving around in slow, distracting circles. "I know it's early yet, but I do appreciate the way you've all been with Jack and Molly. And I might think a nanny is overkill, but the nursery you arranged for Timmy is pretty spectacular." She looked around. The nurse had left her station and was nowhere in sight. "I know it's for appearances, but still. Thank you."

"It's not all appearances, Amelia."

The amber flecks in her eyes seemed to multiply. "If I let myself start thinking that way, then—"

"Then, what?"

"Then I might start…liking you," she finally admitted.

"We're married," he said drily. "Things would be easier if you did."

"And harder still when it all ends. Not just for the children."

"More of that cynicism of yours?"

"I prefer to think of it as experience, rather than cynicism. But neither really matters. Our agreement has a finite term, remember?"

"And if it didn't?"

She smiled skeptically. "Then neither one of us would have agreed to it. We're—" she hesitated, searching for a word "—useful to one another for now. That's all."

Gray couldn't argue with the very argument he'd used to convince her to sign away her singlehood.

"In any case, my sister spoke today for the first time in more than three months. And Molly, too…" She lifted her hands. The skepticism faded from her smile, and she was simply a woman whose faith in her sister's recovery had received a well-needed boost. "Whatever I agreed to was worth this. So." Her dimple winked at him again as she stood on the tiptoes of her navy-blue shoes and pressed an unexpected kiss to his cheek. "Thank you."

He couldn't help himself. He turned his head and covered her mouth with his. Swallowed the sexy little gasp she gave and made himself stop the kiss before he forgot where they were.

She went back down on her heels, looking suddenly shy.

"I, um, I'd better go back to Daphne."

"Yes."

She flushed a little. Then turned on her heel as she headed toward her sister's room once more.

Watching her go, Gray wondered if her gratitude would last long enough to survive Harry's suspicion where Daphne's baby was concerned. If it would survive his own suspicion that was occurring to him now, thanks to Jack's comment about that birthmark. A suspicion that would complicate the situation even more if Gray was right.

He doubted it. And the fact that he wished her gratitude would last—that it *could*—disturbed him more than anything.

"Amelia," he called suddenly.

She stopped. Looked at him. Ran the tip of her tongue over her lower lip. "Yes?"

"You want to go running in the morning?"

Her lips parted. "I, um, I'm really not much of a runner," she admitted.

Given the situation, he'd suspected as much. "Is that a yes, or a no?"

He saw the swallow that worked down her long throat. The look she gave toward her sister's room. The uncertainty in her eyes when she finally looked back at him.

"Yes. I'd like that."

Chapter Fourteen

"Happy birthday, Amelia, happy birthday to you!"

Amelia laughed and leaned over the enormous birthday cake that was decorated with about a million and a half yellow icing roses. She took a deep breath and blew out the candles.

All thirty-one of them.

Around the big dining room table in the main dining room, the guests they'd invited to the birthday celebration that Gray had insisted on cheered.

Even Daphne, sitting between Amelia and Molly clapped. The motion was stilted and awkward, but Daphne managed it. And the smile on her face was slightly crooked. But it was still a smile. It was her first visit to the shack, and as far as Amelia was concerned, it was a raving success. She hoped they'd be able to repeat it soon, but Dr. Jackson was still urging some caution where Daphne's long-term memory was concerned.

"Well, let's not just admire the cake," Cornelia said humorously. "Let's *have* some." She lifted the mother-of-pearl-handled knife that one of the maids had brought to the table along with the cake. "Shall I?"

Amelia happily waved away the duty to her. She sat down next to Daphne and squeezed her hand. Daphne's squeeze in return was weak, but it was there.

"Here." Gray, sitting on the other side of Amelia, slid a slender box onto the table where the maids had already cleared the table to make way for dessert.

She looked at the box—clearly a jewelry box. "But you already gave me a birthday present." It sat, gleaming red and sleek, in the driveway outside their wing. She'd nearly fallen over in her tracks when he'd presented her with the keys to the fancy little car.

In the days since he'd taken over Harry's position at HuntCom, they'd only seen each other on the mornings he'd been able to fit in a run. The rest of the time he'd been dealing with the changeover at HuntCom. He was always up before she woke and didn't come to bed until after she was asleep. The only proof that he'd been there at all was the scent of him on the dented pillow beside her. But he never failed to call and talk to the kids at least once a day and now that they were on their summer break from school, both Molly and Jack raced for the phone when it rang in the middle of the afternoons.

And those predawn runs with him were becoming dangerously addictive for Amelia.

"Consider this a one-month anniversary gift," he said.

"You going to be that attentive after a few years?" J.T. asked humorously. Only Justin and Lily hadn't been able to make it for Amelia's birthday. They were at the ranch in Idaho with little

Ava, who was suffering from chicken pox, though they expected to make it for HuntCom's official reception honoring Harry's retirement that was being held in a few weeks. The planning for it had been in the works for some time, now. Amelia actually found herself looking forward to seeing the house's enormous reception hall put to use. She'd even been able to contribute her part by pulling together a historical perspective of other HuntCom celebrations. Ones that weren't already chronicled in the gallery above the reception hall.

She'd thought she'd have time heavy on her hands without her position at Brandlebury. But Gray had been right. She seemed constantly on the move and had to work hard to keep time reserved for the children.

"Aren't *you* going to be that attentive?" Amy challenged her husband and everyone laughed.

"You going to open it or just look at it?" Jack wanted to know, peering across the wide table at them.

Flushing, avoiding Gray's eyes, she pulled off the gold bow and paper and flipped open the box.

Everything female inside her sighed at the lovely diamond pendant nestled against the white velvet lining. "I don't know what to say." Mindful of Harry watching from his position at the head of the table, she leaned closer to Gray. "It's beautiful. Thank you."

"I was able to find the same designer who did Cornelia's necklace from George. I thought you'd like it."

Her lips parted. "You went to that trouble?"

He smiled slightly. "Had to, since Loretta's been so busy working on Harry's reception," he murmured before brushing his lips over hers a little more slowly than he needed. She felt herself flush and busied herself lifting the necklace from the box. She held it out to show Daphne. Her sister's eyes smiled more easily than the rest of her, but the smile was still that of one to a virtual stranger. Daphne recognized her and the children as family only because she'd been told it so often. But the "connection" was still missing. Amelia was facing the likelihood that it would remain lost.

"I might never take it off," Amelia warned, fitting the clasp around her neck. The delicate pendant settled like a tiny, warm caress in the hollow of her throat.

"Like your A pin. Did you get something for Uncle Gray?" Molly asked above the collective oohs from the women around the table. She hadn't returned to her whispers-only habit since they'd visited her mother that day with Gray. She had to speak up to be heard because not only were Amy and P.J. there with their husbands, but Paula and even two of Cornelia's four daughters had been able to make it. It was Amelia's first chance to meet "the cousins" as Gray called the women, since none had been able to make their hurriedly scheduled wedding. All four would be officially on hand for the HuntCom event, though.

"I should have thought of something," Amelia answered Molly.

"I don't think your uncle Gray is too worried about it, honey," Frankie said, looking amused. Fortunately, for the sake of the youngsters, she refrained from speculating what sort of gift Gray could expect from his new wife.

"Hush your mouth," Cornelia scolded lightly as she passed out china plates laden with hefty slices of the moist, white cake. She gave Amelia the first slice. "There you go, dear. I hope the coming year holds everything you deserve."

"I'll second that." Harry lifted his champagne flute. "We need some refills, here. Corny, where'd that maid get off to?"

Georgie, Cornelia's eldest, rolled her eyes and went to the sideboard to retrieve two bottles that had been chilling on ice. One champagne, and one sparkling cider. "We can rough it," she said drily, and handed one of the bottles to Gray, who sat closest to Harry. Twin pops filled the air as they uncorked them almost simultaneously. Then she began working her way around the table, filling the crystal flutes set near each place. The children automatically received cider, as did Amy, whose pregnancy was just now a soft bump beneath her eyelet sundress.

When Georgie reached for P.J.'s glass, though, the redhead slid her hand over the top. "I'll have cider, too," she said, then seemed to color at finding herself the center of all attention.

Amelia tucked the tip of her tongue between her teeth. She'd noticed that P.J. hadn't drunk the wine she'd been served with dinner but had said nothing. But now—

"No alcohol for me," P.J. admitted, looking toward her husband for some assistance. Gray's middle brother just sat there looking like the cat who ate the canary, and tossing up her hands a little, the woman looked around. "And before anyone gets too excited, we're just *trying* to get pregnant. It's a long shot."

"But even if we don't," Alex added, his gaze on his wife, "we've gotten our names on several adoption-agency lists."

"Wonderful." Harry exclaimed, looking more satisfied than Alex, if that were possible. "Well done, son. P.J., you'll be a fine mother, whenever the day comes. I for one couldn't be happier." He lifted his champagne glass in a toast. "Unless—" His crafty gaze turned toward Gray and Amelia.

From the top of her head to the bottom of her feet, Amelia felt her skin heat. Beneath the cover of the heavy linen draped over the table, Gray closed his hand over hers. "Unless nothing, Harry," he warned easily. "Good luck to you both. I know my brother can't be unhappy at all that trying." Laughter circled the table once more and Cornelia settled a piece of cake in front of Harry, which seemed enough to distract him from further speculation.

Before Amelia knew it, the evening had slipped away. Daphne had been returned to the care center along with the private nurse that Gray had arranged to accompany her on the outing. The children had turned in and a look in on Timmy assured her that the baby was still asleep, as Bonny had reported before excusing herself for the night.

Her finger drifting over the diamond at her neck, Amelia headed along the hallway to her own bedroom. As usual, Gray was not there. If he *was* home in the evening hours— which was fairly rare—he spent most of his time working in his study. Tonight, she found herself wishing he weren't.

Oddly agitated considering how long and busy the day had been, she went into the en suite bathroom and flipped the bronze handle that sent water coursing into the mini swimming pool that passed for a bathtub. She tossed in a generous portion of bubble bath that Paula had urged her to buy one afternoon when they'd been visiting, and left the water running to retrieve her robe.

Still her aging pink terry cloth one, though she now had several replacements hanging unused in her closets thanks to the personal shopper Loretta had recently sicced on Amelia to bolster her wardrobe up to Hunt standards.

Her hair was already pinned up from dinner and she slid off her deep ochre dress and slid instead into the water, nudging a thick folded towel behind her head. Sighing, she closed her eyes and sank a little deeper into the water, swishing her hands through the froth of lilac-scented bubbles building beneath the rushing water.

"The first night I talked to you on the phone you were in the bath."

Amelia's eyes flew open.

Gray was leaning his shoulder against the archway leading into the bedroom. The jacket and tie he'd worn at dinner were missing and he'd rolled up his shirtsleeves.

Her mouth dried at the wholly masculine sight he made. "I remember."

"I wondered then if you were a bubble bath type."

"It's a good thing I am," she managed. As it was, she was barely shielded by them in the rippling water still rising in the tub. "Is something wrong?"

"Should there be?"

She let her shoulders inch farther below the water. "You're usually working at this time of night."

"I'm usually avoiding this bedroom at this time of night," he corrected. He straightened and slowly crossed the thick Aubusson rug that prevented the travertine-tiled room from feeling cold.

"I'm sorry."

"For driving me to distraction?" He sat down on the wide ledge of the tub.

She swallowed. "You're in an odd mood."

"The judge called me this morning about Jack's hearing."

She started to sit up straighter, but caught herself. "It's scheduled?"

"It's dismissed."

"Part of me is relieved. Another part thinks he should have to face the consequences of his actions."

"Don't we all?" He leaned over and slowly turned off the water. The sudden silence around them loomed tight and heavy, broken only by Amelia's heart pounding in her ears and the faint, whispering rustle of bath foam settling. "I think he realizes the error he made. I don't think you need to worry that he's going to graduate to armed robbery or grand theft auto anytime soon. He's a good kid." His brooding gaze drifted over Amelia. "He'll grow up to be a good man."

"I hope so," she whispered faintly.

He leaned across the tub again, this time to pick up the tall, thin bottle of bubble bath. He opened it. Smelled it. Closed it again. "This is why you always smell of lilacs."

"I didn't think it was noticeable. Gray..." But she broke off, not knowing what she wanted to say. Only that *something* needed to be said. Done. Because he was killing her by slow degrees.

He carefully set the bottle aside. "This isn't working."

She froze. Slow degrees? This was a swift guillotine. "I warned you I was the wrong choice. You—you should have chosen someone like Marissa."

His brows drew together in a quick frown. "Jesus. I'm as bad as Harry." He pushed to his feet and rubbed his hand over his raspy jaw. "I want you in my bed, Amelia."

"I...I am."

His lips twisted. "You take up about nine inches on one side of the bed. Even sound asleep you don't budge from that narrow slice. Regardless of who keeps it there—you or me— I'm tired of the ten feet of space between us."

"It's a big bed but not *that* big." Her attempt at humor fell flat. "What do you want me to say?"

He turned away from the tub and planted his hands on the

marble vanity. His head lowered, his shirt straining over his wide shoulders. "Damned if I know."

Amelia looked at his reflection in the mirror above the vanity. He looked oddly worn and her heart squeezed. What had he done since they'd met but protect what he cared about? He even wanted to protect her and the children. There was not a day she went out when she wasn't discreetly trailed by the men in that black SUV. He'd even gone beyond the terms of their agreement when it came to the children and though she knew that was no financial hardship to him, he'd given them time and attention—and those things *were* a premium in his life.

His brothers could make fun of his workaholic nature, but she'd never known anyone to show such dedication to anything.

"Gray."

He lifted his head and looked at her through the mirror.

Praying that she wasn't making the biggest mistake of her life, she drew up her knees, braced her hand on the wide ledge, and slowly rose to her feet. Water and bubbles streamed down her limbs. "I, um, I'm not very good at this."

Gray turned to face her. A muscle flexed in his hard jaw as his gaze burned down the length of her. "Don't underestimate yourself." He plucked a thick towel off the folded stack that was faithfully replenished every day and shook it out. "Come over here."

She felt exposed in a way that went much deeper than nudity. "You come over here."

A glint of surprise lit his eyes. "Negotiation, Amelia?"

She lifted her chin a hair, emboldened by the rushing in her veins. "I'm the one standing here wet and shivering."

His gaze lingered on her. "A valid point." He tossed the towel back onto the stack and kicked off his shoes and Amelia forgot the art of breathing as his shirt and slacks followed. He stripped off his socks, shucked what had to be navy silk boxers and straightened. "Feel more even?"

Her lips parted as her parched lungs sucked in oxygen. There was no hiding the fact that he was as affected as she. But it wasn't only that evidence that turned everything inside her weak and yearning. It was the cording along his shoulders. It was the swirl of dark hair over his wide chest. It was the roping muscles working down his thighs. The way his hands were curled into fists. The way his bare feet looked amazingly sexy.

Mostly, it was the way his hungry eyes looked back at *her.* As if he couldn't tear his eyes from her any more than she could from him.

"Halfway?" Her voice was husky.

"Fair enough." He picked up the towel again and took a step toward her.

She took one toward him. Then another.

A last step. Her breasts, aching and tight, grazed his chest. And he, oh dear heaven, *he* grazed her hip.

"Terms agreed?"

She looked up at him, mute. She lifted her hands and gingerly settled them on that wide chest.

He let out a hissing breath. "I'll take that as a yes." His arms came around her, pulling her tightly to him. He dragged the towel down her back, only to drop it and tempestuously repeat the motion, from her nape to her bottom, with only his widespread hand.

Amelia gasped. She felt his heart charging against her palms as she worked her hands up the crispy soft whorls of chest hair until she reached his shoulders. Wound behind his neck.

"I want you." His words rasped against her temple. His breath burned against her neck as he tipped her head back. "I have for days. Weeks."

Her shaking fingers sifted through the short, thick strands of his hair, finding it even silkier than she'd expected. "You didn't say anything. I thought…I thought you'd changed your mind." She pressed her mouth to his bicep. Touched her tongue to him. Slightly salty. Addictive. "It's happened before."

He crushed her loosely fastened chignon and pins scattered, pinging against the tile. "Look at me."

Her dazed eyes focused on his and she felt scorched to the center of her being.

"It's not happening with me." His deep voice was low. Soft. It still echoed around her. Echoed through her. "Not now. Not ever. So change *your* mind now if you have to, Amelia, or accept that fact."

Her fingertips flexed against him. "I don't want to change my mind." The admission sounded raw. Felt raw.

He exhaled again. Pressed his forehead against hers for a breathless minute. Then his hands dragged down her spine again and he suddenly lifted her off her feet and carried her to the bed, impatiently throwing aside the heavy ivory-and-black bedding before lowering her onto the cool, smooth sheet. Joining her, pulling her deliberately to the center of the wide, wide bed, heedless of the water still clinging to her.

Need tangling inside her, she shifted beneath the long leg capturing hers. Found the slide of her smooth shin against his hairier one too tempting to resist, and repeated the motion.

"I should be wining and dining you or something," he murmured.

"We did that earlier." She dragged her hands down his spine. Back up again. Her mouth blindly sought his.

He groaned a little and deepened the kiss until she couldn't form a single coherent thought that didn't center around him. In the center of her.

When he finally lifted his head, she hauled in a hoarse breath, trying to drag his head back to her. But he was moving again, dropping his lips to her shoulder. "Impatient, Amelia?"

She couldn't manage more than an incoherent moan. Not when his kiss was drifting down to her breasts, not when his tongue teased her nipples into even tighter points and she felt as if the sensations inside her couldn't be contained by her too-tight skin.

She twined her legs around him, moaning his name, uncaring that she sounded desperate. Or impatient. She was both. And it felt like she'd been that way for a lifetime. "Please—"

His fingers slid around her wrists, capturing both in one hand, and drawing them above her head. "I want everything you have to give," he murmured, pressing his other hand flat against the rocketing beat of her heart. "Everything, Amelia."

She sucked in her lower lip. Swallowed. But she was still parched for him. "Gray—"

His hand slid down from the valley between her breasts to the flat of her belly. She jerked a little and he let out a low, masculine sigh, and glided lower. She bit back a cry then, as he slowly, achingly slowly, sought out the very heart of her.

"Everything," he murmured again, and he brushed his lips across hers, just as delicately, as maddeningly as his fingers glided, slick and tempting.

"Then don't tease me," she begged hoarsely, twisting her

hands free only to gasp and grab hold of his shoulders when his teasing did stop, and his hand moved with deliberate intent and she hurtled abruptly into a shuddering, quaking climax.

"You called my name," he murmured when she finally managed to pull in a breath and open her eyes to look up into his.

"I couldn't help it." The admission came without thought, sounding foolish to her.

But he didn't seem to think so.

His eyes were so fierce, his expression so intent, she forgot words altogether, and she stared up at him, unable to look away as he shifted, settling against her.

Motionless, she felt her heart beating with his until they were no longer distinguishable.

Her skin was his.

His breathing was hers.

And just when she thought she'd scream from the agonizing anticipation in that endless moment, he brushed his lips over the diamond—his diamond—that lay against her throat.

Emotion tightened her chest and she knew she was well and truly lost.

His lips worked up her chin and slowly, gently brushed over hers. "Happy birthday, Amelia."

A tear slid from the corner of her eye. He kissed it away. Sighed her name and slowly, unforgettable made them one.

And then Amelia cried out yet again because all there *was* motion.

His.

Hers.

And the awesome wonder that caught her in an even stronger grip, sending them both headlong into the whirlwind. And when it was her name that escaped Gray's lips, she didn't even notice her tears that spilled over.

She just exhaustedly closed her arms around his broad, broad shoulders, and fell asleep with his head against her breast.

Chapter Fifteen

There was no light seeping through the drapes hanging at the tall windows of their bedroom when Amelia woke. A glance at the clock on Gray's nightstand told her that they still had a few hours to sleep.

Only her body didn't seem to want any just then.

So she lay there, her head resting on his shoulder, one leg draped between his, her fingertips slowly drifting over his chest. He made a soft noise, closing one hand over hers. "Baby's crying." His voice sounded rusty. Exhausted.

She sat up, pushing her tumbled hair out of her face. "I didn't even hear him," she admitted, feeling guilty. She scrambled off the bed and snatched up her robe, tying it around her as she dashed down the hall to the nursery. Amelia had insisted that Bonny not worry about tending the baby during the night.

But it was rare, indeed, for Timmy to even wake in the middle of the night anymore.

This time, however, he was wailing but good when she lifted him out of his crib. She cuddled him against her, carrying him to the changing table, flipping on one of the small lamps that were conveniently placed around the nursery.

"He hungry or something?" Gray had followed her, wearing nothing but a loose pair of sweats hanging low over his hips.

"Probably." She dragged her eyes from the distracting sight of him and quickly finished changing the baby before lifting him to her shoulder once more. "Bonny said he didn't finish his bottle before he fell asleep." She went to the refrigerator the nursery was equipped with, and pulled out one of the bottles stored there.

"Here." Gray slid his hands around the baby, brushing against her breast as he lifted Timmy. "You get the cow juice. I'll hold him."

She pushed the bottle into the warmer. By the time she turned it on, Timmy had stopped crying and was slapping his hand against Gray's chest, seemingly fascinated.

She knew the feeling. She was pretty fascinated by the man's chest, too.

"He's gotten heavier," Gray murmured.

"Mmm, hmm." The bottle warmer hissed a little as it worked. "He's on the high end of the length chart and the low side of the weight."

Gray's long fingers spanned the width of the baby's back. "You still think he's mine?"

The question came out of nowhere, nearly making her legs go out from beneath her. She stared at him in the soft light, her mouth parting, but no words coming. Her eyes suddenly stung, because believing him meant she didn't believe her sister and she badly wanted to believe him. "No," she finally said, painfully honest. "But I want to believe you both."

He hefted the baby up to his nose. "She doesn't trust easily, does she, Tim."

"Neither do you," Amelia pointed out. She crossed her arms and wished the warmer would finish its work more quickly.

He lowered the baby to his shoulder once more and prowled with him around the nursery, and despite the turn of the conversation, Amelia couldn't help but feel the powerful punch of the sight. A man and baby. How had she gone so long in her life thinking that she didn't want both of those things?

Now, she had them, but they weren't hers to have. Timmy *had* a mother. One who was fighting to make her way back to them all. And Gray—despite making their marriage a reality—was only hers for the duration of their agreement.

"Harry didn't teach a lot of it. Christina—" He didn't bother finishing that. "Then there was Alex's mom. She's probably the least objectionable of them all, but she was no picnic. And J.T.'s?" He shook his head. "Don't ask. Justin's mom was so vindictive we didn't even learn about him until he was about Jack's age. It takes a lot for *any* of us to trust."

"They trust their wives. It's evident in every breath they take."

"Fortunately, they're not Harry Juniors like I am. And they're in love with their wives."

"You're entirely different than Harry." Gray wasn't in love with her. He didn't have to state that particular fact when she was already painfully cognizant of it. Just as she very much feared she was in love with *him*. She didn't know when. Or how.

She just knew it was there. Inside her. A part of her. "You must have loved Gwen."

He hesitated for a moment. "Somebody's been gossiping," he finally said. "Because Harry kept it out of the papers back then. So who was it? Cornelia? Loretta? One of the cousins tonight at dinner?"

"Does it matter? Losing her must have been very painful."

"Is that bottle ready?"

Swallowing the disappointment that he wouldn't share even something so distant in the past, she plucked the bottle from the warmer and shook it, testing it on her wrist. "Warm enough." She held it out to him.

He looked startled and she was ashamed of the stab of satisfaction that at least there were a few things beyond his comfort zone. So she held out both hands. "I'll take him, then."

His lips tightened a little. He went to the rocking chair by one of the windows and sat down on it, juggling Timmy around.

Amelia softened right back up again. She suspected that would be the case more often than not where Gray was concerned. She went over to him, perching on the padded window seat beside the wooden chair. She tucked the nipple into Timmy's greedy mouth and adjusted the baby more comfortably in Gray's arms. Timmy sighed hugely around the nipple, sending out a bubble of milk, and then settled on it in earnest. She rubbed her fingers along the silky tufts of hair he'd grown in the past month. It was darker than either Jack's or Molly's hair, though it still held a similar reddish cast.

"Daphne never lied about anything in her entire life," Amelia said softly. "Not for any reason and certainly not for money. So why would she do so where Timmy is concerned?"

Gray took her hand. His fingers toyed with the ornate engagement ring he'd given her not so long ago. "Turn on the lamp."

She frowned a little but reached behind his chair and turned on the matching lamp that was situated on the narrow bookcase filled with stuffed animals. "What's the matter? You want to see if any diamonds have fallen out of the ring? There'd still be plenty left to fund a country," she assured, deadpan.

He shifted the baby to his other side. "Look at my shoulder."

"What?" Her gaze automatically shifted to his shoulder.

He angled it toward her. "A little on the back side."

She leaned over, humoring him. "Am I supposed to be oohing and ahhing?" She could certainly do so. His muscles were amazingly well-defined. His warmly tanned skin stretched smoothly over them. One day she'd have to ask him how he managed to get any sun when the only time he seemed to spend out of doors was their early-morning runs.

"The birthmark." His flat voice put an end to her meandering mind.

And there it was. In plain view for anyone to see if they ever bothered to look. If they ever had an opportunity to look.

A small, diamond-shaped smudge of darker-tinted skin.

Just like the one she'd kissed a hundred times on Timmy's little arm right above the crook of his elbow.

She sat back, covering her mouth with her hand, struggling for composure. "You want me to believe that's a coincidence?" she finally managed to ask. "You've known this all along?"

Gray sighed. Timmy was sucking so hard on his bottle, it was already nearly empty. "No. Harry noticed it, right off. He said something to Jack."

Jack? What must he have thought? Her stomach tightened. "No wonder your father's been so welcoming. He thinks—"

"It doesn't matter what he thinks." Gray cut her off. "Timmy is *not* my son." His voice held so much conviction she wanted desperately to believe him. Wanted to know—

without question—that she hadn't stepped into Daphne's shoes where Gray was concerned.

"Then why point out the birthmarks?"

"It was a matter of time before you noticed it yourself. Now that—"

"Now that I've slept with the man who tossed aside my own sister."

He grabbed her hand, squeezing it so tightly the rings seemed to cut into her fingers. "*I* didn't. But I think I know who did." He looked pained. "Gerry."

She slowly exhaled. "Your…half brother?"

"All my brothers are half brothers," he reminded. "Gerry's just not my brother on Harry's side."

"And he has this, this birthmark."

"I don't know," he admitted. "The only thing I share with him are some genetics."

"Daphne's not a fool. She wouldn't have mistaken him for *you*."

"He's done it before. Used my name. You saw him yourself." Gray shook his head. "The bastard can pass for me when he tries."

Amelia pressed her fist to her lips, too many emotions coiling inside her to focus on just one. "But if Daphne met *you* in person, she'd have known."

"She never had an opportunity. Marissa saw to that. Look, I know it sounds harsh. But Marissa was doing her *job* protecting me from what seemed to be just one more scheme against HuntCom."

"Daphne didn't claim HuntCom fathered Timmy," Amelia murmured. "She claimed it was *you*."

Gray snorted softly. "Is there a difference?" He held

Timmy out to her. "You'd better take him. Doesn't he need to be burped or something?"

She gathered the baby against her and rubbed his back. To her, Gray looked more uncomfortable than Timmy. "I thought you were doing fine with him."

"Give me computers and contracts," he said. "More my speed."

She disagreed, but wasn't going to argue the point. If Gray was right, he was Timmy's uncle. "What am I supposed to do with this information, Gray? You want me to question Daphne about it?"

He shook his head. "Hell no. She doesn't need to be upset by anything when she's doing so well." He snapped off the second lamp. "I just didn't want you thinking I was…holding out on you."

Her vision blurred. Against her shoulder, Timmy let out a thoroughly dignified burp. "It seems we're trusting each other more than we intended."

"If I'm right, Daphne would have a legitimate claim against Gerry."

"If you're right, Daphne wouldn't want Timmy to ever be influenced by a man like that. She thought she was notifying *him* about her pregnancy when she sent you those papers. She never saw him again after he dropped her. He probably has no idea whatsoever that he even has a son."

"I wish I could tell you that I knew him well enough to predict what he could do with the information. The only thing I can go on is his behavior where I'm concerned. And it isn't admirable. He'd use Tim for whatever gain he can get. But the decision isn't mine to make. *You* are Timmy's guardian. Whatever happens where he is concerned is your call."

She wished it weren't a decision she'd have to make. And she knew that Gray could easily have gone around her to have Timmy's DNA tested without her even being aware of it. But he hadn't. He was leaving the decision to her. "You really got more than you bargained for with us, didn't you?"

"That works both ways." In the soft light from the single lamp and despite Timmy leaning his satisfied and sleepy head once more against her throat, the way Gray's gaze drifted over her seemed dauntingly intimate. "It's not all bad. Is it?"

"No," she admitted.

"He going to go back to sleep now?"

"Probably." She brushed a kiss over Timmy's forehead and settled him inside his crib. Such a tiny person to have to overcome so much havoc. She wound up the mobile that hung over the crib and a soft lullaby sounded from it.

The baby's eyelids were already closing.

Gray slid his hand over her shoulder. His long fingers grazed the curve of her breast through the robe. "It will be all right, Amelia."

"You said that to me before." She was no more certain now than she had been when she'd agreed to marry him that he would be right in the end.

"I know."

"So far, the only thing that is remotely turning out all right is Daphne's recovery."

"That's not the only thing." His fingers brushed against her again. Not a coincidence, then. And she was shocked at the ready response of her body to the caress.

If she'd ever had such responses to John, the man would probably never have needed to find more excitement elsewhere.

For the first time, she realized how lucky she was that he

had or they'd have both ended up in a marriage that would have been thoroughly and utterly lackluster.

"Come back to bed, Amelia," Gray whispered against her ear.

Shivers danced down her spine. Nothing was going to be solved about Timmy that night.

She turned her head and found Gray's lips with her own. And when they finally broke apart, dragging in long breaths, it was Amelia who took Gray and led the way down the wide, silent hall to their bedroom.

"Retirement looks better on Harry than I thought it would."

Gray was standing near the bar set up in the bustling reception hall with his brothers. It was two weeks since Amelia's birthday. Two weeks of sharing their bed. In every way. No more ten feet of space between them.

He'd begun to realize that he wanted no more space between them anywhere.

Now, Gray followed J.T.'s gaze, looking over to where their father stood.

Still head and shoulders above most of those around him, still wearing his trademark glasses, Harry's head was tossed back in laughter at something being said.

It was Harry's final hurrah as the departed chairman of the board of HuntCom and the gowned and tuxedoed guests milling around the reception hall before they were seated for dinner seemed to have come from every corner of the world to share the moment.

"You going to hang on until you're seventy before you do the same?" Justin sent a sideways look toward Gray.

"You know me. Just like Harry," Gray drawled. He lifted his drink and tossed it back.

J.T. gave him a sharp look.

"I never thought I'd say it—" Alex broke the silence between them "—but his plan where we were concerned turned out pretty well." He nodded toward the far side of the room. "Our bride hunt yielded something I never expected. Look at them. Have you ever seen anything that looked *that* good under this roof?"

Near the head table, their wives were a collective vision, not merely because of their designer gowns that ranged from Amy's timeless black and P.J.'s rebellious fuchsia to Lily's shimmering bronze and Amelia's ivory confection. It was the women, themselves. Character. Grace. Strength.

"Not in my lifetime," Justin agreed. His lips quirked. "In fact, standing over here with you while they are over *there?* No contest." He headed off through the crowd like an arrow set on its course.

"Sorry, guys. He's right. Pretty as you both are, they're prettier." Alex grinned and picked up the soft drink he'd come to the bar to retrieve for his wife and headed after Justin.

"So," J.T. murmured softly when Alex was gone, "you want to spill what's bugging you?"

"Nothing." Gray slid his hand into his pocket. Felt the ring he'd tucked there hours earlier.

"You're gonna take a cell phone call *now?*"

Gray pulled his hand back out. Empty. "I stopped carrying it."

J.T.'s brows shot up. "Since when?"

He shrugged. But he knew exactly when. The night Amelia had told him he wasn't at all like Harry. "Habit sticks, though. They make a patch for people who want to quit smoking. What do they do for people who are connected to their phones?"

"Put research and development on it," J.T. suggested blandly. "They'll come up with something. Another gadget that'll raise profits even more. So, how many crazies have come out of the woodwork since you've taken over as chairman?"

"No more than expected," Gray said absently. "Just the usual e-mail threats about us trying to take over the world and anonymous letters we've always gotten from those who think computers are going to be the downfall of humanity. Security has been beefed up as a precaution with the changeover, but we'll probably lower it again to normal levels in a few months. Did you tell Amy about the guards?"

"I didn't want to spook her, but yeah. She knows. Alex and Justin told their wives, too. Everybody's covered. Nothing's going to happen to anyone, Gray. Nothing like before. You're in love with her, aren't you."

Gray exhaled. "How are any of us supposed to even know what that is?"

J.T. smiled slightly. "I think even Harry's learned a few things along the way this past year. God knows I have." His gaze was focused across the room. "You just have to let them in. And believe."

"You think that will last?"

"Amy and me?" His brother didn't seem surprised by the question. He looked at Gray. "Yes. We're going to make sure of it." He clapped his hand over Gray's shoulder, then he, too, headed for his wife.

"Son." Harry stopped next to him. The glass in his hand would have held vodka a year ago. These days, Gray knew, it held sparkling water. "I want a word with you."

Gray looked across the room again. Amelia was listening to something Georgie was going on about, not even looking his way. She'd fretted about feeling out of place at the reception, but from Gray's observation, his wife was handling herself more than capably.

If anything, she outshone every woman there with that intriguing combination of shyness, intelligence and wit.

He slid his half-filled glass on the tray of a passing waiter and followed Harry out of the hall and took the wood-paneled elevator up to the empty gallery above. "What is it?"

Harry wandered along the gallery several feet before stopping in front of one of the black-and-white photos. He rocked back and forth on his heels, looking casual as he studied the print. "I want to know when you're going to tell me the truth."

Gray went still. "About?"

"You always were a tougher nut than your brothers."

"And you're usually not so cryptic."

"I knew you'd finagle your way around our agreement."

"Our *agreement* felt more like coercion and you damn well know it." He kept his voice neutral. He still wasn't certain exactly where Harry was headed or just how much he thought he knew. "Ironic, really, since we know how you refuse coercion yourself." Gwen's kidnapping might have been faked, but they hadn't known that until the dust settled on her casket.

Harry shot him a look that was filled with an anguish that Gray never expected to see. "You want me to admit that I wish I'd have paid Gwen's ransom? I should have. Maybe you wouldn't have found out until after the baby was born what she was like. Maybe everything ever since would have been different. Maybe you wouldn't still hate me." He ran his hand down his face. Looked at Gray. "This isn't twenty years ago, though. This isn't Gwen. You married that girl to get her boy."

"Tim is Amelia's *sister's* boy."

"Her sister who'll never be able to care for him on her own again. Amelia is his legal guardian."

"She's guardian of all three. You knew that Jack would pass on your suspicions to me."

"He's young. I remember what you all were like at that age."

Gray snorted. "You barely noticed what we looked like when we were that age."

"And I'm paying the price," Harry said. He exhaled. "I didn't marry the right woman when I had the chance, either, and I've paid the price for that, as well. Your brothers are going to be fine. Better than fine, because they've already broken the pattern I set for them. But you—" He shook his head. "You always have to break the rules. Create new ones that you think will better suit you."

"It's that kind of reasoning that had you start up HuntCom."

"Yes. And as we both know, I've made plenty of mistakes, and you're all set to repeat them. I admit I wasn't the best father. But one mistake I didn't make was not claiming my own sons. When I knew they were mine," he added before Gray could challenge the declaration. "Amelia is a nice girl. I don't even need Cornelia's opinion to know that. Does she know about the boy? Know that she was your method of hedging your bets?"

"She knows more than you," Gray assured evenly. "It's a helluva thing, Harry. You really think I'd actually ignore my own child?"

"No wife, no children, no inheritance. Remember? You can have as many or as few children with Amelia as you want, but Timmy is a Hunt, too. He should have the Hunt name."

"Trot out all the reasons you want, Harry," Gray snapped.

"There will never be *any* children with Amelia. Not any of mine. I had a vasectomy when I was twenty-two!"

Harry stared at him. "What?"

But it wasn't Harry's voice he heard. It was Amelia's.

Gray spun on his heel to see her hovering behind them, one hand holding open the elevator door that she hadn't even quite exited. Her brown eyes looked huge in her face that had paled to the same shade as her gown. "Cornelia sent me up," she said. "They're seating for dinner now." She pulled back into the elevator.

The doors were already closing before Gray could stop them.

Swearing, he glared at Harry. "You don't know what you've done."

His father looked pained. "Are you so sure you do?"

Gray wasn't going to stand around and argue the point. He started around the gallery for the staircase on the other side.

But when he finally made it to the main floor and managed to circumnavigate the crowd that was settling itself around the crystal-laden tables, he saw no sign of Amelia.

No sign at all.

Chapter Sixteen

Amelia pounded her hand on the door, praying that Paula would be home. If she wasn't, Amelia didn't know where else to go.

They'd spent the night in a hotel that had used up all the cash Amelia had been able to grab on her rapid escape from the shack. She'd been more concerned with gathering up Molly and Jack and Tim and getting out of there than she had with details that only a few months earlier she'd never have ignored.

"I don't like this," Molly whispered behind her. "I want to go home."

Amelia's eyes burned. "Don't worry, honey," she managed, and rapped her knuckles on the door once more. It was early in the morning. Maybe Paula hadn't awakened yet.

"Why didn't we get to bring any of our stuff?" Molly repeated the question she'd asked several times already.

"'Cause," Jack answered. He was carrying Timmy and he looked no more happy than Molly about being dragged from the shack. Particularly when Amelia had made him leave behind his handheld gamer.

The door suddenly opened and Paula stood there, eyeing them with sleepy, surprised eyes.

"Can we hang out here for a while?"

Paula's expression fell. She silently pulled the door wide and they trooped inside. But not until the children were sitting at the table, distracted only somewhat by breakfast and the television, did she drag Amelia into the relative privacy of her bedroom where they could talk.

"What happened?" She sat down on the padded stool she used at her small vanity table.

Amelia paced. "Nothing I shouldn't have expected," she admitted painfully. She rubbed her fingertip over her bare wedding ring finger. She'd left the rings behind, along with everything else except the children and a handful of cash.

"Gray isn't Timmy's father," she added after recounting the whole story. "At least he didn't lie about *that*." She pressed her fingertips to her aching eyes. As for everything else he'd said, done, she couldn't bear to think how easily she'd fallen into his deception.

He hadn't needed just any wife. He'd needed a wife who came with a child. And she—given the situation—had filled the bill just fine.

How many times had he told her he was just like Harry? *He'd* taken his sons from his ex-wives.

Had that been Gray's plan, all along? Not to satisfy an old man's wishes for family, but to protect his inheritance? If Timmy was his nephew, he'd certainly be able to convince a court that he would be the better guardian. All he'd have to do was buy off Gerry—who'd already proven his only interest was money.

"Did you *talk* to him?"

Amelia shook her head.

"So he doesn't even know where you are?"

"I just…ran." It had been surprisingly easy, actually. Everyone in the house had been focused on the reception.

"Well, now what?"

"I have to go back. I know that." She crossed her arms over her chest, blinking hard.

"You think he'd stop paying for Daphne's medical care?"

"Yes. No. I don't know. He lulled me into thinking there was…something more…than just that hateful agreement. I could have handled the two years, you know." She dashed her hand over her cheek. "I could have handled anything but—"

"But falling in love with him," Paula finished softly. She handed Amelia a box of tissue. "Lie down before you fall down," she suggested.

"I need to get Tim's bottle going. He's probably starving by now." She could hear him beginning to fuss from the other room.

"I think I can manage," Paula said gently. She pushed Amelia onto the bed and closed herself out of the room.

She pretended not to notice the way Jack, looking guilty, quickly set down the telephone.

"Where is she?" Gray said the moment Paula opened her apartment door to him. She held Timmy in her arms, his hands eagerly clasping his bottle.

"In the bedroom. I think she might have fallen asleep."

He exhaled slowly. Ran his hand down his face, trying to

brush away one of the worst nights of his life, then looked over at Jack and Molly, who were sitting on the couch, looking dazed.

"You did the right thing, calling me," he told Jack.

"She's gonna be mad. Last night she made us promise not to make *any* phone calls."

"It's okay." He tossed Jack's gamer to the boy. When he'd found it, he'd looked at the most recent game he'd been playing. Math Crusher. "You're nearly at the top level. You're not going to have any problems in math next year, are you." He crouched down in front of Molly. "Are *you* okay?"

Giant tears welled in her eyes. "I was scared," she whispered.

"I know, sweetheart." He gently tugged the end of her very lopsided braid. "I'm sorry. It's my fault."

She scooted forward on the couch and twined her arms around his neck. "It's okay," she said softly and patted his back as if he were no bigger than Timmy.

He had to swallow, hard. He kissed her cheek. Pushed to his feet and cleared his throat.

"I'll just take Timmy and the kids down the street to the park," Paula suggested. "She's in there." She nodded toward a closed door leading off the hall.

"Thanks." But when they'd left, all he did was stand there and stare at that door. Afraid of opening it. Afraid that she'd turn him away.

Or worse, that she'd go back just because of the commitment she'd made signing that godforsaken agreement.

And then it didn't matter, because the door creaked and she was suddenly standing there. Her pink T-shirt was wrinkled and her hair was a mess of curls from her hairstyle of the night before. Her eyes were bloodshot. Her nose red.

And she was still the most beautiful woman he'd ever seen.

He'd met with heads of state and negotiated deals worth billions of dollars and thousands of livelihoods. But never in his life had he felt so uncertain as he did facing the woman who was his wife across that apartment. "I'm sorry."

Even across the room he could see the glisten of tears in her eyes.

He reached in his pocket and pulled out her pearl pin. "You promised never to go out without that."

Her lashes swept down.

"We were worried. After the third bus transfer you made, we couldn't pick up your trail. It's a wonder Harry didn't have another heart attack."

Her lashes lifted, a spark of temper glimmering. "That's completely unfair."

"Yeah," he agreed. He tossed the pin onto the table next to the couch. "Unlike my brothers, I'm a completely unfair bastard. I know it. And now you know it, too."

Her lips twisted. "I didn't want to be found."

"Obviously. Be angry with me all you want. Just—" He broke off, looking away. He propped his hands on his hips, grappling for composure. "Just keep yourself safe," he finished roughly.

"Worried about losing track of the tickets to your inheritance?" Her caustic voice broke midway through.

"Worried that I'll be burying another woman I...I care about."

Her lips parted. Her jaw worked. "You don't care about me. You didn't even marry me to make your father happy. It was all about your inheritance."

"Not in the way you think. Harry doesn't have to leave me a cent. He knows it. It was HuntCom. He threatened to sell it off."

"And you'd all still be rich as Midas. Big deal."

"The deal is that if HuntCom were sold, it would have been sold in pieces. Hacked up into small enough portions that *could* be bought. And at least half of the thousands of employees we have would have been out of jobs."

"Why would your father have done that? HuntCom was his brainchild. His—"

"His life," Gray finished. "And you're right. He wouldn't have done it. He couldn't have, any more than I could chance it happening. At least that's what I believed before he started meeting with potential buyers. I also knew my brothers didn't deserve to lose what mattered to them on the chance that I was wrong about Harry, and we *all* had to meet his terms."

"That seems…extreme." Her voice was faint.

"Yeah, but my father can be a man of extremes. He's a genius, but not when it comes to people."

"He's been nice to me," she murmured.

"He nearly died. He's working on 'nice.' But HuntCom—" He exhaled. "It's been my life for as long as I can remember. I didn't care about anything else. I didn't… *need*—" his jaw tightened painfully at the admission "—anything else. *Anyone* else. Until you."

The tip of her straight little nose reddened even more. "What you *needed* was a child. How ironic that I was the one who kept trying to believe—and trying not to believe—that you already had one. Wouldn't it have just been easier if you'd said he was?" Her lashes flickered. "After…our pretend marriage supposedly fell apart, you could have ensured that Timmy would never have left your clutches. You could have followed so…admirably…Harry's methods."

"Dammit, I didn't *want* to be like Harry." He shoved his hands through his hair. "After Gwen—" He broke off, swearing. "I met her in college. And I fell hard. I thought she was the answer to everything that was wrong in my life. So we were going to be married. No big announcements. No huge affairs. Just go off and get married at the end of the term and get on with life together. Only a few weeks before we could, she was kidnapped. Harry refused to pay the ransom."

Amelia paled. She pressed her fingertips to her throat, covering the diamond he'd given her.

The fact that she hadn't taken *that* off, too, gave him some strength to continue. "He had the FBI handling it from his end. Acting as negotiators. The kidnapper had to show proof of life. So Gwen was put on the line. She only had time to tell me she was pregnant before the call was cut off."

Amelia took a step forward, as if she couldn't help herself.

"After that I didn't care what Harry wanted to do or not do. I didn't care that they believed the ransom wouldn't get Gwen back. I pulled together every cent I could, and I went to the drop. Only the FBI was following me, too. The kidnapper picked up the money. The feds followed. But the kidnapper panicked and made a run for it. The car he was driving flipped down an embankment. When the bodies were recovered that's when we discovered the truth."

"What?"

"Not only was Gwen in the car, she was in on the plan. She'd set me up from the very beginning. Had binders of research about me before we ever even met."

Amelia moaned and slid her spine down the wall until she hit the floor, hands covering her face. She could hardly bear to listen. But Gray continued, his voice so raw she wanted to weep.

"Everything we seemed to have in common, everything

that I believed made her so perfect, had only been a well-executed plan."

"And the baby?"

He shoved his hands in his pockets. "That turned out to be true. She *was* pregnant. Autopsy tests proved it was mine." He looked out the window and his profile was as stark as his expression. "You want to know how powerful Harry is? Try to find some public record of what happened. There are none."

"No," she agreed faintly. "There weren't." If there had been, she'd have come across it.

"I swore I'd never let it happen again. Never be used. Never let a child of mine be used. I found a doctor who could keep his mouth shut, and that was the end of it. The only person who knew was Marissa, and that was only because of a paternity claim some woman I met in my twenties tried to bring."

"Naturally you knew Timmy couldn't be yours, either."

He picked up the pin and studied it for a moment. "I never let myself care about anyone enough again to be truly concerned with their safety. To be in a position where they could be used as a tool against me. Against HuntCom. And then you and the kids came along. Hate me if you have to, Amelia. I won't kid myself that I don't deserve it." He knelt down beside her and slowly, carefully, pinned the tiny *A* to her shirt. "But…please…"

Her eyes burned. "I was—" angry, her head said "—hurt." Her heart had her admitting the truth, instead. "I thought you'd planned it all along. That marrying me wasn't as much about making Harry happy as it was about keeping your inheritance."

"Harry doesn't have to leave me a cent. I have more money on my own than I'll need in ten lifetimes and he knows it. It was never the money. It was—"

"HuntCom," she whispered.

"He thinks I hate him." Gray's voice was low. Rough. "Would be easier, sometimes, if I did. But he's Harry. He's my father."

"And instead of being the perfect son to him—when he barely noticed his sons—you became the perfect successor to him."

"Yeah. Only now that I've got what I always wanted, I'd give it up in a second if it means keeping you."

She sucked in a shaking sob. Dashed her hand across her cheeks. "Oh, Gray. What a mess we've made of things."

"Too big a mess to clean up?"

She bit her lip. Struggled to get the words out, but it was so hard to trust, to believe. "I—"

"Wait. Here." He pulled a wrinkled, well-folded sheaf of papers from his back pocket and fresh tears hit her eyes when she saw the unsteadiness of his hands. He unfolded it, but she already knew what it would be.

Their marriage contract.

He grabbed the top edge and rent the pages in two. Turned them and tore again. And again. Until nothing remained but a litter of confetti lying around his knees.

She lifted a handful of shredded paper. "I can't believe you did that."

"Do I need to go find a huge roll of tape?"

She gave a shaking laugh at his suddenly grim expression. "No." She let the scraps drift through her fingers. "No more legalese. I don't want you to give up anything for me."

"I would. In a heartbeat. I love you, Amelia. And I never thought I'd say that to a woman again. Whether you have guardianship of Daphne's kids or not, it doesn't matter to me. I want you with them. I want you without them. I already knew it, but until you disappeared last night—" He shook his head. "I had half the city looking for you. The guys we sent here called me only a minute before Jack did. I know I'm not their father, but I swear, I can be the next best thing. If you'll help me."

Her lips parted. She didn't know what to say.

He grimaced. "I know I'm hardly a catch." He lifted his hand when she made a strangled sound. "The vasectomy, for one thing. I can't give you one of your own children. I should have told you, but—"

She covered his lips with her fingers. "There were lots of things we should have told each other."

He pressed his lips to her fingers, then drew them away. "If I could rewind time, do anything so you wouldn't have had to overhear the way you did, I would." His voice was hushed and so un-Gray-like that her heart cracked wide.

"I know it was childish of me to run. I scared the life out of the kids."

"I didn't lie about Gerry. Until Daphne can confirm it or not, it's the only reasonable explanation."

"Then we will just have to wait until she's able to make a decision about telling him herself."

"She may never get to that point," he said gently.

"I know. We'll just have to figure it out as we go along."

"We?"

The uncertain hope in his blue-green eyes finally gave her the courage she needed. "I love you, too."

His eyes closed. He leaned forward, pressing his forehead to the palms in her lap.

Tears slid down her cheek. Fell on his thick, rumpled hair. "Oh, Gray."

He straightened. Didn't even try to blink away the moisture

in his eyes. He reached into his pocket and drew out two rings. "Will you marry me?"

She already had. "Yes," she breathed.

He took her hand. Slowly slid the slender platinum wedding band into place, followed by the second narrow band.

Her fingers curled around his. The diamond baguettes flanking a simple square sapphire glistened in the morning light. "That's not the engagement ring you gave me before."

"You hated that ring. You were right to. It wasn't you."

"And this one is?"

"Both of these," he said quietly, "come with my heart. I love you, Amelia White. I will for the rest of my days. Everything I have, everything I am…is yours."

She felt the promise of it to her very soul. "That's Amelia Hunt," she corrected softly and pressed her lips to his.

His arms swept around her, pulling her tight as he kissed her as if he never wanted to stop. But eventually he did. Lifting his head. Searching her face. "Are you sure? What about kids? What about—"

"What about taking us all home," she suggested, smiling a little. "Where we belong. For now, that's the only plan we need."

His frown slowly disappeared. His lips curved. He pushed to his feet. "Home." He took her hands and slowly drew her up beside him. "For the first time in my life, that sounds perfect to me."

Hand in hand, they went downstairs, collected the children, and they went.

Home.

* * * * *

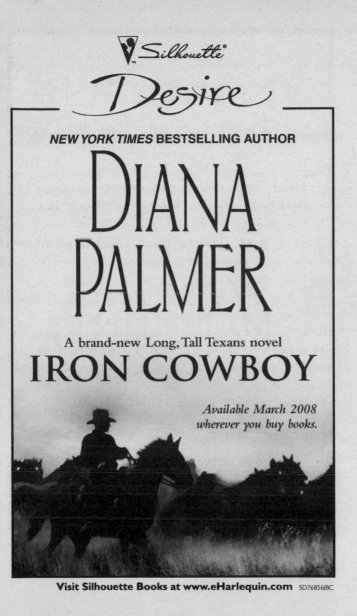

™ *Silhouette*®

Desire

NEW YORK TIMES BESTSELLING AUTHOR

DIANA PALMER

A brand-new Long, Tall Texans novel

IRON COWBOY

Available March 2008
wherever you buy books.

HARLEQUIN® Romance.

MEDITERRANEAN DADS

In the first of this emotional Mediterranean Dads duet,
nanny Julie is whisked away to a palatial Italian villa,
but she feels completely out of place in Massimo's
glamorous world. Her biggest challenge, though, is
ignoring her attraction to the brooding tycoon.

Look for

The Italian Tycoon and the Nanny

by Rebecca Winters

in March wherever you buy books.

HARLEQUIN®
Live the emotion™

$1.00 OFF

The bestselling Lakeshore Chronicles continue with *Snowfall at Willow Lake*, a story of what comes after a woman survives an unspeakable horror and finds her way home, to healing and redemption and a new chance at happiness.

SUSAN WIGGS

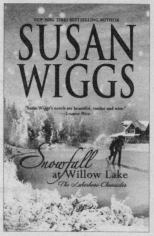

On sale February 2008!

SAVE $1.00

off the purchase price of
SNOWFALL AT WILLOW LAKE
by Susan Wiggs.

Offer valid from February 1, 2008, to April 30, 2008.
Redeemable at participating retail outlets. Limit one coupon per purchase.

52608168

5 65373 00076 2 (8100) 0 11463

HARLEQUIN®
Super Romance®

Bundles of Joy—
coming next month to Superromance

Experience the romance, excitement and joy with 6 heartwarming titles.

BABY, I'M YOURS #1476 by *Carrie Weaver*

ANOTHER MAN'S BABY
(The Tulanes of Tennessee)
#1477 by *Kay Stockham*

THE MARINE'S BABY (9 Months Later)
#1478 by *Rogenna Brewer*

BE MY BABIES (Twins)
#1479 by *Kathryn Shay*

THE DIAPER DIARIES (Suddenly a Parent)
#1480 by *Abby Gaines*

HAVING JUSTIN'S BABY (A Little Secret)
#1481 by *Pamela Bauer*

Exciting, Emotional and Unexpected!

*Look for these Superromance titles in March 2008.
Available wherever books are sold.*

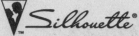
COMING NEXT MONTH